THE FIGHTER

A SAM POPE NOVEL

ROBERT ENRIGHT

For my girls,

CHAPTER ONE

THREE YEARS AGO...

'Good luck, Amara. Thank you for everything you've done for me.'

Amara Singh couldn't take her eyes from Sam. He'd given her the respect of full eye contact, and the matter-of-fact tone to his voice had told her that this was where they parted ways. The whole year had been leading up to this point. Ever since she'd been hand selected by the now fired Assistant Commissioner, Ruth Ashton, to lead the Sam Pope Task Force. When that moment had arrived, Singh had felt her stomach flip. As an Indian woman, she'd taken her fair share of misogynistic and racist bullshit as she'd quickly climbed the ranks of the Metropolitan Police Force, but working so closely with Ashton should have been the making of her career.

The whole country was looking to her to see if she had the capability to bring to justice a man who had decimated a criminal organisation along with uncovering high-level corruption within the Metropolitan Police Service.

DS Colin Mayer.

Inspector Michael Howell.

An ambitious politician, Mark Harris, had hitched his mayoral campaign to the task force, and with the pressure building, Singh allowed the idea of catching Sam Pope to become an obsession.

But then she saw the truth.

With the whole force focused on him, Sam was focused on finding a teenage girl who'd been kidnapped. With his help, Singh was able to save Jasmine Hill, and three others, from a fate worse than death by the hands of the Kovalenko crime family. Not only did Sam bring down their entire people-trafficking empire that stormy night in the Port of Tilbury, he'd also saved Singh's life with one shot of a sniper rifle.

From there, Singh's obsession turned to appreciation, and while she sought the truth about Sam's past, she'd soon been caught up in a dangerous game of cat and mouse with General Ervin Wallace, who wanted Sam silenced. As their quest for justice grew, so had their affection for one another, and Singh had often wondered what life would have been like if she'd turned her back on the law the same way Sam had and joined him by his side. It was a pointless exercise, because despite the very real feelings she had for the man, there was only one love in her life.

The law.

The clear definition between right and wrong.

And while she'd grown to love Sam and understand that he wasn't a bad person, he still existed in a world where that line was too blurred for them to ever be on the same side of it.

Sam knew that too.

It was why he'd been willing to sacrifice his life for hers

in a violent confrontation with Wallace's henchman, and why, after he'd won, Sam had been willing to give up his freedom for her. He had handed himself over to her, the only way to keep her from being arrested for collusion. But things had a funny way of working out, and with the help of Sam's ally, Paul Etheridge, she'd been fundamental in Sam's escape from The Grid, a maximum-security prison that existed off the books and housed the worst criminals the country had ever seen.

Sam had been sent there to die.

Or so Singh thought.

It was upon discovering that Sam and Etheridge had concocted the plan of surrender as a way to get Sam inside that she knew she and Sam would always be apart. The fight never ended for him, for reasons she knew and respected, but it meant that their attraction would only exist for that one evening of passion.

And now, as she looked at Sam, her heart ached for something she could never have, and she feared the worst for what Sam was doing. He'd just been through the emotional rollercoaster of killing his old friend, Matthew McLaughlin, a comrade he'd thought long dead.

His world was spinning, but now, sitting in the commissioner's office at New Scotland Yard, Sam seemed as content as he'd ever been.

On the other side of the desk, Commissioner Stout was sitting back in his chair, his fingers pressed together, and a look of intrigue spread across his face. It was the other man, standing before them, leaning against the edge of the wooden desk, that seemed perturbed by Sam's response.

Director Blake.

No first name given.

Moments earlier, Sam had referred to the man as a 'spook', which Blake himself hadn't denied. Working for

Directive One, the man was shrouded in mystery. The bespoke, expensive suit that clung to his impressive frame screamed wealth, and he had the swagger and charm of a spy. Singh wasn't naïve to the fact that the government had people who worked off the books, but she'd never encountered someone so brash about it before. The man's cocky smile was semi-permanent, continuously flashing across his handsome, clean-shaven face at regular intervals.

He'd offered them both a job, wanting to utilise Sam's incredible talents and Singh's unrivalled tenacity to do some good on a global level.

Singh had jumped at the chance.

Sam had quickly rejected it.

Blake had seemed exasperated at the rejection, clearly not used to being denied what he wanted. Singh had audibly gasped, knowing that her time with Sam was rapidly vanishing. Stout had watched on emotionless, as if he'd expected the outcome. Sam's reasoning had been fair, having been betrayed by his government while working for Project Hailstorm, but this was his chance of freedom.

If Blake walked out of the room without Sam in tow, then Sam would spend the rest of his life in prison.

She'd begged him to reconsider. But he'd just wished her luck and with a firm nod, told her he was comfortable with his choice.

Comfortable in giving up his freedom.

Comfortable in giving up her.

'We'll be in touch.' Blake broke their moment with a curt retort, glaring at Sam before storming from the room. As he slammed the door, Stout gave an audible yawn and then leant forward with a fatherly grin.

'It's late. Singh, why don't you head home? And keep this to yourself. Those guys don't exactly like gossip.'

She stood, the chain of command still beating through her veins.

'Yes, sir.' She turned to the door, and holding back the tears that were forming in the corners of her eyes, she reached out and rested her hand on Sam's shoulder. 'Goodbye, Sam.'

As Sam reached up and squeezed her hand, Singh felt a tear slide down her cheek.

'Good luck.'

Those were the last words she heard from him as she marched to the door and yanked it open, stepped out into the hallway and headed for the exit. She had no idea what would await Sam, but she knew as the door closed behind her, that it was the full stop on their time together.

She was heading to a new life now.

As Singh made her way through the empty building, she thought about what Sam had said to Blake as he'd rejected the offer.

'Let me guess. This will require us giving up all forms of identity, residence, the works. Then we would be assigned undercover missions, where the only directive is to ensure it's completed.'

Blake had all but confirmed it, and Singh was lost in her own thoughts as she stepped through the glass doors and out onto the street. The summer evening was warm and welcoming, and as she began to question the decision she'd made, a voice snapped her from her thoughts.

'Don't rethink it.' It was Director Blake. He was leaning against a jet-black 4x4. The driver sat idly behind the wheel. 'It's a scary notion, but it's worth it. Not just for you. But for them.'

'Is it forever?' Singh asked, her eyes wide with hope. She was certain that Blake had had this conversation countless times before. Agent after agent would have, at one time or another, been visited by Blake and asked to give up their life for their country.

He offered a warm smile as he opened the door and climbed into the back of the car.

'Spend some time with them,' Blake suggested. 'Like I said, we'll be in touch.'

The door slammed shut, and the car sped off, disappearing into the city that had been rocked by the terrorist attack on University College Hospital London just a few hours before. For a few moments, Singh stood in place, gazing out over the River Thames and the surrounding iconic landmarks. Her mind was racing, but through all the noise and the indecision, she could feel the grip of sleep reaching out to her.

It had been a wild day.

She'd broken Sam out of prison.

Made love to him.

Watched him walk willingly into a terrorist's firing line and finally give her up so she could have a life without him.

Tears rushed forward, but she didn't care. Usually so guarded with her emotions, Singh knew that she needed to grieve for Sam and what he'd become for her, and the only way to push past it was to weep for it.

The other stages would follow, and she hoped that they'd be quick.

Despite the expense, she ordered an Uber on her phone to take her all the way back to Canon's Park, where she hauled her shattered body to her apartment.

Somehow, she fought off the exhaustion until she collapsed on her bed, and she was asleep before she could even crawl up to the pillow.

The brightness of the morning burst through her window, and Singh cursed not drawing the curtains before she'd collapsed. It was early, and although she hadn't touched a drop of alcohol, her head pounded like she'd knocked back twenty shots. The previous day was clinging to the edges of her mind, feeling like a dream that she'd been watching through someone else's eyes.

Everything was coated with guilt.

She'd made a selfish decision, one that she probably wouldn't understand the ramifications of until a few years down the line. But she'd made it, and as a woman of the utmost conviction, she knew it was the right one. By seven thirty that morning, Singh was out, pounding the pavements and trying her best to shut away the gravity of her decision as she ran through the streets of Edgware, before returning home for a long shower. As the water crashed down on her from the waterfall tap above, she thought of Sam.

Where was he? Was he okay?

It had only been twelve hours since his hands were caressing her naked body, but it felt like a lifetime ago.

One single moment of passion. It's what would bind them forever, but if anything, it was a perfect way to say goodbye. The thought of the man rotting away in a prison brought a tear to her eye, but she soon composed herself. After quickly drying and getting dressed, she set out to follow Blake's instructions.

She didn't know how long before the call would come, but when it did, Singh would be taken off the map. A lie would most likely be fed to her family, and they would have to make peace with losing her.

Within five minutes of arriving at her sister's house in Barnet, Singh began to have doubts. Her sister, Priya, lived a life of luxury thanks to the law practice that was run by her husband Ravi. Despite not needing to, Priya was always dressed to the nines, decked out in stylish, designer clothes with her make-up immaculate and her hair perfect. Singh always felt intimidated by her. She'd tried to pass it off that she didn't really care, preferring the comfort of her gym clothes, but a little part of her was always envious of how amazing her sister looked. Their children, Deesha and Ava, were her carbon copies, and just watching her nieces play and knowing it would be for the final time brought on a sense of broodiness that Singh had *never* experienced.

She'd always been focused on her career.

Married to the job.

But knowing she was walking away from the prospects of a normal life suddenly made it all the more appealing, and Singh tried to hide her discomfort.

'What's up sis?' Priya asked, her well-groomed eyebrows raised.

'Nothing.'

'Oh, come on.' Priya laughed. 'I've known you your whole life, remember? I know when something is wrong.'

'It's just work…'

'I hear they caught Sam Pope again,' Priya said encouragingly, still under the impression that her sister was leading the task force. 'That's amazing, right?'

'It sure is.' Singh sighed, glancing out through the patio doors at her nieces who were playing with their dolls on the decking. 'So, I got a promotion…'

'Oh, well done,' Priya said, seemingly distracted by the food she was preparing. She called in the girls who ran through, picking up their fruit bowls, before scurrying back to the garden. As they rushed past their auntie, Singh reached out and stroked their hair, her mind rushing to thoughts of what type of women they would grow to be. She felt her eyes water.

It was too hard to say goodbye.

'I have to go…' Singh finally managed, choking back tears. Priya frowned with concerned.

'Amara, what's wrong?'

Without a word, Singh threw her arms around her

8

sister and held her as tightly as she could. The second thoughts were gaining traction as they rolled through her mind, and as she held onto her older sister, she began to shake. With their sisterly bond eternal, Priya didn't say anything. She just wrapped her arms around her little sister and held her for as long as she could.

As if she knew.

Without another word, Singh kissed her sister on the cheek, and then headed for the door. It was only mid-morning, but the day was already weighing heavy on her mind, as she thought about plucking up the courage to either tell her parents goodbye, or to try to contact Director Blake to politely decline the job opportunity of a lifetime. In a confused haze, she drove back to her flat, battling the continuous stream of tears that flowed down her cheeks.

She thought of Priya and the girls, and their wonderful life.

She thought of her parents, who had supported her through everything.

She thought of Adrian Pearce, and how he'd guided her through the noise.

She thought of Sam. Her Sam.

They would all be consigned to the past, different chapters from a previous life.

She had a new path now, one which she would dedicate herself to and finally find the purpose she was looking for.

Amara Singh did not fail.

With a new and powerful conviction pumping through her veins, Singh stepped out of the car, ready to begin her new life.

She didn't hear the truck until it was too late, and as she turned, the two balaclava-clad men were already in arm's reach. She remembered them placing the black sack over her head.

She remembered the Eastern European accents.

Then everything went black, as a hammer of a fist rocked into the side of her head.

It had taken four seconds for them to abduct her.

CHAPTER TWO

The errant drip of a tap was the first thing that came into focus, and its repetitive crash against the concrete summoned Singh back to consciousness. She tried to blink herself awake, but as soon as she opened her eyes, the bright light that was trained on her soon snapped them shut again. Her head spinning, still reeling from the clubbing blow that had shut her lights off, and it felt like her brain had been knocked loose.

With a concerted effort, she focused on her breathing, shutting out the pain and panic that was shaking through her like a tremor.

Then she felt the ice-cold water crash over her and her eyes opened wide with shock, her body tensed, and only then did she realise that she was bound to a chair. The leather straps around her wrists and ankles kept her locked in place, as the ice-cold water slid under her clothing and caused every muscle in her body to tighten.

'Wake up, bitch.'

The man's accent was thick, and the words were laced with disgust. Singh took a few calming breaths and then raised her head, squinting into the spotlight that was aimed at her. Behind it, she could make out two figures, both broad and imposing. One of them stood further back in the shadows, his arms folded, while the other stood beside the tripod that held the light. Swinging from his hand was a metal bucket. Both of their faces were hidden by a balaclava.

'Where am I?' Singh eventually asked, peering around at the derelict concrete room. Beyond the chair she was strapped to and the light fixture six feet from her, there was little else.

'Is not important,' the man said as he dropped the bucket, the clang bouncing off the walls and burrowing into her skull. 'Who is director of Directive One?'

The question was spat at her like an accusation, and with the fuzziness finally leaving her peripheral vision, Singh tried her best to peer beyond the harsh light and at the man before her. Beyond the cruel intent in his eyes, there was nothing she could detect.

'I don't know.' Singh was surprised by her resolve. The man grunted, stood, and then lifted the bucket. He sauntered across the room to the dripping tap and turned it. As the bucket began to fill, he whistled idly. On the far side of the room, the other man kept his eyes on Singh. The man eventually turned off the tap and returned to his position before her.

'I don't believe you.'

As Singh went to respond, the man hurled the water from the bucket directly into her face. The cold blast was instant, and with her mouth and nose unprotected, Singh began to cough and splutter. She felt her body go rigid from the cold, and after a few moments, she slumped forward against her restraints, trying to focus on.

Who were these men?

Associates of Kovalenko? Singh had been instrumental in helping Sam take down their empire, and while Sam had taken the fight to Ukraine to finish the job, there was always the possibility that someone from within the organisation was out for revenge.

Was looking to seize power.

But their focus on Directive One threw her mind in a different direction, but she wasn't sure of the destination. As she finally steadied her breathing, she lifted her head up once more in defiance. She was soaked through, chilled to the bone, and her short, brown hair was plastered across her wet face.

The man once again dropped the bucket, clasped his hands together, and spoke.

'I ask again. Who is director of Directive One?'

Singh spat on the floor before him.

'Fuck you.'

The man smirked; his mouth visible through the balaclava. Before he could react, his associate pushed himself off the wall and stormed towards them. Singh watched as he pushed past his comrade, and the last thing she saw was his fist rushing to meet her face.

Then everything went black.

There was no way of knowing the time or how long she'd been unconscious. As she blinked herself awake, Singh could feel the coldness of the concrete floor, which merged with the chill that had gripped her body. She'd been stripped down to her underwear, and with her entire body pulsing with agony, she had no idea what they had done to her.

They had wanted her to feel weak.

They had succeeded.

The remnants of the freezing water still clung to her body, and as she pushed herself to a seated position, her body shook involuntarily. Her head was heavy. The blows she'd received were causing the room to spin, and it took everything in her power not to collapse to the hard ground again. She pressed a hand to her eyebrow and felt the sudden twinge of pain and the sticky feel of blood.

There was one light in the room, hidden behind a metal grate in the ceiling that was too high for her to reach. Beyond that, the cell was empty save for the metal bucket that had been generously left in the corner for her to use when needed. Four concrete walls and a hard stone floor were all she had, with a thick metal door built into one of them.

Time passed.

How long, she didn't know, but eventually she heard the clomp of footsteps approach the door. As they grew nearer, she shuffled towards it, and slammed her fist against the metal.

'Help me,' she cried, her desperation taking control as she hammered the door with her fist.

A slot at the bottom slid open, and a bowl fell through, spilling some of the beige porridge onto the ground. A wooden spork followed.

'Eat.'

The voice was the same as the one who had demanded information she didn't have.

'Please,' Singh yelled. Tears rolled down her cheeks. 'Let me go.'

The slot slammed shut, and the footsteps marched away from her, finally disappearing and leaving her completely alone. Defeated, Singh slid down the door and then sat. She eyed the bowl beside her, but any appetite had deserted her. In her fury, she hurled the bowl across the room, and it hit the wall with a splat. Porridge smeared down the wall and Singh closed her eyes, pressed the back of her head against the door and began to accept that she was in a lot of trouble.

The process was the same every day.

Singh had lost track of how many days she'd been captive, but she was certain it had been nearly two weeks. With no natural light, the time of the day had long since been lost, especially with the broken patterns of sleep and the regular bouts of unconsciousness, whether through pain or fatigue.

The only things that were certain were the two bowls of porridge every day, the two plastic bottles of water, and the emptying of her bucket.

And the torture.

It had started off lightly for the first few sessions, with Singh being strapped to the same chair as before, subjected to ice-cold water being thrown at her and the occasional punch to her solid stomach. It was uncomfortable, but she knew she could make it through. After those sessions still yielded nothing more than a 'go fuck yourself', her captors upped the ante. Singh was once again strapped to a chair, only this time, two more balaclava wearing members of the group tipped the chair back, holding it in place. Another wrapped a towel over her face, and then the ice-cold water was poured over the fabric.

It gave Singh the sensation of drowning, and as she gasped for air, her captors took her to the absolute limit every time, before sitting her back down, removing the towel, and asking her once more for information about Director Blake and Directive One.

She gave them nothing.

They waterboarded her over and over again. Each time, they would haul her roughly from her cell, dump her in the chair, and work through the horrifying process. Singh was weakened, but she refused to break.

Then came the music.

Whenever she was able to calm herself to the point of a viable sleep, loudspeakers were set up outside her door, the slot was opened, and the music blasted through. It was a playlist of kid friendly songs for toddlers, all of them filled with loud instruments and repetitive lyrics. The words reverberated around her cell, and when one song finished, the next began.

For hours on end.

The same songs on a cycle. They tormented her so much with it that Singh knew the play order and would begin singing the next song before it had even begun.

She still did not break.

They reduced her meals down to one bowl of cold porridge per day and limited the emptying of her waste bucket.

Again, they asked for the information, and despite her malnutrition and her aching to return to her life, she refused. She hadn't even been recruited into Directive One yet, but her refusal to give up information was the only thing she had to hold on to.

They beat her.

After failing to crack her with days of water boarding and childish songs, they strapped her to the chair once more and allowed their strongest member to work her over with a series of right hooks. Her blood spattered the floor, but she refused to talk, telling them to eat shit before another fist rocketed into her jaw.

Then they left her for a few days, lying in her cell as the bleeding stopped and the bruising swelled.

She thought of her family and locked her thoughts onto Deesha and Ava and the amazing things they would be doing. Lying on the ground, she was aware of the smell that emanated from her. It had been weeks since she'd bathed, and since they had rationed her water, she wasn't able to use half a bottle to splash on her face, armpits, and private parts. The hair on her legs was prickly, as was under her arms, and she'd never felt more in need of a hot bath and a good meal. Her ribs were beginning to show through her skin, and the once lean, muscular body was reducing into a weakened shell of what it once was.

Then came the humiliation.

Singh was carried to another room and dumped on the ground, where a large metal drain sat in the middle. A woman's voice, thick with the same accent as the rest of her captors, demanded she strip her filthy underwear and place on the floor beside her.

Singh saw no sense in arguing. If her captors were going to sexually assault her, they would have done so by now, but that threat never materialised.

Standing, naked and filthy, Singh screamed in shock as a powerful jet of water crashed into her, the temperature freezing her to the core and the force of the impact knocking her to the floor. The water crashed into her like a million little fists, each one sending an icy shock down her spine. The woman aimed the hose at every square inch of Singh's body, hosing her down like a filthy animal.

Then the water shut off.

Lying naked and soaked, Singh tried to catch her breath, before another burst crashed into her, the coldness causing her to scream as the water pounded into her like a relentless current.

Then it was shut off.

She was tossed an old medical robe to put on to maintain her modesty before she was taken back to her cell.

They asked for more information.

She refused again.

The cycle continued, and Singh's naked body was

pulverised by the jet of freezing water. After one long, constant pounding from the water, Singh wasn't given her clothing back or taken to her cell. She was left to freeze in the wet, dank room of her hosing, her naked body shaking as she struggled for warmth.

But she would not break.

Days, weeks. Whatever. She'd lost all recollection of time. She hadn't seen the sun in an age or breathed the fresh air of the outside world. If she was going to die in these cells, she would at least do so with the defiance that had kept her going for this long.

Then the day came when they opened the door and tossed her the clothing they'd stripped from her. They demanded she got dressed and then they marched her to the room and threw her into the chair. She was so weak that the restraints weren't necessary. The spotlight was placed on her once more, and then came the footsteps. Singh held her hand up to block the brightness, and through her bony fingers, she saw the figure emerge and cast a shadow over her. Backlit, it was hard to make out too much, but Singh could tell it was the man that had been there on the first day, who had watched from the back of the room before introducing her to his fist.

He regarded her coldly, then, with a muscular arm, he lifted a gun and pressed it against her forehead.

'One last time. Who is the director of Directive One?'

The metal pressed into Singh's skin, pushing against the bone of her skull. She looked up at the man, her eyes meeting his.

'Fuck you.'

'So be it.'

Singh closed her eyes and images quickly shot through her mind.

Her parents.

Their pride as she passed out as a police officer.

Priya. The girls. All of them laughing and smiling.

Sam.

The man pulled the trigger.

The gun clicked. Empty.

Singh's eyes opened in shock, and the man pulled the gun away and nodded with approval. He turned back to the spotlight and shut it off and then motioned for someone to restore the lighting to the room. Swiftly, the bulbs burst into life, and Singh, weary and aware that she'd just accepted death moments earlier, looked around in a panic. The man turned back to her, reached up and pulled off his mask.

Her eyes widened with shock.

When he spoke, the European accent was nowhere to be found. Only the rich, articulate accent that had spoken to her the night he'd offered her a job.

As tears flooded down her cheeks, Singh looked up at Director Blake, who gazed at her with the pride of a father watching his daughter take her first steps. He held out his hand to her.

'Welcome to Directive One.'

CHAPTER THREE

The following week was purely focused on getting Singh back to full strength. After the blind rage and feelings of betrayal had subsided, Singh soon fell in line and followed Blake and his associate through the dreary corridor and up the stairs to the sunshine. As soon as the warm glow of the sun hit her, and the fresh air swept into her lungs, Singh dropped to her knees and wept. Blake would later inform her that she'd been underground for nineteen days, a record for a new recruit. It was a scant consolation, and although Singh would soon realise the gravity of what Blake had done, at that moment, her faith in the man had all but eroded.

But like her, that faith would be rebuilt.

Singh was introduced to Foster, a woman of similar build, who apologised to her for having to hose her down. Only then did the dots connect for Singh, that she was never naked in a room with another man for the entirety of her captivity. Singh grunted her acceptance, but the shrug from Foster told her that they had expected her disdain. It wasn't unreasonable, and Foster showed Singh to her quarters within the Directive One base of operations. It was a studio apartment with the amenities needed for her to live comfortably. The double bed called to Singh, but not before she took a long and purifying shower. Never had the feeling of soap on her skin felt so good, and she spent over an hour just allowing the warm water to cleanse her from her ordeal.

Then she slept.

She slept for nearly a full day.

When she was woken the next day by Foster, she groaned at the hunger and then argued about the meagre portion of eggs and toast that had been brought to her. Foster made it clear that they needed to be sensible with introducing the amount of protein and carbs back into her body and promised that each meal would build upon the previous.

After three days, Singh was eating better than she ever had, with the freshest of vegetables, along with rich proteins that filled her with joy. It was a long way from a cold bowl of porridge, and on each visit from Foster, she opened up a little more. A polite greeting soon turned to a conversation, and while Foster wouldn't give her much detail about what lay ahead, Singh could already feel the seeds of a friendship beginning to grow. By the end of the week, Singh was amazed at how bright and ready she felt, and when Foster invited her out for a brisk jog around Regent's Park, Singh jumped at the chance. Sportswear and running trainers were provided, and Singh ventured out of the Directive One building, which sat just a few streets from Great Portland Street Station, hidden among the private hospitals and international embassies.

'Hiding in plain sight.' Foster had called it, and the building looked as nondescript as every other. They made their way through the streets and fell in line with a group of other joggers, all of them trying to get their runs in during their lunch breaks. As Singh and Foster ran, they spoke intermittently about a few things.

Foster confirmed to Singh that she'd been essentially erased by the Metropolitan Police, and that steps were in place to inform her family that she'd been recruited for an overseas security firm. They would probably hate her for abandoning them without a goodbye, but Singh knew it was for the best. Foster made it explicitly clear that in their line of work, having people who you cared for only made you vulnerable, and Singh's heart broke at the thought of never seeing them again.

She asked about Sam and was devastated to hear that he'd been found dead in South Carolina. There was no rhyme or reason as to why he would have even been in America, but they had DNA records to confirm that the body they found matched Sam's. Singh tried hard to hold on to an element of doubt that Sam was dead.

Sam was built to survive.

When they returned to HQ, Foster left Singh to her lunch, and after she'd showered and dressed in a comfortable tracksuit, Singh ventured further into the building. Most of the rooms were locked, the doors windowless and secured by a thumbprint scanner. The hallways were narrow, a blueprint of the old, Victorian buildings that had been renovated by the influx of cash into the city. The winding staircase led up to an open common room, with sofas, a wide-screen television that was displaying a twenty-four-hour news channel, and a pool table tucked away in the corner. A kitchen unit ran along the far wall, with a kettle, coffee machine, and a toaster atop it, alongside a large steel fridge that housed plenty of snacks and drinks.

Singh made her way to the coffee machine, kicked it into life, and waited for the expensive beans to be ground down and liquified into her mug. With a scowl, she tried to operate the milk frother.

'Here, let me help.'

She spun in surprise at the Welsh accent and came face to face with a well-built, handsome man who offered her a friendly smile. He held his hands up in surrender and then reached past her to take control of the machine. His thick, dark hair was cut short, and his jaw was lined with thick stubble. He took the milk and tipped it into her mug and handed it to her.

'Thanks,' she said, eyeballing him with curiosity.

'The name's Brady,' he offered. 'I guess I owe you an apology.'

Singh was getting used to every greeting being followed by an apology, and she tried to guess what role he had played in her torture.

But it was all part of the process.

He made himself a coffee and then followed her to the sofa and sat down. Unlike her, he was dressed for action, wearing combat boots, jeans, and a black T-shirt that clung to his toned body. They sat in awkward silence for a few moments before he offered her another smile.

'So, regretting it?'

'A little,' Singh admitted, more to herself than to him. 'But I guess that passes.'

'It does.' Brady took a sip of his coffee. 'The first part is always the hardest.'

'You had to go through that as well, huh?'

'We all did. Blake might be a bastard, but he's the best there is. There will probably be a part of you that hates him for the rest of your life for what he's put you through. But you'll get over it. In time. Or at least make peace with it.'

Singh looked at Brady, instantly taking a liking to the man. Hidden under the collar of his shirt was a scar, but she couldn't tell what from.

'So, it's worth it?'

Brady smirked into his mug and then took a sip.

'Put it this way, there's a reason why the government has him running this place and leaves him alone to do so.' Brady shook his head. 'The things we've done. That we've stopped from happening. Blake might be a prick, but he's the best prick this country's got.'

'Thank you, Brady. How sentimental.'

Blake's voice boomed from the doorway and Singh and Brady both spun on the sofa. Instantly, Singh stood, a sign of her adherence to command. Brady remained seated, that part of him having been beaten out of him long ago.

'Sorry, sir,' Singh stammered.

'Please, if anything, he was being generous,' Blake said with little emotion, walking past the sofa and taking a seat on the chair opposite. Unlike Brady, Blake was dressed in an immaculate suit that had been tailored to fit his body perfectly. He seemed older than he had done when Singh had first met him, and the flecks of grey in his hair seemed more prominent. 'Tell me, Brady, how long have we been working together?'

'I'd say eight years or so.'

'Eight years,' Blake repeated and then blew out his cheeks. 'Singh, did you know eight years ago, it only took me five days to know that this man was at breaking point? You, nineteen. What resolve you have.'

'Resolve?' Singh felt her anger flare slightly. 'You stripped me. Beat me. Waterboarded me.'

Blake held up his hand.

'Now, now. Foster stripped and hosed you. Amos beat you, and your new buddy, here, he was the one who spent days waterboarding you.'

Singh spun in her seat and Brady shrugged.

'Sorry, mate.'

Blake leant forward in his seat and met Singh's furious gaze without flinching.

'Listen to me, Singh. What we do, it goes beyond the law. Beyond anything you can imagine. We don't just respond to problems, we snuff them out. We go where the government needs us to go but doesn't want to know about it. To do that, we need a certain type of person.'

'Like Sam?' Singh asked. Blake shrugged.

'Perhaps. But he made his choice and from what I've read, it was a fatal one. The type of person I need, Singh, is someone like you. The fighting. Guns. Surveillance. All those skills can be taught to you, and by the time my guys are done with you, everything will be second nature. No, the reason I put you through what I did, and the reason I put all my guys through it, is to measure what's in here.' Blake tapped his chest with his fist. 'Most people break, Singh. Most people give my name up after a few days and they go back to their lives, thinking they've escaped death and happy I never come knocking. But you. You proved to me what I needed. You'd rather die than give in. That makes you unbreakable. That makes you perfect for Directive One.'

Blake let those words fester for a few seconds before he slapped his thighs and stood. He nodded his goodbyes to both of them and then made his way to the door. Just as he was about to leave, he stopped and called back.

'Zero six-hundred-hours. Brady will be taking your first session.'

Blake stepped through the door, leaving Singh to turn to Brady, who was grinning.

'Session of what?'

The grin turned to a full smile.

'How hard can you punch?'

25

The next six months moved at such a pace that Singh didn't even realise her birthday had passed. A relentless regimen of early starts and long, hard days meant she collapsed in her quarters shortly after dinner and was awoken the next morning to repeat the cycle. After the first month or so, her body clock became finely tuned to the schedule, and she was up before the call, putting her body through a rigorous morning warm up before the day ahead.

There was hand-to-hand combat training with Amos, a man in his early thirties who reminded Singh of Adrian Pearce, with his dark skin and neatly groomed hair and beard. Amos never apologised for the beating he gave Singh in captivity, and his ruthlessness shone through during their sessions. Krav Maga was the basis of their training, with Amos showing little restraint when teaching her the fundamentals of grappling and striking to disable. Her body was battered and bruised, but it soon hardened, especially after her daily session in the in-house gym with Foster. Foster also schooled Singh on the inventory and the network they worked from, providing her with access to the databases and systems they used to circumvent usual security protocols to infiltrate companies and syphon the information they needed.

Nowhere was off limits. However, any misuse of the information carried repercussions that Singh didn't want to imagine.

The final member of the team that Singh was eventually introduced to was Hun, whose cockney accent was in stark contrast to his South Korean heritage. Always bubbly, he greeted Singh with the same enthusiasm every day, and seemed to generally love his work. When it came to surveillance, the man was at the top of his field, and there was no security system he couldn't breach or a person he couldn't follow. Everyone had their specialisms within the unit, but Blake was adamant that everyone should be cross trained across all of them.

'It's what made each member of Directive One a valuable weapon in the fight to keep the country safe.'

Singh's diligence and determination had marked her out as a field agent, and along with Brady, would be one of Blake's assets out in the field. Amos and Foster would provide back-up, while Hun would usually input from afar.

Blake ran the show.

Along with being Blake's number one agent, Brady was also the weapons expert of the group, and as he and Singh spent hours together in the shooting gallery beneath the building, a friendship grew between them. Singh trusted the man, despite being waterboarded by him, and Brady made it clear that out in the field, he would gladly die for the cause. As the months passed, Singh found herself adopting the same feeling.

Six months of intense training.

Six months of blending into the team, so much so that she soon couldn't remember a time when she didn't know them or trust them implicitly.

Six months of being part of something bigger than herself. Than her career.

And six months of following the one rule that bound them all together.

There was no talk of who they were before they refused to give up Blake's name. Whoever they were before that moment stayed before that moment. The whole team had been given a fresh start or an opportunity to be the best version of themselves.

Singh looked at herself in the mirror and was proud of what she saw. Her arms were now sculpted with lean, hardened muscles. She could run five miles without breaking a sweat. She could dissemble and reassemble an assault rifle in seconds. She never missed the targets.

She was becoming a special agent, and the pride of her work shone through in the smile on her face.

She'd left her old life behind, sacrificing a good career with the Metropolitan Police and a happy family life to do something more.

Be something more.

Amara Singh was now an asset for a secret, elite agency that existed in a world that she could never have imagined.

She was ready to go out into the field.

And Amara Singh didn't fail.

CHAPTER FOUR

TWO YEARS AGO...

For six months, Singh had cut a frustrated figure alongside Blake, as Directive One pushed on with their investigation into a London based terrorist cell. Despite showing impressive aptitude and capability, Blake was hesitant to push Singh out into the field before she was ready. Every remonstration by Singh was pushed back under the notion of 'walking before running', but Singh felt like she was crawling.

Brady was on point for the most part, backed ably by Amos and Foster, who were always floating around the edges, hidden from the naked eye. There had been a few close calls, and one of them involved Brady having to break the neck of an attacker, but it would be swept under the rug.

With the information the team had been able to pull together, along with Hun's expertise, they had been able to narrow down their suspected leader of the group.

Bhavin Kahn.

The man led a squeaky-clean life, leaving no footprint beyond the good work he did for the community and the accountancy firm that he ran. But there were too many links to shifty people, all of whom had either been investigated or interrogated by Blake's outfit, and all roads led to Kahn. With the net closing in on him, Kahn had been spooked and had acted accordingly.

Five flights booked from five different airports, all leaving on the same day, all headed to different countries.

A Eurostar ticket to Lille.

Two separate coaches, one leaving from London Victoria and the other from Golders Green Coach Station.

Blake and Hun had worked through the weeds of it all, in the limited time frame they had, while Brady, Amos, and Foster all hit the streets, rattling the cages of Kahn's known associates to try to pinpoint his departure. Despite Blake's links to MI5, there was no way they would offer up the manpower to cover every viable exit route from the country, which infuriated Singh.

But Blake explained that the head of MI5 didn't necessarily approve of the team's existence, nor their methods.

It was Hun who made the breakthrough, two hours before the supposed departure time of the train, that a shell organisation that funnelled money through Kahn's practice had a safe house in Lille. Blake assembled the team, and Brady, Amos, and Foster went ahead to St Pancras International Station, blending into the crowds of commuters who congregated on the concourse and packed out the numerous eateries that lined it.

Blake and Hun took the van, parking it up on a side road off Euston Road, where Singh sat on her hands, trying to fight off her impatience. All six of the team were connected via radio, their wireless earpieces also working as functioning microphones for them to communicate as they searched the building.

'Eyes.' Amos's voice cackled through, and Hun swiftly pulled up the live CCTV footage, which he'd hacked into. Singh leant across Blake to watch, and sure enough, Kahn, flanked by two of his devoted soldiers, was hurrying across the platform, heading for the Eurostar entrance that sat in the heart of the station.

'Engage as peacefully as possible,' Blake authorised.

'*Copy that.*' Brady's unmistakable Welsh accent filtered through, and on the laptop screen, Singh watched as Brady slid out of the crowd and fell in line behind Kahn, covering the distance between them as quickly and discreetly as he could. Opposite the entrance to the Eurostar, a crowd had gathered around a public piano, where an old gentleman was charming them all with his talent. Kahn and his men roughly shoved their way through the crowd, and Brady slipped between the onlookers. Just as their target was reaching the entrance to the security, Brady made his move.

'Bhavin Kahn.' Brady flashed his badge. 'You need to come with me.'

The gunshot sent the entire station into a panic, and before she even knew what she was doing, Singh threw open the door to the van and was racing towards St Pancras International Station, with Blake's fury echoing behind her.

All she could hear was Foster's panicked voice over her radio.

'*Agent down.*'

The station erupted with fear, with people hitting the ground or running in every direction away from the gunshot. Brady stumbled backwards, his hands pressed to his stomach, trying to stop the warm blood that was pumping through the gaps of his fingers. Terrified screams echoed from every direction, and Khan turned and ran as fast as he could, heading away from the Eurostar platform that would have provided nothing but a dead end. As he raced towards the crowd that was headed to the London Underground station nearby, his two henchmen stuck as close to him as they could. The high-vis jackets of the police came into view, and carelessly, Khan unloaded another two rounds in their general direction, not caring who or what he hit.

More screams.

One of the officers hit the ground. His partner rushed to his aid.

Through the chaos, Foster pushed past the terrified civilians to Brady, who was lying prone on the concourse, his eyes rolling backwards as she cried out for help. She pressed her hands to the bullet wound, trying to apply the pressure that Brady couldn't. She screamed for help, demanding one of the concerned commuters call for an ambulance or find the paramedics. As they scuttled off, she screamed at her colleague to stay with her, refusing to let him give up the fight.

But Brady needed help, and quickly.

Khan was hammering the concourse with wide strides, with people moving out of the way of the gunman as he made his way through to the Underground tunnel that connected St Pancras International with Kings Cross St Pancras Underground Station. He had no destination in mind, only to get out of the station as quickly as possible.

One of his henchmen raced ahead towards the brick archway that led to the tunnel, only for a clubbing forearm to crash into his throat, taking him off his feet and crashing hard to the concrete.

Amos stepped forward, and Khan swiftly changed direction, heading instead for the side exit of the station, which would take him to the new housing developments that surrounded the station. Amos made an effort to tackle Khan, but the other henchman dived forward, slamming his shoulder into Amos's stomach and sending them both crashing to the ground.

The panic rose audibly around them, and the henchman tried his best to wrap his meaty hands around Amos's throat, his eyes wide with murderous intent. After a brief struggle, Amos managed to drive his knee into the man's spine, sending him rolling to the side, and as the two men got to their feet, the henchman pulled a knife.

More screams.

More terror.

Amos lifted his hands, ready to deflect any blows, but as he did, the other henchman snatched him from behind, locking his arms in place, and offering Amos's body up for a sacrifice. The knife wielding henchman launched forward, but at the final second, Amos dropped his body-weight, falling to his knees and pulling his captor forward. The knife embedded into the henchman's shoulder and he roared with pain, relinquishing his grip and stumbling to the ground. As Amos got to his feet, the reckless henchman swung a knee at him, but he blocked it, then cracked the attacker with a swift right that sent him back a few steps.

Then came the cavalry.

Armed police swarmed onto the concourse, weapons up, and their commands for everyone to get down on the ground sending the entire station into a terrified silence. The sight of several locked and loaded assault rifles being held by men with itchy trigger fingers was enough for the terrified public to hit the deck, and Amos held both his hands up in surrender. One of the henchmen was on the ground, crying with agony at the stab wound that was pumping blood all over the concourse.

The other henchman, defiant to the end, took a few

steps towards the nearest armed officer, and after one warning, was sent spinning to the ground by a bullet that ripped through his shoulder.

He'd live.

Amos obediently lowered himself to his knees and clasped his fingers behind his head. He peered through the carnage towards the Eurostar entranceway, where he could see a team of paramedics frantically trying to save his friend's life. With a gun pushed to his head, Amos lowered himself to his stomach, allowed the officers to slap cuffs around his wrists, and knew that within the next five or so minutes, they'd be taken off with an apology.

And with his friend on the cusp of death, the station ground to a halt due to what would be put out as a 'terror threat' and the public terrified, Amos felt his fists clench in anger at the fact that Khan had got away.

With the armed police now swarming St Pancras International Station, Bhavin Khan had fallen in with the wave of people who had barged their way through the exit and out onto the surrounding London streets. Traffic had come to a standstill as hundreds of commuters flooded out, all of them in varying stages of panic. Dressed in his smart casual wear and with the gun tucked into the inside pocket of his coat, Khan looked like just another scared citizen. Calmly, he made his way through the congregation, smiling politely at the other civilians who were all sharing their thoughts and feelings about what they'd just been through.

Like a snake in the grass, he slithered through the group and made his way off into the side streets, just as the police were beginning to round them up.

The plan had been scuppered, but at least he was free.

His two followers would likely go down, but their loyalty to the cause would guarantee their silence and all he would need to do was regroup, shift his location, and continue with the work that he and the hundreds within the terrorist cell believed in.

His heart pumping with adrenaline, Khan rounded the corner and made his way down a side street, the newly laid road weaving through a recently constructed housing estate, with its fresh paint and planted trees. He chuckled to himself as he walked, and it was only when he heard the footsteps picking up pace did he turn.

He reached into his pocket for the gun.

He aimed it.

He pulled the trigger.

Singh pushed his arm upwards just in time, sending the bullet skyward, before she drove her elbow into Khan's forearm, sending the gun sprawling across the pavement. Angered, Khan swung a hard right, but Singh's training kicked in. She dodged the fist easily, drove a knee into the man's side, grabbed his arm with both of her hands, and flipped him over her shoulder. He crashed hard on the concrete, groaning with pain as the air shot from his lungs, and before he could scramble to his feet, she drove her boot into his jaw, sending it and Khan shaking to the ground. With the terrorist lying prone, she retrieved the fallen handgun and then spoke into her mic.

'I have Khan.'

She trained the gun on the man, who was woozily surveying the area, his jaw laying slack. All around her, she could hear the pandemonium from a few streets away, with the honking of car horns and the wailing of sirens polluting the air of the city. A few teenagers had watched the events unfold at the end of the housing estate, and they were excitedly recording Singh on their phone.

She didn't mind. Blake would ensure that those phones

were confiscated, and any video that made its way into the fickle world of social media would soon be removed.

Right on cue, the Directive One van turned onto the side street, thundering down the road and pulling to a stop a few feet from where Singh was standing. Blake killed the engine and stepped out, his face like thunder as he rounded the vehicle and approached.

'Sir, I've got him,' Singh said proudly.

'Lower your weapon and get in the van,' Blake demanded, as he stomped towards the groggy terrorist. With one flick of his boot, Blake flipped Kahn over onto his front, and then bound his hands behind his back with cable ties. 'Now.'

'But, sir, I…'

'You failed to follow an order, Singh,' Blake said as he took the gun from her. She looked beyond Blake to the two police officers who were racing up the road. 'I'll handle things from here, and I'll deal with you later.'

'Sir, I'm sorry,' Singh said, baffled. Blake sighed.

'You need to be gone. We were never here, and the longer you stand around the harder it makes it for me to prove that.' Blake nodded to her. 'Now, move.'

Understanding the urgency, Singh darted to the van, jumped into the driver's seat and brought the engine to life. As she pulled away, she rushed through the gears, with Hun throwing out a stream of expletives at the speed she was going.

In the rear-view mirror, she could see Blake already weaving his magic over the officers. He'd make their presence nothing more than a rumour, but as she pulled out onto Euston Road, Singh felt a sea of worry wash over her.

Brady had been hit.

She'd disobeyed a direct order.

Despite catching a dangerous terrorist, Singh began to realise that no matter how hard she tried, success within

Directive One would never be without cost. As she pushed her foot down on the pedal, she asked Hun to hack into the emergency services to find an update on Brady. Then, as he told her what hospital Brady had been taken to, she prayed to the gods she'd long since abandoned that her friend would still be alive when she got there.

CHAPTER FIVE

SIX MONTHS AGO...

Life moved so quickly that the fallout of the Khan operation soon dissipated. Thankfully, Brady had survived the gunshot, but Singh had noticed a change in the man. The usual, bubbly Welsh welcomes when she walked into a room had all but disappeared, and instead, the man seemed to be racked by the continuous thought of his own mortality. The risk involved in their line of work was palpable, and whether it was sneaking into a building, maintaining a cover, or confronting a suspect, there was always an element of danger lurking in the shadows.

Singh had negotiated a few near scrapes. There was a time when she was undercover as a waitress in an exclusive gentleman's club, during a meeting between two Kosovan gangsters who were concluding a business deal. One of them had taken a liking to her, but when she rebuffed his advances, he soon grew agitated. Considering the women who worked there were encouraged to make the clientele as comfortable as possible, Singh stood out like a sore thumb. Thankfully, Amos, who was also working the operation as one of the security guards, stepped in and ended the matter within seconds.

Blake had become a mentor to her, which had surprised Singh due to the man's reputation. The team constantly spoke of Blake as being a bastard at the best of times, but he seemed to have a genuine interest in Singh's career. After disobeying his orders at St Pancras eighteen months before, Blake had sidelined Singh for three months, giving her nothing but paperwork and menial tasks. It was a tough lesson for her to learn, especially with Brady fighting for his life, as Directive One felt like it'd slowed to a crawl. Foster and Amos were capable of working in the field, but they both offered such expertise elsewhere that Blake was hesitant to put them front and centre.

Brady and Singh were his field agents, and for a while, they both were out of action.

But the water soon swept under the bridge, and with the severity of Brady's injuries requiring intense physiotherapy, Singh soon became the jewel in the Directive One crown. With the help of Foster and Hun, she successfully brought down a corrupt politician who was dealing with a right-wing group. It should have been almost impossible to get close to the man, considering his racist inclination, but Singh had managed it.

What surprised her most of all was the lack of action.

When she'd been approached by Blake two and half years ago to join his covert group, she had fantasies of car chases and shootouts. Of explosions and spy gear.

But it wasn't the case.

Her skills as a detective were put to the task on an almost daily basis, with Blake gathering the team in the briefing room to walk through their operations in meticulous detail. Often he would ask her theorise a motive, and Singh soon realised that while Brady was the action hero of the group, she was the criminal mind. They would call on her to look deeper into the details, and she found herself working in tandem with Hun and Foster more regularly.

Brady was back in the field, but the swagger of the man had depleted. He was now ruthlessly efficient as opposed to charmingly effective, and Singh knew that trauma could change a person.

Like it had changed Sam Pope.

It was on a routine surveillance mission alongside Foster that the name Vladimir Balikov first entered their domain. They were tracking two Russian diplomats, who'd been exonerated of corruption by the UK government, but, as Blake put it, hadn't had their names taken off the shit list. Three weeks of dull meetings and stops at restaurants uncovered little, until Singh, sitting discreetly at the table beside them, heard the name Balikov.

It went on the board.

Soon, one of those diplomats was found in a public toilet, his throat slashed and his trousers around his ankles. What had been staged to look like a secret sexual encounter gone wrong was clearly a murder, so Blake had demanded they dig deeper. Brady went to work, rattling the cages of the Russian mafia that now dominated the wealth within London. Amos provided security, as always.

Foster kept track of the other diplomat, who was now under the watch of a militant security detail.

Hun worked his magic, trawling through the depths of both the internet and the dark web to discover more.

All of them came to the same conclusion.

Balikov was a ghost.

Singh had pulled all their information together to form an impressive white board display, but there was nothing of substance.

A muttering here.

A potential business deal there.

But for a man with an estimated fortune of over three hundred million pounds, Balikov left no footprint. Which didn't sit well with Singh.

Nor Blake.

As always, the head of Directive One used his turn of phrase to dismiss notions that Balikov was just another oligarch.

'If you hear hooves, think horses.'

Singh had smirked at that one. Blake had the same command over words that he did of people and was always on hand for a slick saying when the voices began to escalate in the room. But Singh agreed. There was too little they knew about a man of such power and influence, and his name was beginning to bounce across criminal activity like an echo in a cave.

It was Brady who made the first significant breakthrough.

Hun had tracked a shipment to an independent delivery service in East London, that had been sent by a company with links to one of the many organisations they'd attributed to Balikov. Under the guise of a Russian thug, Brady had successfully intercepted it, but not before rendering the original delivery man unconscious in a fistfight.

Inside it was a pressure gauge, with an inbuilt shut down mechanism. It was an impressive piece of kit, and Hun had a field day examining it before his presentation showed them all the severity of the problem. The gauge would be affixed to a canister and would send a digital reading to a connected app, which would monitor the levels within. If the levels reached a certain point, the mechanism would auto-lock the canister.

When Blake asked what the gauge measured, Hun's response sent the room into silence.

Radiation.

Although they had nothing but breadcrumbs and the mere whisper of the man's name, all of them were of the belief that Balikov was funding a project to build and arm a nuclear bomb. With the international relationships across Europe strained with Russia, the theory was that the rich and powerful patriots of the country were looking to take back some power. The fact that they only had one piece of the puzzle was enough to send everyone into overdrive, and through tracing the journey of the package, Hun was able to pinpoint three locations with solid links to Balikov.

Foster was able to get a photo of the man, found by traipsing through records of the University of Moscow, which then allowed Hun to find several more through facial recognition and his adept skills with a computer.

Through hard work and diligence, the team managed to build a picture of the man, his fortune and the lengths of his influence. What was startling was how much of that influence was in their very own country, and Blake knew, much to his chagrin, that they needed to inform MI5.

He and Singh took the information to their head office, but it was dismissed as nothing more than a theory. Singh pleaded their case, but Blake steered her away.

'They don't know their arse from their elbows.'

The director of MI5 wasn't the biggest fan of Directive One's rogue nature, and what had been a genuine attempt to bring them onboard had led to nothing more than a bit of dick swinging.

Singh went back to the information they had, combing through it once more, and then found a loose connection. Two trips to Budapest, over the same weekend, two years on the trot.

It wasn't much, but it was a thread, and as was her nature, she began pulling at it with every fibre of her being. Soon she found a third trip.

Then a fourth.

With the team gathered in the briefing room, she laid out her information on her neatly decorated board and turned to them. Brady watched with his newfound intensity. Hun and Amos, an unlikely friendship but one Singh very much enjoyed, were sitting casually behind one of the desks. Foster sat upfront, glasses on and notepad in hand.

This was Singh's show.

'Every second weekend in August, Balikov visits Budapest for a three-day period.' She tapped some of the documents on the board. 'No idea why, but—'

'That's six months away,' Blake interrupted, his hands on his hips.

'Shit timing.' Amos chuckled, and Hun joined in. Brady scoffed.

'Yes, sir,' Singh said, adamantly. 'But it's something.'

Blake smiled.

'I'll give you two months to figure out why.'

PRESENT DAY...

Singh took a deep breath as she watched Blake follow Agent Renée Corbin into the coffee shop. The warm glow of the Parisian sun basked down on her uncovered shoulders, and she looked up at the clear sky. The market was busy, with local sellers all trying to barter with those who gathered around their stalls, and Singh admired the beauty of the place.

If she'd taken a picture of the moment, she could have sold it as a postcard.

The stereotypical French scene.

The glorious buildings of the surrounding streets

loomed large in the background, and a relaxed atmosphere flooded through the marketplace.

Blake had accompanied Singh to the French capital, signing it off with those who were interested as a goodwill gesture amidst the political turmoil the country was in. After Ducard had been ruthlessly taken down by Corbin, the country's political landscape was full of potholes, but their interest was in one of the details that had been kept from the public.

Sam Pope had been the one to do it.

When Sam had returned from the dead a year or so ago, Singh had felt her heart stop for a second. She'd cared deeply for Sam, and his death had silently hit her when the news broke. Hun had been keeping track of Sam, monitoring the increase in attacks against organised crime to paint a picture of his activities since his re-emergence.

The death of Daniel Bowker.

Slaven Kovac, a man who had been on Blake's shit list.

Dana Kovalenko.

They each had Sam's fingerprints all over them, but Singh knew first hand that Sam was a hard man to find.

When he inserted himself into the Ducard situation, a light bulb had gone off in Blake's head. All their hard work over the past few months had led to this point, and now, with a viable route to Balikov, they were just missing the final piece to their puzzle. Singh had pushed back against Blake for the first time in the three years they'd worked together, but her boss was unrelenting.

Half of what he said made sense. The other half, Singh theorised, was because Sam had curtly turned down a job offer three years prior.

But it was a way back for Sam, an opportunity to take back his life and leave behind his war. All he had to do was to join them for this one mission. Singh had waited long enough, and she made her way into the coffee shop, where

Blake had already turned on the charm and was chatting with Corbin. The agent had her back to Singh, but on the few times Singh caught a glimpse of Corbin's side profile, she could see she was a beautiful woman.

Singh ordered a coffee and waited, her ears trained in the direction of their conversation.

'Well, what makes you think he will listen to you this time?' Corbin asked, her perfect English wrapped in an alluring French accent.

'Because I won't be the one asking.'

Blake looked beyond Corbin and right at Singh, which caused Corbin to spin. Singh took her coffee from the counter, thanked the barista, and took a step toward them.

'Who are you?' Corbin asked, a hint of betrayal in her voice.

Singh took a sip of the piping hot coffee and smiled.

'Amara Singh.'

The name seemed to evoke recognition from Corbin, and Singh was surprised at how happy that made her. The agent shook her head.

'Let's not talk here.'

The matter-of-factness of her movements only played up to the French stereotype, and as she made her way down the street towards her car, Blake and Singh walked in tandem a few steps behind. Eventually, she stopped beside the car and placed the two coffee cups on the roof. As she shuffled to the boot of the vehicle, Blake chivalrously leapt forward and took her bags, placing the groceries into the car and then closing the boot. He then nodded to the coffees.

'They'll be getting cold.' He smiled. 'Shall we have this conversation back at yours?'

Corbin sighed and shook her head.

'Sam is a good man. What he has done for me and my country, we will never be able to repay him. Because the country will never know.' She looked at both of them. 'Sorry, but I can't just hand him over to you and let him rot in a cell for the rest of his life.'

'Like I said, we don't want to arrest him…' Blake stammered, a flare of irritation in his voice. Singh stepped forward.

'Agent Corbin. I know you know who I am. I saw your eyebrow twitch when I told you my name.' Corbin looked equal parts impressed and frustrated. 'So, if you know who I am, you know what I mean to Sam. What he means to me. I wouldn't be here if the idea was to take him out of here in cuffs.'

A silence stood between the trio, and Corbin looked up and down the quaint street, her gaze falling upon the hustle and bustle of the market at the far end of the road.

'Then what do you want with him?' Corbin finally relented.

Singh offered her warmest smile.

'We want to give him a way back home.'

CHAPTER SIX

It had been a long time since Sam Pope had been on holiday.

As he stood at the end of Corbin's garden, he gazed out over the surrounding fields, basking in their tranquillity. A rolling wave of different shades of green stretched all the way back to the horizon, with the various fields sectioned off by old, wooden fences. A few of them were being patrolled by farmyard animals, all of them roaming the grass like gangs. The sun bore down on everything, offering a warmth that was welcomed by human, animal and plant alike. The fresh smell of the cut grass wafted on the faintest of breezes, and now and then, Sam would get a whiff of a farmyard that would rock his senses.

It was as near to a holiday as he could remember.

His life with Lucy and Jamie used to feel so close to him, as if he could reach out and touch it with his finger-tips, but now, those days were drifting further and further away. It made him question at what point did recent memory turn to distant? Those moments and memories, where the Popes were a happy family, were blurred around the edges now, and he cursed himself for sometimes misre-membering things.

The sound of Jamie's voice.

The colour of Lucy's hair.

It had been over six years since everything had been taken from him, and he knew that eventually, all that would remain would be a hole in his heart where the two of them once existed. The finer details would trickle away and only their absence would remain.

They had never been on a family holiday when they were together, with Sam's job keeping him away for long periods of time. He and Lucy had discussed taking Jamie to Disney World, but wanted to wait until he was old enough to fully appreciate it.

It was just another layer of guilt that Sam would have to live with.

He'd accepted his son's death. Grief was a concept that had been marketed into stages, but there was no true blue-print for it. Nobody could ever dictate the impact of loss, and Sam knew that for years, he refused to accept it. The guilt of not stopping Miles Hillock, the drunk who had run over his boy, would claw at Sam until his dying day, but for years, he let that guilt manifest as rage.

The pain of Jamie's death had fuelled his one-man rampage against organised crime and corruption, but Sam was finally at peace with his loss. Jamie's death was no longer the reason why he fought for those who couldn't fight back.

But it would always be the catalyst.

And Sam hoped beyond hope that he could cling onto those finer details a little longer.

His fingers gripped around the mug of tea, and he lifted it to his bearded face and took a sip. Agent Corbin had made him feel more than welcome in her home, and apart from one drunken stumble where she made a pass at him, they had become firm friends. The woman was as strong as he'd ever met, and as they'd dropped their guard around each other, she'd informed him of the promotion she was receiving for her stellar work in taking down Pierre Ducard.

Sam was happy for her to take the credit.

A month had passed since he'd interjected in Olivier Chavet's quest for justice, after his father, a French Diplomat, was abducted and murdered over a decade ago. Ducard, the *Chef d'État-Major des Armées* at the time, had insisted he'd done everything in his power to bring Chavet's father back alive. In reality, Ducard had sanctioned the murder himself, and had aligned himself with General Ervin Wallace to at least keep up the pretence that he was acting in Chavet Snr's best interests. That meant Wallace had sent a team of four into the Amazon to bring the already dead man back alive, but he really had sent them to die.

Three of them did.

Only Sam survived.

Seeing the opportunity to avenge the deaths of his three comrades, Sam's intervention spiralled into an all-out war with Ducard that not only claimed the lives of Olivier Chavet and another DSGE Agent, Martin Agard, but it brought an end to Ducard's seemingly inevitable rise to the presidency.

Whilst the country was in a political tornado, with different parties scrambling to try to take control, Ducard was awaiting sentencing for his war crimes. Corbin, who had been investigating Ducard for years, was right by Sam's side through it all, and it was she who arrested the man and brought him to justice. In exchange for his help, Corbin had given Sam sanctuary in her home on the outskirts of Paris, allowing him to heal from his wounds and to give them enough time to figure out a safe way to get him out of the country. Both the French and British governments had made it clear that Sam was a wanted man, and after how hard he'd fought for the truth, Corbin had told Sam that she believed he deserved the chance to walk away as a free man.

He stretched his back and winced.

The scar that ran across his broad shoulders had healed, and slipped seamlessly among the others that littered his body. The wound had been inflicted by a broken bottle, swung by the murderous hand of Ducard's Head of Security, Laurent Cissé.

As was the scar that now ran the length of his right cheekbone, which Sam himself had joked made him look like Action Man. Corbin hadn't understood.

The stiffness in his back had come from years of war against crime, and the countless fights and falls throughout, and as Sam stood, gazing across the stunning landscape, he wondered if maybe he'd done enough.

Maybe it was time to bring it to an end.

His friend, Paul Etheridge, a man who had been off the radar for three years, had left Sam a sizable fortune to continue his fight, having found his purpose in working alongside him. Etheridge had served with Sam years ago but had found his calling in cyber security and had amassed an eye-watering fortune through his businesses. But it had led to an empty life full of loveless marriages and materialistic dependence and had left Etheridge directionless. It was only after Sam had called on him for help that he'd found something to dedicate himself to, and after a year of working diligently alongside Sam, Etheridge had gone dark after springing Sam from a police convoy.

The money was Sam's to do as he pleased, and part of him tried to convince the other that he'd done all he could.

That he deserved to disappear and see the world and leave behind the pain and the violence.

But Sam knew he couldn't.

Despite his body constantly aching and the scars stacking up, Sam knew that he was too far gone to turn back. He'd lost too much to not see it through. His best friend, Theo Walker, a man who had served with him for years as a military medic, was killed trying to keep an innocent woman safe. His mentor, Sgt Carl Marsden, had died to show Sam the truth of what Wallace truly was, the horrible things he'd ordered Sam to do. Amara Singh, like Etheridge, had been MIA for over three years and the only person who had been a rock to him, Adrian Pearce, had banished Sam from his life after Sam made him dip his hand into the criminal world one final time.

Then there was Mel.

A woman who had, for four months, given Sam a reason to give it all up. Sam's travels had taken him to Glasgow, where he met Mel one night at the small bar that she ran. It was quiet and quaint, and Sam had soon found himself falling for the woman. Her teenage daughter, Cassie, proved to be just as witty and charming as her mother, and for the first time in nearly a decade, Sam had felt the touch of family life.

But he was who he was.

A billionaire's son, Jasper Munroe, had escaped punishment for yet another sexual assault, and Sam, to prove to Cassie that the world could sometimes correct itself, set out to put things right. But in doing so, he put both Mel and Cassie in danger, and for that reason, Sam had to move on.

He left Glasgow, leaving behind fond memories and the hope that one day he would return, and hopeful that Mel would still be holding the heart he left with her.

If he couldn't turn away from the fight for love, then turning his back on it to see the world was out of the question. His time with Corbin was coming to an end, and he would be eternally grateful for everything she'd done for him. But, as he looked across the sun-drenched fields, he knew that beyond the beauty he was appreciating, the murky world still existed.

It was still dominated by those beyond reproach and still designed to keep its boot on the throat of society. People like Olivier Chavet, who had been willing to die to prove that the rich and powerful were corrupt and complicit. Sam felt a twinge of guilt for the man's death, but Corbin had reassured him that it wasn't his fault.

Without Sam, Chavet would have been killed sooner, and because of Sam, the death of Chavet's father had been avenged. It was scant consolation for the young man's death.

The sound of tyres crunching over gravel echoed gently in the distance, and Sam headed back towards the house, passing by the rows of flower beds and fresh vegetables that Corbin kept. She argued that gardening was something that took her mind off the job. He stepped back into the house and through the long, neatly decorated kitchen that was the centre of Corbin's house. Distressed wooden panels ran the length of the kitchen, and in the middle was a large island, a ceramic sink, metal hobs and an array of chopping boards and cooking utensils. The agent, it turned out, was an excellent cook, and Sam's stomach was already beginning to rumble as his mind raced to dinner. With his intention to leave clear, Corbin had demanded she cook him one more meal and had been out all day at the market to get fresh produce. French cuisine was something Sam had always marvelled at, as if it was ingrained in every French native to be a superior cook. He dumped his empty mug in the sink and then walked to the windows that overlooked the gravel-laden driveway that looped around the corner and joined the gravel path that cut through the nearby woodlands. Corbin's house was discreet and tucked away in a beautiful rural wonderland on the outskirts of the metropolis of Paris. It not only provided her with the peace and tranquillity that Sam had been absorbing all morning, but it also gave her the perfect place to lie low if needed.

To disappear off the grid.

Sure enough, Corbin's sleek, black Peugeot sports car rounded the corner and slowed to a stop on the driveway. She stepped out of the driver's seat swiftly, holding two cups of coffee, and Sam smiled. She looked up to the window and Sam waved, but then caught himself as he noticed the concern on her face.

Then a black 4x4 came into view as it rounded the corner and pulled up behind Corbin's car. The windows were tinted, and Sam found himself already headed to the front door. He was a wanted man, and if their luck had finally run out, he would face the consequences with his head held high and with Corbin nowhere near the firing line. He knew she wouldn't allow him to take the blame, but she had a life and a career that she'd dedicated herself to, and Sam wasn't going to allow her to sacrifice it for him. He opened the front door and stepped back out into the sun, squinting as Corbin stepped forward and handed him a coffee.

'Are you okay?' Sam asked. Corbin smiled. Once again, Sam had proven that everybody came before him.

'Yes, but, Sam, you need...'

Sam's focus was gone. His eyes were drawn to the 4x4 as the passenger door flew open, and out stepped a well-built man, wearing a smart, casual suit and an open-collar shirt. His eyes were shielded by a pair of expensive aviator shades and his slick hair, neatly combed, showed flecks of grey as it shimmered in the sun.

Blake.

Floods of memories washed over Sam's brain until it clung to the one in Commissioner Stout's office, where

Blake had stood, oozing with cockiness, and had offered Sam and Singh a job working for the shady organisation he claimed to be a part of. Sam had promptly shut him down, but that night was the last time he'd heard from or saw Amara Singh.

Sam's throat felt dry.

Blake looked at Sam, held up a welcoming hand, and nodded to him.

Sam stepped past Corbin, ignoring the coffee she was holding out to him. His eyes were locked on the driver's door, which flew open.

For the first time in years, Sam felt his heart rate increase as a strange feeling sat in the pit of his stomach.

He saw the foot crunch down on the gravel, then the other, before the door slammed shut and he felt his heart stop for a second.

He felt the air rush from his lungs.

Amara Singh smiled at him.

Blake had already taken a few steps towards Sam, extending a hand of presumed friendship, but Sam just walked by him, not even acknowledging him with a look. With powerful strides, Sam headed straight to Singh, and without a word said between the two of them, he wrapped his muscular arms around her.

She reciprocated and for two whole minutes, the two of them clung to each other as if for dear life.

Feelings of pain, fear, attraction, love and friendship swarmed around the two of them, as they shut out the world and for those few moments, they held each other.

They were both still alive. It was clear that the other was thrilled to see that. Then, reluctantly, Sam relinquished his grip and stepped back, unable to keep the smile from his face.

'Good to see you.'

Singh gently touched Sam's arm.

'You too.'

Sam shot a glance at Blake, who stood, hands on hips, and clearly bored with the whole situation. He turned back to Singh, who now wore a more serious expression.

'What's going on?' Singh bit her lip in anxiety. 'Amara?'

Blake stepped forward, his shoes crunching the stones beneath and cutting through the silence.

'Sam, we need to talk.' Blake shrugged. 'Shall we?'

He motioned to the door of the house, and Sam glanced at Singh, and then to Corbin, who offered him a reassuring nod. Eventually, Sam exhaled and nodded, and then turned to fall in line behind Blake as they headed to the house. As they did, Singh stepped next to Sam and interlinked her fingers with his and then squeezed.

Sam smiled.

But part of him knew, as she held his hand, that he was being led into an ambush.

CHAPTER SEVEN

The three years had been good to Singh.

As soon as they'd entered the house, she'd relinquished her grip on Sam's hand and stepped into the kitchen. Sam cast his eyes over her. The summer dress clung to her well-toned frame, and Sam could see the clear definition in her arm muscles. There wasn't an ounce of fat on her, and Sam knew that whatever fitness regime she was following, it was certainly a strict one.

But there was something else beyond the stylish haircut and the designer dress. Beyond her athletic body.

Confidence.

The first time Sam had met Singh had been on a rainy night over three years before, when she'd been tasked with taking Sam down. Appointed as head of the 'Sam Pope Task Force', Singh had been an ambitious detective trying to climb the corporate ladder in an attempt to spit in the face of the sexism and racism she'd encountered on her climb. She was a prodigal police officer and had drawn scorn from a number of others who envied her ascent. Sam had only just begun his war on crime, and the Met wanted to cut him out below the knees before it gained any momentum. That night, he'd managed to evade an Armed Response Unit that had swarmed Etheridge's house and had then cuffed Singh as she swore revenge.

Ever since then, and up until the moment he'd said goodbye to her in Commissioner Stout's office, he'd always seen a hunger in Singh's eyes. Something that betrayed the powerful and industrious detective. It was a need to be seen for what she was, and the years of a system that put up blockers based on her gender, or her skin colour, had only stoked the flames of her need to be accepted.

But that neediness was gone.

Sam could see it in the way she moved and the way she carried herself. Whatever had happened to her over the last three years, it had been for the best.

Blake stood against the worktop that ran the length of the back wall of the kitchen, his arms folded across his chest. He had removed his sunglasses, and they hung from the open button of his shirt. His eyes glanced around the kitchen, appreciating the tasteful décor and he nodded at Corbin who was shuffling anxiously. Singh took a seat on one of the leather stools that lined one side of the island, crossed one leg over the other, and then turned to Sam, who remained in the doorway.

'Please sit down,' she asked him with a smile that couldn't hide her sorrow.

'Agent Corbin, if you wouldn't mind.' Blake turned to the French woman with a smile.

'No,' Sam said curtly. All eyes fell on him. 'Whatever you have to say to me, you can say in front of her.'

Corbin smiled her thanks to Sam, who nodded. Singh seemed taken aback by their bond, while Blake seemed pleasingly irritated.

'Fine.' Blake cleared his throat.

'So...' Sam shrugged. 'I take it this isn't a social visit?'

Blake stepped forward, asserting his authority as he commanded the attention of the room.

'I'm afraid not. Sam, I have a job for you.'

'Like I told you the first time, I'm not for hire.' Sam looked at Singh, then back at Blake. 'But thanks, though. I appreciate you keeping me in mind.'

'You know, I could have you marched out of here in cuffs…'

'Am I under arrest?'

The two men were slowly edging closer to each other, neither one backing down. After a few steps, their noses were a mere inch or two apart and their eyes were locked in a fierce duel.

'Come on, Sam. If I wanted you arrested, I would have had you in a cell the second you took down Ducard.' Blake smirked. 'You think you're in control, Sam? But understand this, you have no idea of the contacts I have or how far my reach goes—'

'You know what? You sound like Wallace—'

'Stop it!' Singh's voice sliced through the rising, palpable tension and both men turned to face her. She scowled at them both and shook her head. 'If you guys want to put your dicks away, we came here for a reason.'

The two men maintained eye contact for a few more tense moments before Sam sighed and finally took his seat at the island.

'Fine.' Sam relaxed and placed both hands on the marble. 'What's going on?'

Singh regarded Sam for a few moments, unable to keep the smile from her face. She reached across and placed her hand on his forearm.

'It really is good to see you. I wish it was under better circumstances.'

'Meaning?'

'Meaning the shit's hitting the fan in a big way,' Blake

interjected, drawing another scowl from Sam for his troubles. Singh patted Sam's arm to steer him back to her.

'About six months ago, the name Vladimir Balikov fell into our orbit. Nothing too sinister, but during a routine operation involving Russian diplomats which I can't go into, the name Balikov began to pop up. Then, when one of the diplomats ended up murdered, we did some digging. Despite being one of the wealthiest Russians on the planet, the man is essentially a ghost. No known address. No links to any known or registered business. But from what we have been able to gather, he's sitting on a fortune that could buy half of Europe without making a dent.'

Sam looked at Corbin, almost for assurance. She shrugged.

'It's not a name the DGSE has on its radar.' Corbin admitted.

'I'm not surprised.' Singh continued. 'The places we've had to go to dig up some dirt on the man haven't been pretty, but we have been able to build a pretty solid picture, not only of the man and his wealth but also his allegiances. It appears that Balikov belongs to a powerful cabal of older Russian men who still see their motherland as the Soviet Union, and are pretty pissed off with what they believe to be the unfair treatment of their country. To make matters worse, they don't seem particularly pleased with the way their country has handled its exile and—'

'They want to fight back.' Sam finished the sentence, nodding his understanding of the situation.

'Exactly,' Singh confirmed. Sam sat back in his seat and blew out his cheeks.

'I'm not sure I can help. My Russian is a little…non-existent.'

'Very funny,' Blake said dryly. Singh ignored both of them and continued.

'A few months ago, we intercepted a package that our

analyst was able to trace through a number of dummy identities to Balikov that we believe was intended to be part of a prototype bomb.' Sam sat forward, his concern rising. 'It was a pressure gauge, used to arm and detonate a device based on radiation levels.'

'Jesus,' Corbin exclaimed involuntarily.

'Luckily, we took it out of play, but a man of Balikov's resources will just find another. We don't know when or where, but we know it's coming.'

'So, take it to MI5?' Sam suggested with a shrug. 'Surely they would be a better bet than me?'

'This may not come as a shock to you Sam, but there are people at MI5 who don't exactly approve of how we go about our business,' Blake said grimly.

'You're going off the book?' Sam asked with a raised eyebrow.

'Right now, everything we have has been either been dismissed as circumstantial or batted away as nothing more than a theory.' Singh, once again, took control of the conversation. 'But we know that if we don't somehow find a way to Balikov, then this is only the beginning. We can intercept as many packages as we can, but it won't make even the slightest dent.'

'But you don't know where he's based or how to find him?' Sam asked. Singh shook her head. 'Then what?'

'We have a pattern of behaviour. Every year, for the past four years, Balikov has been in Budapest for a two-week period in October. The dates vary ever so slightly, but close enough for it not to be a coincidence.'

'Maybe it's an annual city break?' Sam turned to an already irritated Blake. 'I hear the kebapche is to die for.'

'Well, you will have to let me know…' Blake said with a wry smile. 'Have you ever heard of *Boytsovskaya Yama*?'

Sam shook his head and turned back to Singh.

'Our analyst did some digging, and it appears that

every year, Budapest is the host of an event known as 'The Fight Pit'. Or, as Blake said, *Boytsovskaya Yama*. Sixteen fighters are handpicked from various prisons around the world, each one sponsored by some rich prick with too much money and serious issues. The winner gets to fight with the champion—'

'Balikov's guy?' Sam deduced, and Singh nodded.

'Again, our intel is just made up of fragments of a breadcrumb trail, but considering no one is giving us any support, it's our best shot at getting to Balikov.'

'Hell of a risk,' Sam said as he folded his arms.

'Well, the risk only depends on whether you're as good as people make out, isn't it?'

'Excuse me?' Sam turned to Blake, who was smirking. Singh stood from her chair and reached forward. She wrapped her fingers around Sam's hand.

'For the past few months, I've been working undercover as a Qatar-based heir to a billionaire that our team has created. I've attended events, rubbed shoulders with some, let's say, pretty shitty rich people. But I've got a seat at the table. We've been able to redirect funds from a global terrorist network to pay the entry fee, and in four weeks' time, I'll be in Budapest. We won't know the location until the day before. We won't have any back-up, but like I said, it's our only shot.'

Sam retracted his hand in horror.

'Jesus, Amara. Do you know how much danger you're putting yourself in?'

Singh smiled.

'It's my job, Sam. I'm good at it, too.' She looked at Blake, and then back at Sam with a hopeful look. 'I just need a fighter.'

Like a gavel hitting a judge's desk, the reality of the situation came down on the entire room. Corbin shuffled uncomfortably, her worrying piercing through Sam as she looked at him. Singh's eyes were full of hope as she looked at the man who had saved her life all those years ago. Blake, revelling in his role as the man in charge, stood with his hands on his hip.

Sam chuckled.

'You are kidding me, right?'

'Sam, look at me,' Singh begged. 'I wouldn't be here, asking you if this wasn't the only chance we had to bring this man down.'

Sam turned to Blake, who hadn't budged. He looked at Sam with a rigid glare of authority.

'Why don't you just use one of your own guys?' Sam shrugged.

Blake stepped forward.

'Because each fight is to the death and—'

'And I'm expendable?' Sam cut in. He shook his head in disbelief and then stood. 'It's been nice seeing you, Amara.'

Sam withdrew his hand and stormed across the kitchen, past Corbin who looked on the verge of tears. He threw open the door and marched across the freshly cut grass towards the fence and gazed out once more over the vast greenness of the rolling hills. His fists clenched with anger until his knuckles grew white, and he did his best to calm his anger. As expected, he heard the sound of someone behind him, and the gentle rustle of paper. He turned to find Singh approaching, her hands filled with photos that she'd pulled from the envelope.

'Sam, I'm sorry. But Blake won't sanction this with one of the team.'

'So you thought of me? I'm flattered.' Sam grit his teeth and looked away from her once more. 'I know it's been three years, Amara, but I thought you would have seen me as more than a disposable body for you to throw to the fucking wolves.'

'I'm doing what I have to. Whatever it takes.' Singh's voice boomed with defiance. 'You taught me that. You showed me that sometimes, you have to get a little dirty when you get down in the mud, so don't lecture me on right and wrong, okay?'

Sam turned to her, his body relaxing.

'That's fair. Only difference is, Amara, I did everything to keep you *out* of harm's way.'

Sam looked beyond her to the backdoor of the house where Blake appeared, his hands on his hips and a look of intrigue on his face.

'Look, it's not a one-way street,' Singh said quietly. 'You might have already made your mind up about Blake, but he is one of the good guys. He's willing to put in some calls and give you a little leeway from now on.'

'Leeway?' Sam scoffed.

'Keep the police and the government off your back. Let you clean up the streets while they look the other way.'

'Thanks, but I don't need permission.' Sam looked back out across the field. 'And I'm not going to ask for it now. Like I said, it was nice to see you, Amara.'

Singh sighed and then slapped the photos into Sam's chest.

'This was the result of the last weapon test we could link to Balikov.' She looked at Sam with nothing but anger. 'We predict the next one will be ten times worse.'

Singh turned on her heel and made her way back up the garden towards the house, where Blake watched Sam intently. After a few moments of watching his friend depart, Sam turned the photos over and felt his stomach flip.

Children.

At least twenty of them, strewn among the bodies of other civilians, all of them burnt or mutilated in some way. There was a timestamp and a location at the bottom, but the words were a blur. All he could see was the death of innocence, and it took every ounce of Sam's resolve not to let his own guilt, pain, and memories come flooding back.

His eyes watered.

Every muscle in his body tensed.

Every sensible thought left his brain.

Every feeling he'd held for Amara Singh evaporated.

After a few more seconds of staring at the black and white depiction of the war crimes by Balikov's hand, Sam scrunched the photos into a ball, trying his best to erase them from existence. Rage coursed through his veins as he marched back towards the house, where a victorious Blake stood proudly, and a sheepish Singh stood to one side. Sam slammed the balled-up photos into Singh's arms.

'Fuck you.'

Singh nodded, accepting Sam's rage at the manipulative methods she'd used. He then turned to Blake, and the two men sized each other up one more time, before Blake reached out and slapped Sam on the side of his arm.

'We leave in fifteen minutes.' He looked into the kitchen, where a sorrowful Corbin was sitting at the island in the centre. 'Get your things, say your goodbyes, and meet us out front.'

Sam wanted to respond with every fibre of his being, but instead, he grunted and then obliged, stepping back into the house and disappearing up the stairs as instructed. Blake turned to Singh and raised his eyebrows, before sliding his sunglasses back onto his nose.

'Well done, Singh.' He smiled. 'Good work.'

Singh nodded, and every step she took towards the car she knew was one step closer to Balikov, and another step further away from Sam.

Her heart was broken.

But she'd done what she'd needed to do.

She had her fighter.

CHAPTER EIGHT

The private jet that left Charles de Gaulle Airport was filled with tension and uncomfortable silence, and Sam had little to say to either of the two passengers who had accompanied him. Ever since she'd manipulated him to joining the cause, Singh hadn't even been able to make eye contact with him, as if she was dealing with the realisation that she'd changed their relationship forever. Blake, on the other hand, seemed to have relaxed into his role as the leader of their mission, and on the journey to the airport, he'd even made some friendly comments about the times he'd worked in the famous city and a few of his favourite places to visit. It had caught Sam by surprise, and the last thing he wanted as he dealt with Singh's betrayal was to find himself liking her boss.

Blake was a government agent. He could dress it up however he liked it, but that was the fact of the matter, and ever since his time in Project Hailstorm and the truths he'd uncovered, Sam was now pre-disposed to not trust anyone.

Once they'd got to the airport, Blake had made it clear that he wouldn't cuff Sam, as they didn't want the attention, but any attempt of fleeing would be met with a gunshot that he couldn't guarantee wouldn't be fatal. Sam was happy to oblige them, and as he carried his bags through the airport, he'd marvelled at how oblivious the world truly was to what went on in the shadows. To the naked eye, the three of them were just a group of friends or colleagues, making their way through one of the cultural epicentres of the world. In reality, he was a wanted man, walking beside a secret agency in a desperate attempt to hunt down and stop a nuclear arms dealer.

The jet was waiting for them at a private hanger and Blake made no effort to hide the smug satisfaction of being able to charter one. It was a flex of the government's trust in him, that it would afford such a budget, and Sam had rolled his eyes as he'd boarded, sitting away from both of them and focusing his mind elsewhere.

He thought about Corbin and the gratitude he had for her. Their mission to take down Ducard had forged a bond between them that would last until their dying days, and he hoped there would be a time where he would stand in her garden once more and breathe in the spectacular view. When he'd walked out of her home with his bag over his shoulder, carrying the clothes she'd kindly bought for him, she'd wrapped her arms around him and held him as tightly as she could. Blake had tutted and dropped into the driver's seat as Sam placed down his bag and reciprocated, holding Corbin tenderly. After a few moments, she'd stepped away, refusing to let him see the tears rolling down her cheeks, and she uttered just two words.

'Be careful.'

He was a long way past that point.

Now, he was sitting on a private plane, in the tentative custody of the UK government, heading to an unspecified location to infiltrate an underground, deadly fighting tournament. Blake had taken the seat opposite Singh further up the plane, and while they engaged in a brief discussion, it was clear that Singh wasn't in the mood for talking. Blake extended the invitation for conversation with Sam a few times, which Sam politely declined by turning his head to the window and casting his eyes out at the clouds.

It was only when they touched down at Belgrade Nikola Tesla Airport two and half hours later did he know that they were heading to Serbia, and as he followed Blake and Singh down the steps and into the private hanger on the far side of the runway, the gravity of the situation began to hit him.

There was no going back.

If he did, there was little doubt in his mind that Blake would put him in the smallest cell he could find, in the deepest, darkest corner of the globe.

Then there was Balikov. Despite the horrendous tactics that Singh had used, she'd made the point clear enough. The man was a war criminal, willing to sacrifice the lives of thousands of innocent children to breathe fresh life into his own country.

Even if he wanted to, Sam couldn't turn back.

He had to fight.

They quickly boarded another 4x4 and with Blake behind the wheel, they left the airport and began their journey through the city of Belgrade, which resembled most other European capital cities. Tall buildings, all of them filled with the same global brands that dominated every high street in the world. Tourists roamed around in groups, snapping photos of the local buildings and immersing themselves in the culture. The streets were rammed with traffic, with buses, taxis, and commuters all vying for road space as they funnelled through the intricate light system.

Sam kept his eyes on the window, watching the world go by. He could feel Singh flashing a few glances toward the rear-view mirror in a hopeless attempt to maybe lay the first brick of a bridge.

'You ever been to Belgrade, Sam?' Blake asked, cutting through the tension with his eyes still locked on the road.

'I have now.'

'I hear the *sarma* are to die for,' Blake said, then flashed a grin in the mirror. Sam turned and glared at Blake, but failed to stifle the smile that crept across his face.

'*Touché.*'

That was the last word spoken for the rest of the drive. Once they'd escaped the urban labyrinth that was Belgrade, they cut their way through the gorgeous country-side that surrounded the city. Blake knew the way, ignoring the use of the inbuilt satnav that would have been a neces-sity had Sam been behind the wheel. But then again, Sam didn't have a clue where they were headed, only that what-ever was waiting for him was another step towards fighting for his life for the entertainment of billionaires. The world was a cruel and messed up place, and Sam tried to focus on the beauty that was whizzing past his window to calm his mind.

But all he could see were the images of the dead children.

Their scorched bodies.

Their helpless hands, reaching out for comfort that would never come.

Sam's own hands balled into fists, and he kept the name Balikov in the centre of his mind. Whatever awaited him would be worth it if the man responsible for such atrocities was brought to his knees.

The Serbian countryside fanned out as far as the eye could see, and their wordless journey took them through a small town called Lozovik. They continued south, passing through the municipality of Velika Plana, as well as the town itself. Wonderful, white stone buildings lined the few streets, before Blake turned off and back onto the country roads that stretched across the country like veins. They rounded the town of Markovac, and then continued south, past Lapovo, and into Batočin, where they began to drive alongside the Great Morava River that flowed through the country. The further from Belgrade they travelled, the more deserted and derelict some of the villages became, and Sam was in awe of their rustic charm. Free from the craving of tourism, the villages appeared as if from another time completely, with the simplicity of life as obvious as their lack of tourist attractions. They were soon in the heart of the country, and as they arrived in Paraćin, Blake finally turned off the long motorway and joined another, heading east through long, winding roads where civilisation was in short supply. The woodlands were a magnificent sight to behold, and Sam returned to his thoughts of a holiday once more, and how days spent hiking through such trees would be nothing short of bliss.

He'd be alone.

No fight. No reason.

But that wasn't who he was, and by the time they cut through Boljevic, he could feel himself becoming restless. They'd been driving for over two hours, and the silence had become so ingrained that he didn't even contemplate asking for an ETA. He looked across the vehicle to Blake, who was as composed as ever, guiding the car at a high speed, his sunglasses locked on the road ahead. Beside him, Singh seemed to be asleep.

Eventually, they passed through a few small rows of houses that was known as Podgorac and Blake turned off the main road and onto a dusty, unmarked path that ran through the trees that lined the exit of the village. As the car made its rocky way over the stones, they became engulfed in the woodlands and Sam's mind flashed back to Slaven Kovac's grand home that was hidden away in the

Suffolk woods. Singh stirred, awoke quietly and soon, a large, abandoned looking facility came into view, peeking through the trees and exposing some of its worn, stone exterior to the sunshine. As they approached, Sam could tell the building had long been out of commission, and Blake brought the car to a stop alongside another 4x4 that was spattered with dust and dirt from its journey in.

'Here we go,' Blake said to no one, as he killed the engine.

'Looks nice,' Sam said dryly, looking up at the dull, windowless building.

'It's quite homely when we get inside.' Blake turned with a grin. 'Come on, come and meet the team.'

Blake threw his door open and stepped out, followed swiftly by Singh who made no attempt to even look at Sam. Taking a deep breath, Sam opened his door and stepped out, his trainers crunching on the stone forecourt. Blake was marching towards the thick, wooden door of the building, which opened, and he was soon greeting a muscular black man. They shook hands and stepped in for a hug, and Sam felt a warmth from their camaraderie. The last thing he wanted was to enjoy his time with a covert government operation, but Blake was beginning to make that difficult.

A woman also emerged from the door and was quickly brought in for a hug by Blake, who again, was exuding a leadership that betrayed his arrogance.

Sam watched as the two members of the team disappeared into the building, and Blake turned back to Sam and beckoned him to follow.

Sam closed the car door and obliged him.

———

'Fuckin' hell! It's Sam Pope.'

Hun leapt from his chair with excitement and hurried around the table that sat in the dingy meeting room. Sam felt his cheeks go warm with embarrassment, as the man bounded towards him like an excitable puppy. Blake stepped in.

'Sam, this is Hun,' Blake said with a hint of irritation. 'He's a bit of a fan.'

'Oh, thanks?' Sam offered. Hun's smile was infectious.

'A fan? I think you're a fuckin' legend, mate.' Hun reached out and shook Sam's hand. The cockney accent was a strange juxtaposition with his South Korean complexion, but Sam felt a smile creep across his face. 'Did you really beat the fuck out of Jasper Munroe?'

'Hun…come on now,' Blake said sternly. 'You know the rules.'

'I know sir, but that boy is a right cunt.'

Sam couldn't help but chuckle as Hun winked at Sam and then returned to his seat at the table. The chairs were a mishmash of whatever they could find, and Sam was soon introduced to the other members of Directive One. Amos and Foster, who he'd seen at the door, politely welcomed him, along with a Welsh man named Brady, who looked like an identikit spy.

Handsome. Chiselled jaw. Muscular.

But Sam could see a darkness behind the man's eyes, something that he himself had experienced for years. Once they were all seated and the bottles of water were passed around, Blake went through his pre-rehearsed spiel for Sam, explaining who Directive One were and what they were doing. It wasn't too different to what they'd discussed at Corbin's house, but he did pepper it with information such as how they were defying MI5 by being there and an explanation of the rule he'd alluded to earlier.

Nobody spoke about who they were before Directive One.

The past was the past, and that's where it stayed.

Once all the formalities were out of the way, Blake turned to Sam.

'So, I guess you want to know what happens next?'

'You send me to Budapest and hope I don't die, right?'

Across the table, Hun laughed and drew a glare from Brady.

'What…it was funny?' Hun shrugged. 'And so…so wrong.'

'Excuse me?' Sam looked at Singh. 'I thought that was the plan.'

'Not quite.' Blake stood, removing his jacket to reveal a crisp, white shirt that clung to his athletic frame. He rolled up the sleeves and then stood in his customary pose with his hands on his hips. 'Balikov doesn't just let anyone enter his tournament. It's taken us every play in the book just to get Singh through the door, but even then, they'll be checking everything about her chosen fighter. Their past, what they've done. As much as it pains me to admit it, Sam, you've made a hell of an impact on organised crime, and when you took down Kovalenko and then Kovac, too, well, let's just say it sent a few ripples out into the world.'

'Good,' Sam stated proudly. Amos and Brady nodded in agreement.

'Well, it means they know who Sam Pope is.' Blake sighed. 'So, we need to make you very un-Sam Pope.'

'I have an alias. Jonathan Cooper. It's watertight.'

'Yes, Singh has told us about that, and thankfully, the man who pulled that together did an outstanding job of separating you and Cooper entirely.'

Blake flashed a glance to Hun, who nodded eagerly.

'Sorry, I'm not following,' Sam said with frustration.

'Every fighter that appears in *Boytsovskaya Yama* doesn't just walk in with their MMA team. These people have been through hell and plucked out of places worse than that.' Blake smiled. 'Which means, I get to send you to a Serbian prison for a week or so which, I'm not going to lie, Sam, puts a smile on my face.'

Singh turned to Sam for the first time since she took the seat next to him and reached a hand out and rested it on his shoulder.

'You'll be fine…'

Sam shrugged it off.

'I know,' Sam said curtly. 'Let's face it, I've been in worse places.'

'I doubt that,' Brady chipped in. 'This facility is on twenty-two-hour lockdown. The guards hate every single prisoner in there, and with good reason. War criminals. Rapists. Murderers. The prison is rife with assault and sexual abuse and from what our recon has told us, they don't take kindly to international guests.'

'How's your Serbian, Sam?' Blake asked with a raised eyebrow.

'About as good as my Russian.'

Blake smiled, but that was quickly replaced with a serious expression of concern.

'Look, Amos here will get you ready for what they might throw your way. Hun has already created a lovely four-year journey of your prison life, where you've been moved around countries on account of your violent tendencies.' Blake leant forward. 'You go in one week. Then, you have a week to get yourself into the trials that Singh will arrange with the guards.'

'And how do I get myself into those trials?'

Blake smirked.

'Use your imagination.'

Sam nodded, understanding the remit. In seven days, he was going to be airlifted into the jaws of hell and would have another week to cause as much carnage as possible to build his credibility. Then, when Singh, under her cover as a Qatari billionaire, came calling for her fighter, Sam would need to fight with everything he had.

Blake cut through Sam's contemplation with a few more words.

'So, of course, you're going to have to look the part. I hope you're not too attached to your hair because we'll take that off. But keep the beard, though.' Blake chuckled. 'One last thing. How are you with needles?'

'I can't knit you a scarf, if that's what you're wondering?'

Once again, Hun burst out laughing. Amos, Brady, and Foster chuckled, too. A grin spread across Blake's face before he responded.

'You're going to need more than just those scars on your body for this to be believable. Right, let's get some rest and tomorrow, Amos will start your training.'

With a clap of his hands, Blake stood, dismissing the team who all followed suit and lifted themselves out of their chairs. Hun eagerly volunteered to show Sam to his quarters, and as they began to slowly filter out of the room, Sam caught up with Amos.

'No offence, but I already know how to fight.'

A cruel smile fell upon Amos, who raised an excited eyebrow.

'We'll see.'

CHAPTER NINE

It took a lot to catch Sam Pope by surprise.

Considering the situations he'd placed himself in over the years, whether fighting for his country, undertaking a nefarious mission set by General Wallace, or mounting his own assault on organised crime, Sam had prided himself on being prepared. Even when he went into a situation blind, like storming the Port of Tilbury to find an abducted girl, or fighting his way through Pierre Ducard's estate, Sam was always ready.

He knew that he could rely on his training. His physical strength and ability was one thing, but the mentality not to panic had saved his life on countless occasions. He memorised minor details wherever he went, analysing the steps needed to escape or the angle needed to drive someone's head into a wall to render them unconscious.

He was a walking weapon, ready to react at a moment's notice.

But when he squared off with Amos in the makeshift training room, he found himself thoroughly shaken by how out-skilled he was. The room had once been a storage room, based one level underground, and Amos himself had done some work into making a feasible dojo. All the furniture had been removed, along with any décor that had hung from the walls. Now, all that remained were rusty hooks and the clear outline of where frames had clung to the wall. The floor was solid concrete, but he'd done some work in to lining a portion of it with thin crash mats that offered a paltry comfort when Sam was slammed against them.

And he was.

Endlessly.

Amos was a few years younger than Sam but looked easily a decade younger than that. His boyish face wore patchy stubble, and his hair was pulled tight in to a ponytail of dreadlocks that swung from the back of his skull like a pendulum. Physically, the man was a specimen, and Sam understood instantly why Blake had placed his faith in Amos to get Sam ready for what was ahead. Although the one rule of Directive One meant knowing about Amos's past was off limits, Sam could make a reasonable assumption that the man was a former Marine, and based on how swiftly he rendered Sam to a motionless husk on the floor, had an extensive background in Mixed Martial Arts. After the first hour, in which Sam landed just one paltry blow, Amos mockingly asked Sam if he'd had any training before. When Project Hailstorm plucked elite soldiers from the armed forces and into their pool of assassins, they provided extensive hand-to-hand combat training. Sam had quickly taken to Krav Maga, enjoying the defence and strike nature of the discipline, as well as its ruthless efficiency. Coupled with the striking prowess of Muay Thai, Sam had built himself into a capable fighting machine.

Or so he thought.

Amos was quicker and more direct, penetrating Sam's defences countless times, and often dropping Sam to the hard ground with a trip or a hip toss. To his credit, Amos didn't gloat, seemingly seeing Sam as both a trophy and a challenge at the same time. He was schooling one of the most wanted men in the UK, proving that if he was so inclined, he too could fight his way through an army of gangsters.

It made Sam feel useless, and as the fourth hour of the first morning came to an end with a hard crash onto the concrete, Amos squatted down next to Sam's body, his wrists hanging over his knees, and he smiled.

'Having fun?' Amos said lightly.

Sam looked up at and scowled. The air that had been driven from his lungs on impact was trying desperately to return.

'Fuck you,' Sam responded with a grin, and Amos extended a hand and hauled Sam to his feet. 'Where the hell did you learn to fight like that?'

'Uh-uh.' Amos shook his head. 'You don't need to know. All you need to worry about is how you're going to stop me from wiping the floor with you.' Amos strode across the room and hauled a pair of boxing gloves from the sports bag he'd left in the corner. He also collected two bottles of water and returned to Sam. As he did, Sam lifted himself with visible discomfort and accepted the bottle of water.

He guzzled half of it in one go.

'What are the gloves for?' Sam eventually asked.

'They're for you.' Amos slammed them into Sam's chest. 'Pop them on. We've got a whole afternoon of sparring, Grandad.'

'Ha ha.' Sam replied sarcastically. As he slid his hands into the gloves, he frowned. 'Where are yours?'

'Your cell mates won't have gloves.' Amos shrugged. 'So let's get you ready for that, shall we?'

Sam nodded his understanding, slammed the two

gloves together and then stepped out onto the mats, where Amos was already in his stance.

Fists up.

Feet apart.

Coiled like a venomous snake.

Sam fared a little better with the striking, landing a number of blows to Amos that even sent the expert crashing to the mat. But when he made it through Sam's guard, his fists hit like a sledgehammer, and after a few hours of sparring, Sam's mouth was awash with blood and the cut in his right eyebrow had been re-opened. Even when he drilled Amos with a brutal hook to the gut and then a pin-point uppercut, the man dusted himself off and would yell for Sam to come at him again.

There was no animosity between them.

Just blood, sweat, and the painful acceptance that whatever Sam would be facing in a week's time would be ten times worse.

At the end of the first day, with his body bruised and bloodied, Sam was greeted by Foster, who handed him a towel and took him through to a medical room. The sterile smell burnt the back of Sam's throat, but it at least gave the necessary assurances that it had been cleaned. Like Amos, Sam found Foster to be instantly likable, with her charming smile and genuine compassion, and she gave him a quick examination to ensure Amos's training hadn't caused any real damage. She patched up the cuts and made Sam follow her finger, which always sent him dizzy.

'Sit,' she said, patting the elevated chair that rocked back at an angle. Sam obliged, swinging his feet up and wincing at the thought of being in a dentist's laboratory.

He'd faced heavy fire in Afghanistan, was under siege in the Amazon, and had fought multiple people to the death, but the thought of the dentist still sent a shiver racing down Sam's spine. With a cruel smile, Foster brought the tattoo gun to life. The machine buzzing in her hand. Sam frowned and then turned to Foster as she shuffled her stool nearer to him.

'You've done this before?'

Foster brought the needle to Sam's left shoulder and the ink instantly began to burn into his skin, sending a wave of irritating pain through his body. It felt like a deep cat scratch, and Sam knew he just had to grit his teeth and suck it up.

'Nope,' Foster said cheerily.

'Great.'

Sam was surprised at how likable he found Blake's team, and although his disappointment with Singh was rooted in their history together, Foster's dry humour certainly made the tattoo session bearable. After a few hours, she'd added to his plethora of scars. Only these were rich in black ink.

A barcode across his left shoulder.

A crude tally chart on the inside of his right bicep.

A random sequence of numbers down his right forearm.

'That will do,' Foster said eventually, killing the tattoo gun and dropping it onto the metal tray. Sam cast his eyes over her handiwork.

'These look like shit.' He joked.

'Well, prison tattoos are hardly works of art, are they?' She stood and then rummaged in the drawer of the cabinet that held the metal tray. She pulled out a small tube of Bepanthen and tossed it to him.

'Apply it a few times a day.' She shrugged. 'Should help with the recovery.'

'Isn't this for nappy rash?'

'What do I look like, a doctor?' Foster smirked. Beneath her mousey brown pixie haircut, her face was seemingly permanently happy. Her pretty smile seemed as permanent as the tattoos she crudely provided. Sam chuckled and stood, sliding his T-shirt over his body. And he was a little taken aback at how much his arms ached.

'So, is this your role on the team?' Sam asked. 'Sub-par tattoo work?'

'I can also fuck up a piercing if you like,' Foster replied, with a slight hint of flirtation. 'I assist out in the field, but mainly I work alongside Hun doing surveillance. He might be the computer whiz, but I'm the one who picks up the scent.'

'What did you train in before?' Sam asked and drew a scornful look. 'Oh yeah. The rules.'

'Blake might seem like a bit of a stick in the mud, but he's a good man,' Foster stated. 'Whatever he's asking you to do, just know he's doing it because we have no other choice. Anyway, enough of this heavy shit. Fancy a beer?'

'I don't drink.' Sam shrugged.

'Oh yeah.' Foster palmed her forehead. 'Silly me. Well, the offer is there, Mr Boy Scout.'

Sam smiled and nodded his goodbye, before stepping out of the room and back into the corridors of the complex, knowing that the long list of people he'd killed made him anything but.

Four days later and Sam's entire body was at breaking point. The dull, numbing pain of the tattoos had worn off, and the ink itself was beginning to flake and crumble to the floor. The soreness was still very much alive, enhanced every time Amos landed a clubbing blow to one of his new pieces of artwork.

Sam was surprised at how much four days of intense, continuous fighting could condition him, and although his body was screaming for rest, he felt more alive than ever. As he'd begun to understand Amos's techniques and fight patterns, he'd begun to fight back, flooring his new friend a number of times with well-timed strikes or pinpoint throws. Ever the competitor, Amos seemed to relish the challenge, and Sam's body was a battered and bruised testament to the man's skills. There was no malice between the two, and at the end of their sessions they would sit and discuss the mundane aspects of life, always skirting around their respective paths to this moment.

That evening, after Sam had eaten with the team and then taken a shower, he collapsed onto his bed and stared up at the beige ceiling, his eyes scanning over the cracks as he welcomed the sleep that was beginning to envelope him.

Knock. Knock.

Sam stirred from the doze and lifted himself onto his elbows, his bruised torso doing its best to pin him back to the bed.

'Come in.'

The door opened slowly, and Singh poked her head through the gap, a helpless smile on her face.

'Can I come in?'

'Why?' Sam felt his muscles tense, and he swung his legs over the side of the bed. 'I have nothing to say to you.'

Singh stepped in defiantly.

'Oh, come on, Sam. You've not said a word to me since you got here.'

'Like I said, there's nothing to say.' Sam stood, towering over her. He gestured to the door.

'Look, I know what I did was underhand, but—'

'Underhand?' Sam scoffed. 'Using the guilt I have for my dead son as a trigger to get me to do your bidding. I'd say that's pretty far past underhanded, Amara.'

'I had no other choice.'

'There is always a choice.' Sam felt his voice rise.

'Three years ago, *you* chose to join this team, and *you* chose to walk away from everything. From us.'

'You were going to prison, Sam.' Singh could feel her eyes watering. 'There was never an *us*. You know that.'

Sam sighed. Singh was right, and he put his hands on his hips and blew out his cheeks.

'I just never thought you'd do something like that to me, Amara. After everything we've been through.'

'I'm sorry I hurt you, Sam. But I'm not sorry I did it. You're here, aren't you? So now we have a chance of getting to Balikov, and that's what matters. The end goal is all that matters. You taught me that.'

'And you taught me that actions have consequences.' Sam took a seat on the edge of the bed. 'Like I said, we're done.'

Instead of heading to the door, Singh hurried to the bed and took a seat next to Sam, their shoulders pressed against each other.

'This is bigger than us, Sam. Balikov is a monster on an entirely different level to the pieces of shit you put in the dirt. This man has killed hundreds, possibly thousands, and he will kill more. We can stop that. Stop him. And like Blake said, you make it out of this alive, and instead of being hunted by the police, you'll be given a chance to step out of this grey area you exist in.'

'She's right, Sam.'

Blake's voice boomed from the doorway, and both Sam and Singh looked up at him. His arms were folded across his chest and the sleeves of his open collar shirt were rolled up to the elbow. Despite the man's slick demeanour, the bags under his eyes showed his exhaustion.

'I'm not the one who exists in a grey area.' Sam protested. 'I get what you're trying to do, but every government has an agenda. Every move is calculated, and every action has a reaction. With me, it's black and white. Right and wrong. I'm not doing this so you can open up doors for me or keep the heat off my back. I've been kicking down doors and staying ahead of the police for years now. So *when* I make it out of this alive, I'll go my way and you guys can go back to your grey area.'

Angry tears began to form in the corner of Singh's eyes, and she gingerly reached out and rested a hand on Sam's shoulder as she stood.

'Try to stay safe Sam,' she said feebly. 'You fucking arsehole.'

Singh stormed to the door, barging past Blake who made a token effort to get out of her way. Sam watched her leave, shaking his head with anger and regret. Blake raised his eyebrows and stepped into the room.

'Women, eh?' He joked. 'But she has a point, Sam. We have the chance to stop something big from happening. *You* have the chance to be a part of something bigger than yourself.'

'Save the bullshit Blake. I don't need a pep talk.' Sam lowered himself back down onto the bed to indicate the conversation was over. After a few moments, he looked back up at Blake with irritation. 'We're done here.'

'I know.' Blake nodded. 'Just remember, Sam, you're not the only person in this world who's lost someone. Who's sacrificed something. Who's felt pain.'

'What are you talking about?'

Blake took a considered pause before taking a seat on the edge of Sam's bed. Whatever he was mulling over was clearly painful as he stared straight ahead at the wall.

'Do you want to know why I made it a rule that nobody speaks about their past?'

'Not particularly—'

'It's because it's easy to let what's gone before define who we become. Ten years ago, I was leading a team of agents at MI5. Counter terrorism, you know, that sort of thing. We were tracking a terrorist cell that was bubbling beneath London and we thought we'd taken out the ringleader and shut them down. Only, while we were playing checkers, they were playing chess.' The pain in Blake's voice caused Sam to sit up. Blake continued, his words cracking with sadness. 'In an attempt to strike back against us, they stuck a bomb underneath my car. The next morning, my wife took my daughter to her swimming lesson, and the last time I saw either one of them was as she smiled at me through the windscreen as she went to reverse out of our driveway.'

'Jesus,' Sam said. 'I'm so sorry.'

'MI5 wanted me to take a backseat, but I wanted the opposite. I wanted to go further than we had ever done before and *that* was how I pushed through the idea of Directive One. We operate outside of the usual framework, and you know what, Sam, we do a damn good job of it. Like I said, you're not the only one who has lost something, and similarly, you're not the only one who has something to fight for.'

A silence hung between the two men, filling up Sam's modest room like a leaky tap. Eventually, Sam spoke.

'Is it the same for the others?'

'Not all of them,' Blake said as he stood. 'But I went to all of them when they had nothing left to lose. Gave them a chance to be a part of something bigger. I know this is a one and done deal with you, Sam, possibly because you will be brutally beaten to death, but I know the type of pain that courses through your veins. The anger. The hatred. The need to fight. Deep down, you understand exactly why Singh did what she did, because you would have done the same. So, in two days' time, when you're locked inside that prison, I need you to fight with everything that courses through you. Otherwise, a lot of innocent people are going to die.'

Blake headed to the door, and Sam could feel the man's words pumping through his veins like a shot of adrenaline. Whatever conceived notions he had of the man from their first meeting three years ago had vanished. Replaced by a respect based on mutual loss and the need to fix a broken world. Just as Blake was about to exit the room, Sam called after him.

'Thank you, Blake,' Sam said. 'I'll do my best.'

Blake turned back, the grieving replaced with the usual confidence.

'Don't give them your best, Sam.' Blake smiled. 'Give them hell.'

CHAPTER TEN

The rooftop bar was expensively decorated with wicker seats and glass top tables, the sun glistening off the panels in blinding strips. Along the edges of the rooftop, wooden trellises ran the length of the building, all of them coated with lights and flowers. The bar, which sat at the far end of the building, was an arched construction, with the most expensive liquor hanging from the optics in a neat row. Below them, shelves displayed an extensive selection of the very best alcohol on the market, and young, attractive bartenders were busying themselves preparing drinks.

Singh watched from her table in the far corner, admiring the skill of the muscular man who was shaking a cocktail into existence, before a young woman collected a tray of drinks and took them across to a table where a group of overweight, expensively tailored men leered at her.

Their memberships to the club were an annual five figures from their bank accounts, and it boiled Singh's blood that they believed it gave them the right to harass the young woman as she presented their drinks. As one of them briefly caressed the small of her back, Singh had to grip the arms of her comfy chair to stop herself launching across the venue and hurling the man over the side of the building.

But she couldn't blow her cover.

The maître d' knew her as Aysha Al Ansari, the heir to the Ansari Oil manufacturer and a multi-billion-pound fortune. The last thing they'd expect from someone of such stature would be to beat a group of horny, middle-aged businessmen to within an inch of their lives. It annoyed her, but she knew that she would need to look the other way.

There was a bigger prize to play for.

She reached forward and lifted her mineral water, taking a delicate sip before placing it neatly back on the coaster. The black, Versace dress clung to her body tightly, along with the white blazer and black headscarf, both of which were also emblazoned with the prestigious logo. She looked the part, and Singh knew she needed to act it too.

Across the rooftop from her, standing five feet from the entrance, was Amos. Decked out in a dark suit, with an open-collar black shirt, he stood out as her private security, and even with his sunglasses on, she knew his eyes were constantly scanning the rooftop. The two of them had come a long way since he'd beaten her during her induction into Directive One over three years ago, and they both trusted each other implicitly.

Whatever happened, Amos would have her back.

As two suited men approached the hostess standing at the front of the bar, Amos quickly moved forward, walking with a purpose that oozed intimidation. The maître d' waved them through, and Amos gave both men a quick pat down before nodding curtly, and then turned and headed towards Singh. One of the men who followed was Amos's equivalent.

The other was Artem Alenichev.

Balikov's right-hand man.

A well-groomed man with dark, slick hair, Alenichev sauntered towards Singh with the swagger of a man who knew how far his power stretched. He was in good shape for a man approaching fifty, but under the charming façade, was a brutal man who was capable of unspeakable evil.

Singh had read his file.

Amos took his position behind Singh as Alenichev stepped forward with a broad smile across his face. She stood and elegantly extended her hand, which he took in both of his.

'Miss Al Ansari. A pleasure.' His English was nigh on perfect.

'Please,' Singh replied, offering a hint of an Arabic accent, which she'd perfected. 'Call me Aysha.'

'Aysha.' He nodded. 'Then I am humbly Artem.'

'Please, sit.'

Singh guided Artem to his chair and both of them sat at the same time. The waiter approached and Artem ordered a water under the pretence of respecting Singh's religion, but she knew it was for show. They were two people acting the roles they were assigned and would dance through the necessary steps before they got down to business.

Blood and money.

'I must say, there are places in Serbia of unspeakable beauty.' Artem then gestured towards her. 'But none, I feel, that compares to yourself.'

'Flattery is a tool of a weak man, Artem. I know you are not, so let us talk business.' Artem smiled with approval as she continued. 'I must say, I am a little insulted that Mr Balikov has not come to see me in person.'

'He means no offence. Mr Balikov is a very private

man, Aysha, as I am sure you can appreciate. By sending me, he is extending a massive show of respect.'

'Then shall we discuss our business?' Singh asked confidently.

'We shall, but I must ask, why you would be interested in such a venture? Forgive me, Aysha, but we very rarely find that women are interested in the competition Balikov has created. I would have expected your husband to be here, such is the custom in your country.'

Singh paused for a moment and maintained her eye contact. Alenichev was certainly an engaging character, and the glint in his eye told her he was enjoying the interrogation. Blake had prepped her for their meeting. Their extensive research had already prepared her for the man's forthright charm.

'My husband understands my ambition. My security guard, he's a loyal friend of my family, and as long as I have him with me, I have my husband's permission.

Artem flashed a glance to Amos, who nodded to confirm.

'Very well.'

'And as for my wanting to participate,' Singh continued. 'The same reason Balikov has built *Boytsovskaya Yama*. To break down barriers. To challenge the world. Balikov, as you say, is a private man of immense power, and he has chosen to show this by having the rich and powerful pick their fighter, and then pay money to see who has the best one. There are no rules to say that a woman such as myself, a woman with the wealth to buy Balikov *twice* over, cannot get a seat at the table, are there?' Singh stared at Alenichev, who shook his head. 'Then, like Balikov, I want to lead the way. I want to be the first woman, not only to have a fighter compete in *Boytsovskaya Yama*, but the first woman to own the champion.'

Alenichev sat back in his chair and interlocked his fingers in contemplation. Singh didn't know if it was the heat inching through her headscarf or the nervous tension that sent a droplet of sweat slithering down her spine. After a few moments, Alenichev sat forward and smiled.

'Then let us get you a seat at the table.'

Singh nodded, maintaining her cool.

'Let's.'

Alenichev clicked his fingers, and his private security stepped forward and pulled a phone from his pocket. He handed it to Alenichev, who turned it on its side and began to tap his fingers across the screen. Without looking up, he began to speak.

'The fee of entry is ten million euros. This is non-refundable, even if you fail to secure your competitor. Once payment is received, you will receive your invitation by hand delivery at a pre-designated time and place. The fee is non-refundable if you fail to make the meeting. Is this understood?' Alenichev looked up and Singh nodded. He turned the phone to her. 'This is the account to transfer the money to. You have two minutes.'

Singh lazily waved her hand, and Amos stepped forward. Alenichev cast his eye over her hulking security guard and seemingly impressed, he sat back in his seat. As Amos tapped in the numbers and completed the payment, Alenichev didn't take his eyes from Singh. She held his gaze and then, as Amos stepped back, she turned the phone back to him.

Payment complete.

Alenichev clasped his hands together and stood.

'Is this man your competitor?' He pointed at Amos. 'He will need to lose the suit.'

Singh chuckled and sipped her water.

'No. I was thinking of shopping a little more locally.'

'Ah…' Alenichev buttoned his jacket and smirked. 'Then may I suggest Sremska Mitrovica. If you want the worst this country has to offer, the warden can be easily bought.'

'I do not want the worst, Artem. I want the best.'

Alenichev placed a few notes on the desk to cover the drinks and then flashed his well-rehearsed grin once more.

'Trust me. You want the worst.'

He turned and headed to the exit, followed obediently by his attack dog, and Amos followed them, maintaining his role of security and then taking up his previous position near the entrance. Singh finished her mineral water and then stood, clenching her fists as she let out a sigh of relief.

They were in.

All they needed to do now was to make the meeting with the warden, and then get to the try-out.

And all Sam had to do was survive a week in hell.

———

By the time the convoy pulled through the third set of manned gates that led into the fortress that was Sremska Mitrovica Prison, the sun had already set on the warm summer's day, replaced by a shower that peppered the windscreen like a machine gun. Armed guards checked the credentials of the two men in the front of the truck, and one of them turned their torch onto Sam in the back. He squinted through the brightness. Then a few words were exchanged, and the guards stepped back and signalled for the gate to open.

As the metal slowly retracted, creaking woefully against its mechanisms, Sam felt a sense of dread drop into his stomach. The fortified building was a bland, hopeless looking structure that housed the very worst criminals

Serbia and a number of other countries had ever seen. The prison's legacy stretched back over a hundred years, where it trapped war criminals, rapists, murderers and everything in between and shook them together. Over the years, the prison had been under investigation for countless deaths, with reports of 'mock trials' being held by the sadistic guards who dished out their own sentencing.

Inmates were found, beaten to the brink of death, and left to expire in their own piss and blood.

As the final metal gate slowly closed behind the vehicle, Sam cast one glance back to the road beyond, and watched as his path to freedom slammed shut.

He'd entered hell.

It had been a long process to get him into the prison itself, with Blake taking Sam to a police station in Velika Plana, whereupon arrival, Blake presented himself as an Interpol agent. Hun, working his magic back at the compound, had created the necessary paper trail that backed up all of Blake's lies, and the false story that he had Jonathan Cooper, a wanted murderer, in custody. The authority had already been passed through to transport the man to Sremska Mitrovica Prison, where he would see out the sentence that Hun had certified through the Serbian legal systems network, laughing as he danced around their firewalls with minimal fuss. Blake, impressing Sam with his Serbian, charmed the police chief who agreed to have Sam in their cells until he could obtain the authority for the transfer.

Two hours later, they were ready to make the trip, and as Blake led Sam to the back of the 4x4, he uttered his orders one last time.

'Give em' hell.'

The remit was clear, and Sam had kept it at the front of his mind for the entire journey, but now, with the gates closed and his freedom stripped, there was a sense of doubt that hung over everything like a thick rain cloud.

He was the most wanted man in the UK and now he'd been stuffed in the darkest corner of Europe. There was a chance that they could leave him there to rot.

The door flung open and Sam was roughly hauled from the backseat and shoved forward. The chains that locked his hands together were connected to the ones that were attached to his ankles, and he struggled to keep his footing. He slipped on the wet stones and crashed forward, drawing a few chuckles from the guards who watched through the smoke of their cigarettes. One of the guards approached and helped him to his feet.

'You. English?' the man asked with a thick accent that tried its best to overpower his words. Sam nodded. 'Then you are a very long way from home.'

'Tell me about it,' Sam snarled, shooting a glare at the guards and bringing their laughter to an abrupt stop. The rain clattered down around them as the English-speaking guard sized him up.

'Come. Follow.'

He turned and headed towards the front of the facility and Sam struggled to follow through his restraints. The two armed guards who flanked him clearly didn't sympathise, and every ten seconds or so, they roughly shoved him forward to pick up the pace. The English-speaking guard spoke through the radio affixed to the side of the metal door and it was swiftly followed by a harsh buzz. The door opened, and Sam was pushed through, his chains clinking loudly over the grunts of his guards.

The next hour developed as he expected.

There were countless security stops as they descended further into the prison, with each set of guards offering Sam nothing but a look of disgust that harboured a promise of the horror that awaited him. Eventually, they came to a room where he was unshackled and then, at gunpoint, forced to strip off his jeans and T-shirt. While one of the guards gave him an uncomfortable search, the other guard made a comment in his native tongue.

'What did he say?' Sam asked.

'He said you will probably be adding to your collection,' the other guard responded, pointing to the litany of scars that dominated Sam's torso.

'Great,' Sam said with a sigh, and he was then tossed his orange T-shirt and trousers, along with a pair of ill-fitting white plimsols. Nobody had asked for his size, and he was pretty certain they didn't care. They left the shackles off him, motioning to their weapons, which Sam was certain they had no hesitation in using. Flanked by the two armed guards, Sam followed his tour guide further into the prison. As he did, the man relayed the rules to him.

'The prison is on lockdown for twenty-two hours. You will have one hour of outside exercise. You will have two thirty-minute eating periods. Three showers per week. Any acts of defiance towards the guards are met with extreme force. Any acts of violence to prisoners or guards will result in extreme force and solitary confinement. Is this understood?'

Sam nodded.

'I think I got all that.'

'You're surprisingly calm about where you are right now,' the man stated with a raised eyebrow. He unlocked a metal door and ushered Sam inside. A metal bed ran the length of the tiny cell. Opposite was a metal toilet with no seat and a half-used toilet roll. A sliver of a window was built into the wall just beneath the ceiling, offering the faintest hint of the outside world. Sam stepped in and turned back to the three men.

'Thanks for the tour,' he said with a shrug. The

English-speaking guard motioned for the other guards to leave which they did, and he turned to Sam, who had already lowered himself onto the edge of the stone-cold metal slab.

'We bring all new guests in this late. Do you know why?'

'I'm guessing it's not the conversation,' Sam said with a smile. The man scoffed, slightly uneased by Sam's lack of concern.

'It is because we want them to have one last good night's sleep. Tomorrow, you will be moved into your actual cell and then we will do our best, but it is up to the inmate if they sink or swim.' The man sighed as he headed to the door. 'My advice, Mr Cooper, is say nothing. The nationalists do not take kindly to tourists.'

The guard stepped out into the corridor and hauled the thick metal door shut with a clang that bounced around Sam's cell like a ping-pong ball.

'How about some extra security?' Sam yelled out. The guard appeared at the thin hatch and looked at Sam with a forgiving stare.

'I'm afraid we don't offer new inmates extra security. Warden's orders.'

Sam chuckled as he swung his legs up onto the metal and laid back against it, looking up at the ceiling.

'It's not for me.'

Sam's chilling warning stopped the guard for a second, and then after a moment to collect himself, he wished Sam good luck and slid the hatch shut. As the man's footsteps disappeared down the corridor, Sam stared up at the ceiling of his cell.

The lights shut off.

As he stared into the darkness, he took a few deep breaths, contemplated the situation, and then decided to try to get some sleep. As he drifted off, Blake's orders echoed in his mind.

Sam was now locked in hell on earth.

The only way out was to do what he was sent in to do.

Fight.

CHAPTER ELEVEN

A deafening clang of metal cut through Sam's consciousness, and he blinked himself awake. As the sound of the lock twisting signalled the arrival of the guards, Sam yawned, stretched, and then swung his legs over the side of the bed.

His whole body ached.

It had been over a month since he'd fought Laurent Cissé to the death inside Ducard's mansion, but the scars of that battle still remained. Spending a week being beaten from pillar to post by Amos had certainly added to the numbness that was coiled around his spine.

With a tired hand, he reached back and tried to rub the stiffness from his neck as the English-speaking guard stepped into the room. His firearm was strapped to his hip, as were the weapons of the other two guards who stood by the door. The hatred in their eyes told Sam that if he needed any assistance, it wouldn't be forthcoming. The guard stood before Sam, hands on hips, and sighed.

'It is time.'

'Fantastic,' Sam uttered, pushing himself off the cold metal bed, and he held his fists forward. The chains were re-applied, and with a sympathetic smile, the guard turned and led Sam from the safe haven of his cell. With every step, Sam could feel the tension building. The guards became more alert, their movements more precise as they approached the thick metal door that led to the prison. The guard had a brief conversation with the doorman, and then the two keys were entered into their panels, turned at the same time, and revealed another lock. Sam's tour guide stepped forward with the third key and, eventually, the gate to hell was opened.

A rhythmic beating of the metal bars echoed through the corridor like a heartbeat, with angry slurs flying in from every direction. Sam knew he was being paraded to the whole prison. He cast his eyes up past the staircases and walkways, to the three levels of cells, where brutish criminals pressed against the bars, all of them eager to catch a glimpse of the fresh meat that had been brought in for them.

Threats of rape.

Threats of murder.

Threats of worse.

Saliva flew from some of the cells, antagonising one of the guards who barked a threat back at the spitter. The entire facility had erupted into a cauldron of hostility, and Sam knew it was all for him. Considering the sadistic ways of some of the guards, the likelihood of the prisoners being informed that an Englishman had been sent to their turf was high. As they climbed up the steps to the second floor, Sam locked eyes with an older prisoner, whose gaze was locked onto Sam like a heat-seeking missile. The man's head was shaved to the scalp, and a myriad of tattoos ran across his arms and

peeked out from the collar of his shirt.

A swastika was emblazoned on the centre of his throat.

'Look away,' the guard uttered from the corner of his mouth.

Sam waved instead.

The man stepped closer to the bars in an act of intimidation, and Sam offered him a cursory look back as they headed down the walkway, only to be shoved in the face by one of the guards.

More threats were hurled.

Another prisoner urinated through the bars at them. The two trailing guards stopped, unlocked the door, and Sam could hear the viciousness of their strikes and the roar of approval from the other inmates. As Sam was ushered into his cell, he looked back to briefly catch a glimpse of the guards rubbing the bloodied and beaten face of the perpetrator in his own piss.

'Charming,' Sam said with a shake of the head. He stepped into the cell. The walls were made of crumbling brick, which were engraved with etchings from previous occupants. Numerous tallies were scratched into the brick.

A rusty bed sat in the corner, with a mattress that looked like it had been beaten half to the death. There was no pillow or blanket, and beside it, a grotesquely stained toilet hung from the wall. Like the previous cell, a small sliver of light was afforded by a window the size of a brick.

'This is you,' the guard said shamefully. 'Like I said before, just try to keep your head down.'

'I don't think that's going to be an option. Do you?' Sam asked. The silence was an answer enough. The other two guards arrived at the door, smirking from the beating they'd just delivered. The English-speaking guard once again ran through the house rules pertaining to lockdown and behaviour, and Sam nodded half-heartedly. The idea that everyone was kept under lock and key was fanciful. In every prison, there was a hierarchy. Even in The Grid, Sam had been shocked at the preferential treatment of

Harry Chapman, one of the most powerful gangsters the UK had ever known. Considering the prison was supposed to be a fortress, the man had his own private rooms and the freedom of the facility.

Sam doubted that Sremska Mitrovica was any different, and he was certain he'd have visitors soon enough. The idea that the guards ran the prison was a fallacy.

In hell, the devil reigns supreme, and considering the makeup of the prison's residents, Sam was certain that the devil himself was somewhere nearby.

As the guard finished relaying the house rules, he clasped his hands together and blew out his cheeks.

'Before I go, Mr Cooper, is there anything else you may need?'

Sam looked around the pitiful room and shrugged.

'I assume there isn't a Wi-Fi code?'

Again, the guard seemed perplexed by Sam's lack of fear, and he shook his head.

'Good luck.'

The guard turned on his heels and marched out of the room, closing and locking the cell door behind him. The other two guards sneered at Sam before following, and as the three men ventured away from Sam's cell, they were once again subjected to a barrage of abuse. Sam sat on the edge of his bed and looked out through the bars of his cell. Across the chasm between the walkways, he locked eyes with a few prisoners in their cells.

Some of them bared their teeth like rabid dogs.

Others smirked with malicious intent.

Either way, Sam knew they were all working out the best way to get to him, and how much fun they'd have when they did. It made him think of the horror that some other 'tourists' must have faced in the prison, but then remembered the criteria to get in.

If there was a hell, then he was certainly in it.

And as he laid back on the lumpy mattress, he knew that it wouldn't be long until he showed all of those in attendance exactly why he was there.

The morning went by without incident.

Sam spent the majority of the time doing push-ups, dropping to the concrete floor in fifteen-minute intervals and pushing his muscles until they burned. As he did, threats were hurled throughout the prison, the vile words echoing from cell to cell. The time in lockdown didn't bother Sam.

His decade as a sniper had taught him many things, and patience and stillness of mind were two of them. Prison was originally designed as a construct to punish those who broke the law, as much as it was to keep the public safe. Although the violence and sexual assault was systemic throughout every prison system the world over, the biggest punishment was the effect it had on the mind. Squirrelled away in a hellhole, locked behind bars like an animal, was a process designed to cause criminals to crumble.

A person could take multiple hits to the body and recover.

But once the mind was broken, it was permanent.

Throughout his entire tenure as an elite sniper, Sam had been able to keep his thoughts and his breathing in check. He'd spent days sitting in the same place, not moving a muscle, his sole focus on the space where his unfortunate target would eventually take their final step. The only thing that threatened his sanity was Jamie's death, and although Sam ended up clinging to the final strand of his rope, he'd managed to haul himself back to a better place.

It's why he'd given up alcohol.

It was why he'd thrown himself back into the fight.

And it was why he was willing to walk into one of the most dangerous prisons on the planet, with the express intent of causing trouble.

Purpose.

That was what he had that separated him from his neighbours. While they may have carried out their crimes for more sinister pleasures, it was likely that Sam had more blood on his hands than the entire prison roster combined.

But he'd done it for a reason.

He was fighting for something.

During the morning meal break, the guards led the prisoners out in five separate sections, minimising the opportunity of being overrun by the temporarily released inmates and to lower the risk of violence. Sam's venture to what passed as a cafeteria was in the fourth group of the morning, and although all eyes were on him as he slid his tray down the line, nobody made a move.

Sam met every gaze with one of his own, daring someone to make the first move.

Nobody did.

During the hour of exercise permitted to Sam's group, he made his way to the courtyard where a group of tattooed skinheads were hogging the weight bench, grunting and back slapping as they put their impressive physiques through the ringer. The weather had taken a slight turn, and the enclosed quarters of the courtyard offered minimal sunshine and contained the chill of the wind, so it remained constant. Sam took a seat on a bench where he could see the entire courtyard, keeping his eyes peeled for the first person to take a step towards him.

He sat in isolation as he studied the bodybuilders, all of whom shot him menacing glances and paraded their swastika tattoos with pride. It was a show of intimidation, and halfway through the hour, the gate opened once more and the older gentleman who Sam had waved to marched confidently out onto the courtyard. It was a show of power to Sam and the rest of the inmates.

The curfew didn't apply to him.

The adjoining courtyard was sectioned off by another metal gate and behind it, three segregated areas were under lock and key. They were outdoor prisons, lined with a thick tarp that shut off the occupant from the watching world. Sam watched with interest as a guard walked the length of the courtyard to the small cage on the left-hand side and opened it, beckoning a prisoner out. The man was naked, beaten, and in need of a good meal.

'Solitary.' The thick accent of the guard cut through Sam's thought process. Sam turned to the man who had welcomed him to the prison. 'They get half an hour of confined air.'

'Do they get clothes?'

'Sometimes.' The guard shrugged. 'But the cages get very hot.'

'You guys didn't tell me you had a sauna.' Sam joked, before turning his focus back to the group of neo-Nazis. The leader was smirking at Sam with murderous intent.

'That is Ivan Kostić.' The guard warned, his voice shaking slightly. 'He has, how do you say, loyal people?'

'He's a Nazi.'

'He is very powerful.' The guard lowered his voice. 'We try to do what we can, but we have to survive in here as much as the prisoners. A man like Kostic, he has reach outside of this prison that means—'

'That means he can do whatever he wants.'

A shrill alarm cut through the brisk air, signalling the end of the exercise session. As the prisoners began to shuffle back towards the exit, the armed guards made a show of their automatic rifles. Above them, located in strategically placed towers, other guards trained their rifles on the herd. Kostic turned once more to Sam and mockingly reciprocated his wave.

Sam chuckled. The guard stepped alongside Sam as he headed across the courtyard.

'Be careful, Mr Cooper. He is very dangerous.'

Sam clenched his jaw and turned to the young guard.

'So am I.'

The evening venture to the cafeteria felt different.

As Sam stepped through the door, he felt the hush course through the room like a wave. As the voices lowered, all eyes turned to him, as if they were waiting for his appearance with eager eyes. Unfazed, he stepped past the guard, who sneered at him as if he was keeping a secret.

'Evening.' Sam nodded, lifted his metal tray then walked along the metal counter. Behind the plastic coverings, an unhygienic chef lazily lifted a spoon and slapped a beige paste onto Sam's plate, followed by some dry-looking vegetables. Sam blew out his cheeks in bewilderment, his stomach grumbling as it begged him for some normal food.

He collected his thin cardboard spoon and walked to the nearest empty table. Purposefully, he slammed his tray down before glaring at the rest of the room.

A few eyes darted away.

Others watched on with intrigue.

Sam had already clocked Kostic and three of his followers heading his way. Calmly, he shovelled some of the tasteless sludge into his mouth and only looked up as Kostic took the seat opposite him.

'Please, sit down,' Sam said dryly, sitting back in his chair.

Kostic's men spread out slightly. Sam calculated the steps between each man.

Always processing.

'You are lost, Mr Cooper,' Kostic said in an accent heavy enough to drown the words.

'You know my name.' Sam shrugged. 'Call me John.'

'John.' Kostic smirked, revealing his stained mishmash of teeth. 'It is not often we get an Englishman in this prison.'

'It's your lucky day, then.'

'Oh, it is. The last Englishman we had, I spent four months fucking him to death.' Another smile. 'He was very sweet boy.'

'Well, it sounds like you treated him very well.'

'You do not worry that this is your life now?' Kostic chuckled. 'This is my prison, John. These guards, they keep you safe a little, but when the lights go off, the doors will open and then…well…you can decide then.'

'Your English is very good,' Sam said with a mouth full of food. 'Your pick-up lines…not so much.'

'You do not fear me.' Kostic sat back and straightened his neck, making a display of his venomous tattoo. 'That is a mistake.'

'No, Ivan…and yeah, I know who you are, too. You've made a mistake.' Sam could see the man's eyes flaring with rage. 'You've interrupted my first dinner here, and although it is one of the worst things I've ever tasted, I was looking forward to it. Now listen. I'm not interested in joining your little boys' club, I'm certainly not interested in rolling around the bed with you, and I'd highly recommend you tell your friend to stop eyeballing me like that.'

Kostic's snarl flickered, and he gave a curt nod.

The henchman to Sam's left launched forward, his

right hand driving towards Sam's face with a carved shiv intended to maim. Sam arched back at the last second, letting the rough blade skim his cheek before he drove his elbow down onto the man's forearm. As he did, he pulled the arm straight by the wrist with his other hand.

The snap of the bone echoed through the room.

The man's howl of pain was gut wrenching.

Pinned to the table, the man relinquished the blade, which Sam swiped up and then drove into the back of the man's hand, the metal ripping through the skin and cartilage and embedding in the wood underneath.

Shocked, Kostic sat back, and before the guards set upon them like a pack of rabid dogs, he directed another one of his tattooed thugs toward Sam. As the man approached, Sam wrapped his fingers around the metal tray and swung it full force into the man's throat. The impact crushed the man's trachea and as his hands shot to the injury in panic, Sam followed it up with a right hook that knocked the man's jawbone loose.

The entire room shook with the cheers of the bloodthirsty crowd, and before Sam could make his next move, three guards took him off his feet to the hard, concrete floor and began raining down on him with their metal batons. He held his arms up to protect his skull; the pain being absorbed by his thick biceps. He felt himself being dragged away, and as he looked back, he could see the wild eyes of Kostic burning through the crowd.

He heard the utterance of solitary confinement, but as he arched his head up to look at one of the guards, he was met with a hammer-like fist that sent everything black.

CHAPTER TWELVE

'Confined air.'

That's what the boxes were marketed as by the guards, but Sam soon realised they were built for torture. He'd spent his second night at Sremska Mitrovica in solitary confinement after he'd been dragged from the cafeteria. The guards had roughly hauled him down the stairs. The impact on his spine had shunted him back to consciousness. The prison was alive with ferocity, with those in their cells banging the metal bars with excitement, as rumour spread of Sam's defiance to Kostic like a disease.

The dumb Englishman had signed his own death warrant.

Compared to solitary confinement, the main prison was luxurious, as Sam was shunted through two more metal doors to a dark and damp corridor, where a lone bulb hung from a fixture, flicking intermittently. There were three cells, all of them built into the underground foundation of the prison, and before Sam was thrown into one of them and shrouded in darkness, a few of the guards took a few more cheap shots with their batons.

For the entire night, Sam had laid on the concrete

floor, his head sticky with blood and his body humming with pain. The cell was more of a pit, with no light, bed, or toilet.

In the morning, there was no trip to the cafeteria.

Although Sremska Mitrovica stripped back its prisoners' rights to the most basic of them all, even those were denied in solitary.

With no concept of time, Sam was stirred from a hazy doze by the clang of the metal door, and two guards set upon him, hoisting him up from the ground after a few hard kicks and then hurried him back through the prison to the segregated courtyard. Without a word about his wellbeing, they tossed him into one of the tarp-covered cages and locked the door, chuckling as they walked away.

The heat was intense.

The brisk wind of the day before had disappeared, and as the hot summer sun bore down on the prison, Sam's own personal courtyard quickly became a furnace. He peeled his orange T-shirt from his body, the garment heavy with sweat. He took a few deep breaths and then approached the chain-link door, hoping to breathe through some fresher air. As he rested his head against the metal, something slammed against it, shaking the cage and pushing him back. The English-speaking guard appeared from the right-hand side, baton in hand, and a forlorn look on his face.

'You should have listened to me,' he said firmly. 'You are in serious danger.'

'I know,' Sam replied. 'I guess I'm not very good at making friends.'

'This is serious, Mr Cooper. I am here to warn you that Kostic is on his way. Out here, you are sitting duck. The watchers in the tower have taken a break and soon, the gate on the far end will open and Kostic and his men will be let through with the key to this cage.'

'Then stop them.'

'I can't.' The guard shook his head. 'I don't agree with it, but it is safer for us and our families to let Kostic have certain privileges—'

'And letting me die.' Sam slammed his hands against the fence. 'What's your name?'

'We don't tell the prisoners our names—'

'Fuck off. You just told me I'm going to be killed in the next few minutes. At least tell me your name.'

'Goran.'

Right on queue, a guard appeared across the main courtyard, scurrying with fear as he glanced over his shoulder. Trapped within the small walkway between the two courtyards, the guard struggled to handle the ring of keys in his hand, shooting tentative glances over his shoulder before finally finding the one for the lock.

'Goran…' Sam began, but the colour draining from the guard's face told him all he needed to know.

'Oh…shit,' Goran finally stammered. The guard successfully unlocked the gate, shot Goran a worried look, before sprinting as fast as he could up the walkway and back into the prison. Within seconds, Kostic and his men appeared, walking casually through the walkway, their shirtless, ink-covered torsos basking in the sunshine.

'Goran, listen to me. Unlock my gate.'

'I have to go.'

'Unlock the fucking gate!' Sam spat, sweat streaming down his shaved head and losing itself within his beard. 'Please. Give me a fighting chance.'

Beyond the fence, Kostic gave a shrill whistle, an indication for Goran to make his leave. The young guard turned back to Sam, his eyes wide with fear, and he slyly slid the key into the lock and turned it.

The lock snapped open.

'Good luck,' Goran uttered under his breath. Sam

nodded his thanks, and then held the door in place as the young guard scurried across the courtyard, past Kostic and his men and dashed as fast as he could out of sight. Kostic watched him leave, turned back to Sam, and shrugged. Flanked by four, identikit, musclebound neo-Nazis, Kostic began to stride towards Sam's cage, with his henchmen slowly fanning out into a blockade.

They had him penned in.

A lamb to the slaughter.

Sam played along, looking down at the ground in defeat as he clung to the door of his cage, holding it in place. Kostic stopped six feet from the door, clasped his hands together, and laughed.

'What is it you said to me...I made mistake?' Kostic turned to his men who all laughed on demand. 'Tell me, how is my mistake working for you?'

'Look, I'm sorry,' Sam pleaded. 'We don't need to do this.'

'*We* don't. *I* do.' Kostic nodded to the man to his left, who made his way towards the door. 'I'm going to fuck you and kill you, Mr Cooper. I'm just not sure which way round will be the most disrespectful.'

Sam ignored the threat. His eyes scanned the group that were excitedly watching their friend approach the gate, and his eyes devoured as much as they could. One of the gang members was holding a metal pipe. Another had a crudely made shiv. Kostic and the other gang member weren't armed.

Kostic was approximately six feet from the door. The other men, eight or nine.

It would give him a few steps before they set upon him.

It's all he would need.

The sneering skinhead approached the cage and shook his head at Sam, who turned away in pretend fear, ensuring he held the door in place with one hand. With his other, he rubbed his eyes.

Kostic laughed again.

'Now is certainly the time to cry, Mr Cooper.'

As the key entered the lock, Sam let go of the door and took one step back. Kostic's goon turned the key, but his brow furrowed as the sound of the lock snapping open didn't come.

His eyes widened with realisation.

Sam took one step forward, and with all his might, drove his foot into the door. It swung open, the metal bar slamming into the henchman's face and sending him stumbling backwards to the ground. As he crashed onto his back, his hands clutching his obliterated nose, a cloud of dust rose around him, as Kostic and his men watched on in shock. Sam's momentum took him clean out of the cage, startling them all, and he darted towards the lone goon on the left-hand side of their formation. Before they even knew what was happening, Sam drove his elbow into the man's throat, slapped his hand onto the man's sweaty scalp and pulled it backwards. Then, with all his might, pressed his palm to the man's jaw and twisted as hard as he could.

The man's neck snapped like a breadstick.

As the man collapsed to the ground, Sam reached down and lifted the self-made blade that the man had dropped and turned to Kostic and his men. Kostic's jaw was open, and for a split-second, a flash of shock echoed in his eyes.

Then it all turned to a hideous scowl as he yelled his orders in Serbian and the two standing henchmen rushed towards Sam. Sam steadied his feet, and as the two men ate up the ground between them, one of them raised the lead pipe in preparation for a killer blow.

Sam spun the shiv round in his hand and pinched the

blade between his index finger and thumb and then launched it forward.

The blade spun through the heat, slicing through the air and embedded into the man's neck, taking him clean off his feet. He hit the ground hard, gasping for air as the oxygen and blood gushed from the wound and the steel pipe clattered beside him. Sam turned just in time to absorb the other man's shoulder tackle into his stomach, the air driven from his body and the man hoisted Sam off his feet and carried on charging until both men slammed into the tarpaulin covered fence. Sam drove his elbows down onto the man's spine, but they had little effect and the brute drove his shoulder once again into Sam's midriff, before lifting him off the ground and driving him down to the ground. The impact shook Sam's entire body, and as the man reared back to drive both fists down onto him, Sam lifted his leg and slammed his foot into the man's jaw. The man rocked back, and Sam planted his foot on the man's chest and pushed him off and both of them scrambled to their feet, and Sam almost slipped in the blood that had pooled around the corpse of one of the gang.

Kostic had hauled up the man who Sam had introduced to the metal door and barked at him to get involved, and Sam clenched his fists and looked at both men.

One of them had blood dribbling from a split lip.

The other, his nose a shattered mess, had blood smeared across his face and he reached down and picked up the now blood-soaked metal pipe.

Beyond them, Kostic watched on with fascination.

Simultaneously, both men charged forward, and Sam followed suit, weaving underneath the first punch thrown before swinging a hard right into the broken nose of the armed thug. Instantly, he felt the other man latch onto his arms from behind, locking them in place, as the other thug swung the pipe into his stomach. Sam grunted with pain and looked up to see the pipe racing towards the top of his skull.

He dropped to his knees.

The sudden shift in weight caught his captor by surprise and he stumbled forward, lurching over Sam's back and taking the full brunt of the metal on the top of his skull. Sam struggled free, just in time to take a hard right hook to the jaw, followed by another to the ribs. The man who had held him captive was out cold, and now he was under the attack from the final henchman standing. The man drove Sam backwards towards the open door of the cage with a brutal kick to the chest and as Sam stumbled through the door; the man swung another wild punch.

Sam pulled the door shut.

The metal clamped on the man's arm, drawing a groan of anguish, and locked the man in place. With one hand, Sam held the door in place, and with his other, he wrenched the man's arm back against the metal frame. The shoulder dislocated with a sickening pop as the tendons ripped, and the man slumped to the ground in agony.

Sam booted open the door and stared at Kostic.

The man, who had felt invincible minutes before, feebly held up his hands and then, as a last throw of the dice, began to slowly clap.

'Impressive,' Kostic said. 'Perhaps we should talk.'

Sam stepped out of the cage, his shirtless torse covered in a mural of scars, ink, sweat, and blood. Gingerly, he reached down and plucked the shiv from the neck of the dead man and then looked up at Kostic and shrugged.

'You didn't seem to want to talk earlier.'

Kostic's façade fell as quickly as his smile.

'Fuck you. This is my prison.'

Sam adjusted his grip on the shiv and then took a menacing step forward.

A gunshot echoed.

A bullet crashed into the concrete less than a foot in front of Sam, sending a fountain of dust and stone into the air. He looked across the courtyard, where a sniper was situated in the watchtower, his gun trained squarely in Sam's direction.

The wailing of the alarm cut through the air, and sure enough, decked out in helmets, vests, and plastic shields, a swarm of guards began filing into the walkway before bursting through the gate. Kostic smirked triumphantly, and Sam held his gaze for a few more moments before tossing the shiv and lifting his hands above his head. As he lowered himself to his knees, he looked back at Kostic, who stood proudly as the guards moved past him.

Another display of his power.

'Like I said. This is my prison.'

With his parting words, Kostic turned and headed back towards the gate, as Sam felt the full force of the metal batons that rained down upon him. Beaten to the very edge of his consciousness, Sam felt his feet lifted from the ground, and the carnage of the courtyard raced past him as he was hauled back towards the dank, dark pit that would be his home for the foreseeable.

He was holding up his end of the bargain.

But with the very real threat of repercussion for his actions looming as large as the blazing sun above, he hoped that Amara Singh would be able to hold up hers.

CHAPTER THIRTEEN

The city skyline of Moscow always filled Vladimir Balikov with a deep sense of pride. A dyed-in-the-wool nationalist, Balikov had always sought out the beauty of the *Motherland* at every opportunity, and due to the exorbitant wealth he'd acquired over his sixty-two years on the planet, he was afforded more opportunities than most.

He frequented the Kremlin due to his personal relationship with the president.

Every secret men's club was honoured by his presence.

Every door to every exclusive restaurant or venue in the country would be thrown open without so much as a word said.

And as he gazed over the edge of the balcony of his penthouse suite, he blew a victorious plume of smoke from his cigar into the night sky and took in the immaculate view.

He felt his fists clench.

While the city itself was stunning to the naked eye, knowing what ran rife within made his blood boil. Generation after generation of Russians who felt that the world was a better place if everyone worked together. Young men and women who protested against the military. Who slandered the great leader of their country and then protested more when their president reminded them of the power he wielded.

A country that had once been the most feared in the world was now demonised, and the lack of respect shown to his beloved *Motherland* sat like a bad taste in the back of Balikov's throat.

And he was ready to wash it away.

During his twenties and thirties, as Balikov began to attain a level of wealth that would fund smaller, lesser countries, he'd lived the high life alongside his fellow oligarchs, splashing insane sums of money on trivial ventures like yachts and property. What was seen as a show of power was nothing more than a lavish show of emptiness. An expensive life had led to expensive women, and while it was seen as a necessity for him to have a supermodel on his arm, Balikov soon found the love of a woman to be as empty as the life he was living.

He desired purpose.

A meaning.

The ultimate power wasn't what resided within his bank account, but what he could do with it. By the age of forty, he'd funded three covert militia groups, all of whom were designed to shake the foundations of the country to rebuild it as the powerhouse it was before.

He threw his wealth into every cause that would lay another brick for the new Russia they planned to build.

He funded presidential campaigns.

He donated to nuclear research.

Anything and everything to help rebuild the country into the image that it used to have.

Then the world went soft.

Russia became soft.

That was when Balikov realised he would need to take

extreme measures to achieve the change he craved, and it had taken four years of careful and expensive manoeuvres, but they were so close.

Poslednyaya Nadezhda were exactly what they were called.

The Final Hope.

A rebel group that had been formed by disgruntled military veterans, dismissed politicians, and disgusted billionaires such as himself. Men and women who had had enough of the new world and were willing to sacrifice it all to rebuild their great country into what it was and should be.

With Balikov's money behind them, *Poslednyaya Nadezhda* had been able to begin plans on building an undetectable and unstoppable nuclear bomb. The production would take years, especially with the world on high alert for Russian activity, and their operation would be run in the shadows of their everyday lives.

Balikov had to continue as the business powerhouse the world knew him as, and in doing so, continued to maintain his commitments both politically and personally. But the time was drawing near. The auto-engage safety lock for the bomb had been designed, and while a prototype had been intercepted, another would soon follow.

Thousands had already been killed by trials of weapons that Balikov had funded, but they were necessary sacrifices for the cause. Their deaths did not weigh on his conscience.

Nor did the fifty-three people he'd killed over the past three decades, whether it be business rivals or overeager police officers.

Anyone who had tried to take from his table.

Anyone who tried to stop him from his mission.

To make Russia the force it should be.

With a deep sigh, Balikov blew out another cloud of thick smoke and turned as the footsteps approached. He was greeted by the perfect smile of Artem Alenichev, who shook his boss's hand enthusiastically.

'*Welcome back,*' Balikov said with a smile. '*I trust all is well.*'

'*No problems,*' Alenichev responded with a firm nod.

'*And the woman?*'

'*She is most interesting,*' Alenichev said, rubbing his chin. '*For someone we know so little about, she has a wealth that rivals your own. And what's more, she has zero concerns about the nature of Boytsovskaya Yama.*'

'*This is troubling you?*' Balikov said with a raised eyebrow.

'*It is hardly the place for a woman of such standing. To pay millions to watch her chosen fighter beat other fighters to death. It seems to betray her gender and her background.*'

'*Artem. Everyone's background is the same. Although the West believe they are above the executions and laws that other countries press upon their people, their own countries were forged in blood and the barbaric treatment of others. Do not hold her country against her, like the world has held ours against us.*'

Alenichev shook his head and grunted.

'*I just have a feeling—*'

'*That is good. Feelings are good and I suggest you hunt down that suspicion and you kill it stone dead.*' Balikov placed a hand on Alenichev's back. '*That is what I pay you for, and if anything slips through the cracks, then it will be you who pays the price.*'

A silence sat between the two of them, both understanding the power dynamic that had always been there. Alenichev was as loyal as anyone Balikov had met, and there was nobody in the world he trusted more than his right-hand man. But like with everything else, failure to live up to the expectation would result in the most serious of punishments.

As Balikov finished his cigar, both men looked out over the city with pride.

'*It truly is beautiful,*' Alenichev finally said, playing on Balikov's love of the view.

'*It is. Worth fighting for.*' Balikov turned and walked back into the penthouse, beckoning Alenichev to follow. '*Do you know why I started Boytsovskaya Yama?*'

'*Competition?*' Alenichev shrugged as they stopped at the elevator, and Balikov pressed the button. The doors opened immediately, and the two men stepped in, each adjusting the buttons of their sharp suits.

'*No.*'

'*I doubt it is for money,*' Alenichev said with a chuckle.

'*It is for the hunger,*' Balikov said with a glint in his eye. The elevator dropped swiftly through the apartment complex, and then as it slowed to the ground floor, Alenichev frowned as it went one further and then stopped at the basement level. The doors opened upon a dark corridor, dimly lit by crude halogen strips that clung to the ceiling. '*Follow me.*'

Alenichev did as he was told, sighing to himself at the brutality he was about to witness. Over his years serving Balikov, he'd ventured down the corridor numerous times, usually to find a doomed individual receiving the tail end of their torture. As Balikov owned the building, only a designated few people had the privilege of access to the underground rooms, and Alenichev knew the violent nature of that particular list.

'*How is Marko's training going?*' Alenichev asked as they walked together. Balikov's face flickered with pride at the mention of his prize fighter, the man who had won every *Boytsovskaya Yama* tournament since its inception.

And the man who also happened to be Balikov's son.

'*He is ready,*' Balikov said with a dismissive hand. '*When I said earlier it is about hunger, that is something we rarely see. You can watch all the competition or sport in the world, but hunger doesn't play any role. There is too much money and prestige showered upon everyone in this world that the need to succeed has all but evaporated.'*

They stepped through a door into a large, open space, with the dim bulbs offering a shadowy view of the figure who was tied to a chair. The man was shaking with terror, his hands and feet bound to the metal and his mouth gagged. His eyes were red from crying, and the puddle of urine underneath his seat was pungent. Balikov continued.

'Boytsovskaya Yama exists to give those with nothing the chance to fight for something. The men chosen, they are plucked from the edges of places where there is no hope. Only fear. And those men are willing to fight to the death for something more. Forced to live on scraps, these men become wild dogs that will kill to eat. It is fascinating to watch.' Balikov nodded proudly. *'And soon, my friend, we will make that the reality for millions of people.'*

Balikov clicked his fingers, and fifty yards away, a metal shutter designed for a garage door began to slide open. The terrifying growling echoed instantly from the darkness, and sure enough, the rabid, saliva-covered teeth of two rottweilers snapped into view. As the door fully retracted, the hulking specimen of Marko Balikov emerged, his hands wrapped in the thick chains that were holding the blood thirsty hounds in place. Balikov took a few steps to his terrified captive and place his hands on the man's shoulders.

'This is Gorav Kalenkov. A man of significant wealth but minimal guts. Like the world we have now, he has a soft underbelly and lacks the willpower to fight for something. He tried to join the cause, then fear led him to threaten me with betrayal.' Balikov shook his head and stepped back to where Alenichev was standing. *'So now, I will show him how wild a hungry dog can be.'*

Balikov turned to his son and nodded, and simply by opening his murderous fist, Marko relinquished his control of the hounds. As the man screamed in terror through his gag, the two rottweilers charged forward, their eyes crazed and their teeth snapping. The first one barrelled straight into Kalenkov's chest, tipping the chair over and then sunk its teeth into the man's neck. The other made light work of the flesh on the man's arms and within seconds, Kalenko was a twitching husk, as blood gushed across the floor and his skin and muscles were ripped from the bone.

Alenichev watched in discomfort but found the most worrying thing about the whole situation was Balikov's reaction.

The man was smiling at what he saw.

The weak being torn apart by the desperate.

As the dogs ripped the final strands of life away from the twitching corpse, Balikov gave a gentle pat on Alenichev's shoulder.

'Do not let me down, Artem.'

Balikov turned and walked back towards the elevator, as Alenichev watched the dogs tear at the flesh, the grotesque sound deafened by Balikov's warning that rung in his ears.

With every frame of the video that passed, Singh had to swallow her guilt at what she was putting Sam through. Strazar Kolarov's office was in stark contrast to the rest of the derelict prison, with its soft furnishings and array of books that lined the bookshelves. As the overseer of Sremska Mitrovica, Kolarov was a daunting presence. His bald head sat upon a stocky frame that even in his later years, looked as sturdy as the pillars that held up the old building. As Sam's brutal assault of Kostic's men played out on the television screen before them, the Strazar's eyes lit up with excitement at the opportunity before him. Singh felt her muscles tighten with fury at the pleasure the man seemed to extract from the violence that existed within his regime, and Singh couldn't shake the feeling that the man reminded her of General Wallace. Behind Kolarov, a few of his guards stood, arms crossed, and they chuckled and shared words about the brutal beating Sam was administering.

Singh winced.

The five on one ambush soon became a two against one as she watched, through the grey CCTV footage, as Sam killed two men with little remorse.

It had been her idea to recruit Sam for the mission, knowing there was no other path to Belikov. The ends would justify the means, but the guilt sat in her stomach like an undercooked meal, threatening to repeat on her at a second's notice.

Sam was fighting for his life.

Her eyes widened with horror as one of the men took the upper hand, drilling Sam into the cage, before Sam improvised and snapped the man's arm in the cage door. As the footage ended with a wave of guards brutally assaulting Sam, Kolarov stopped the video and turned to Singh with a wide smile and a thick accent hanging from his broken English.

'What do you think?'

Singh shot a glance across the room to Amos, who was expertly playing his role as her personal security. Singh snapped back into her own façade and smiled.

'He is good,' she replied in her faux accent. 'I trust what I have offered is more than enough to cover the technicalities.'

'Oh yes, Mrs Al Ansari, your offer is extremely generous.' The Strazar rubbed his hands with greed.

'Then it is done,' Singh stated with a nod.

'Not quite.'

'Excuse me?'

'The opportunity to fight at *Boytsovskaya Yama* is one

that most of the men in this facility cling to. This is a dark hole in the world and these men have been left here to fade away within it.' Kolarov leant forward, lessening the gap between himself and Singh and treating her to his stale breath. 'The trials offer these men hope. A chance to get out and fight for their lives, something they cannot do here.'

Singh nodded to the screen.

'Some do.'

'Ah, that is fighting to survive.' Kolarov shook his head. 'That is different. Fighting just to carry on is one thing. Fighting for a chance to have your life back? That is something entirely different. Give desperate men a flicker of hope, and they fall in line. They keep their heads down. They toe the line. Remove that hope, and they have nothing. And men with nothing to lose, locked in a place such as this, will become uncontrollable.'

Kolarov sat back in his chair, a smug grin across his face. Singh wanted to slam her fist into it, but she relented.

'Fine.' She waved a dismissive hand. 'But that man there, Cooper, he is the one I want.'

'Then he will have to win the trials.'

'That I have no doubts about. My concern is that I am paying you this money for his freedom, and he may not even make it to the trials.' She flashed a glare at the guards, who stopped their whispered conversation. 'Let's just say I do not hold much faith in your men.'

One of the guards frowned and took a step forward, but immediately stepped back as Amos approached. Kolarov held up a hand to end the potential conflict.

'The trials are in two days. Your quite generous donation more than covers the expense of eradicating the man from our records—'

'If he wins…' Singh interjected.

'If he wins. So as a show of good faith, I will put him

in solitary until then and you have my word that he will be left untouched.'

Singh stood, adjusting her expensive jacket and headscarf.

'You have my money. And believe me, if you renege on our deal, you will have worse than hopeless men to contend with. Is that understood?'

Kolarov grinned a row of stained teeth.

'Loud and clear. I look forward to seeing you in two days, Mrs Al Ansari.' His eyes flickered with perverse pleasure. 'You will be in for quite a show.'

Singh marched to the door flanked by the two guards and followed by Amos. Her heart was thumping in her chest as they rushed through the corridors of the harrowing facility, and all Singh could think about was Sam.

He was a survivor.

Hopefully, she'd brought him a little respite.

In a place like Sremska Mitrovica, that would have to be enough.

CHAPTER FOURTEEN

There were a multitude of characteristics that could have been held up as the standout reason for why Director Blake was given the free rein to develop Directive One. Throughout his career in MI5, Blake had shown an uncompromising dedication to every mission sent his way. He was talented, ruthless, and loyal. His good looks, although beginning to fade at the edges, combined with his charm had earnt him the nickname 'Blake Bond' by his colleagues. He was an expert at hand-to-hand combat, efficient with weapons, and talented behind the wheel of a car.

His years as their top field agent put him in good stead for a senior position, which was what would eventually lead to him becoming a target for powerful enemies.

Enemies that took his family from him.

The loss of his wife and child planted a seed of pain in the man that could have blossomed into something darker, but it sent him spiralling headfirst into his work, and his commitment to the safety of the country was something that couldn't be taught or trained.

But the standout characteristic, the one that caught

everyone off guard and cultivated loyalty from his own team, was his inability to panic. Throughout his years as the director of Directive One, Blake had faced threats to himself, his team and the country that could have sent the country into a meltdown. But throughout them all, he'd remained calm, maintained his borderline arrogant composure, and led the team to an outcome that kept everyone alive.

The man was unflappable.

At forty-eight years old, he was too long in the tooth to allow his emotions to cloud his judgement, and when the worst thing that can happen to a man had already shaken his world to its foundations, Blake very rarely felt out of control.

Until now.

As he marched through the corridors of the abandoned Serbian warehouse that was their HQ, he felt the strange sense of a situation falling between the cracks of his fingers. The mission to get close to Balikov had been a longshot, with so many variables that hinged on factors that Blake knew he couldn't influence.

But too much of it rested with Pope.

Too much rested on that man's ability to survive.

As his footsteps echoed against the cold tiles, he made his way through the facility. The decommissioned base was a gloomy tomb and Blake was looking forward to the team leaving the next day. It had been a long week, and with Singh and Amos offsite, he'd found himself worrying about the mission. From their daily check ins, Singh had delivered everything she'd promised. Thanks to Hun's unrivalled abilities, her entire backstory as Aysha Al Ansari had been accepted. There were pages upon pages of information not just about Aysha Al Ansari, but of her family, their company, and the apparently limitless wealth they had created. Hun had been able to forge standings within the stock exchange and any financial system worth its salt in the world, and it dawned on Blake just how dangerous an asset Hun truly was.

Singh had made her connection with Alenichev, who from Amos and Singh's recounting, seemed to buy their cover and accept their entry to the tournament.

And from Singh's harrowing account of Sam's actions in the prison courtyard, the man was doing his level best to survive.

Not just survive.

Flourish.

Blake walked into the large room that the team had turned into a common room and made his way across the vast space to the kitchenette. The rusty sink jutted out from the wall beside a small counter, which was littered with bottles of water. Blake threw open the cupboard beneath and retrieved a bottle of gin, along with a tonic water, and poured himself a glass. He took a long sip, enjoying the refreshing wave that crashed down his throat before he sighed.

'Pour me one.'

Brady's voice caught Blake's attention, and the director spun on his heel.

'I thought you were packing up?' Brady gave a mock salute to signify the completion. Blake nodded. 'Very well.'

Blake rinsed a glass in the sink and quickly concocted Brady's drink before topping up his own. The broad field agent approached, gratefully accepted, and then offered his charming smile.

'To the Serbian prison system,' Brady joked, and Blake scoffed as they clinked glasses, and both took a sip.

'Tell me, Brady. Do you think this will work?'

'The gin? Depends how much you have—'

'Very funny.' Blake frowned. 'No, this whole mission. I

know we're too far gone for it to make a blind bit of difference now. But what's your gut telling you?'

Brady turned and standing next to his boss, leaned against the countertop, and took a considered swig of his drink.

'My gut says it has to.' Brady shrugged. 'We've all seen the pictures. Whatever Singh and Amos need to do, they need to make sure they do it. Otherwise, a lot of innocent people are going to die.'

'I know. But it just feels too…too—'

'Reliant on Sam Pope?' Brady offered, knowing full well it was the right answer.

'Exactly.' Blake finished his drink and went about making another one. Despite being less than two years from fifty, he was still in fantastic shape, and stood next to a man over a decade younger, he looked it. 'There are certain limits we have here at Directive One. I know we're not exactly doing this one by the book, but then that's what we were designed for. MI5 will shit a brick when they finally cotton on to what we've done, but at least when it's with my team, I know what to expect.'

'You don't think Sam will come through?' Brady asked, his eyebrows raised.

'Have a little faith, boys!'

The cockney voice boomed as Hun exploded into the room, his face beaming with a huge grin. Both Blake and Brady couldn't help but feel the mood lift as Hun's youthful exuberance and positive outlook warmed the atmosphere.

'Drink?' Blake offered, and Hun nodded. The director began the now tried and tested process.

'You think Sam will pull through?' Brady asked and Hun turned his nose up at him.

'Come on. Of course he will. That man will rip that prison a new arsehole.'

'I forgot you're his biggest fan,' Brady said with an eye roll. Hun slapped Brady's solid stomach.

'You jealous, babe?' Hun chuckled as Brady swatted him away. 'I've followed Sam since he took down Frank Jackson. He gets shit done.'

'True.' Blake agreed as he handed Hun his drink. 'But the man works alone.'

'I bet he feels pretty fucking alone right now.'

'Are you able to hack into the prison CCTV?' Brady asked and Hun shook his head as he took a sip.

'Already tried. Funnily, the Serbian hell hole isn't up to code with its security monitoring. Funny that.'

'I don't think any of it is funny…' Foster cut into the conversation, seemingly sneaking up on the group as they all turned in surprise. 'One of you boys going to make me a drink, or what?'

'Barman.' Hun chuckled as Blake turned to make the final member of his team a drink. Very quickly, all four of the remaining members of Directive One were standing in a circle, surrounded by the emptiness of their temporary base.

'Well, to our last night,' Blake offered, and all three followed and tipped their glasses to each other.

'How's Singh doing?' Brady asked, a quiver of worry in his voice.

'Fine,' Blake said firmly. 'As I expected. That woman is made of stern stuff.'

'She's bulletproof,' Hun added, and then turned quickly to Brady. 'No offence.'

'None taken.' Brady smiled painfully. 'She's the best we've got. Even my ego can accept that.'

'Plus, you'd make a pretty shit Qatari woman.' Hun joked, and all four of them chuckled. The pressure of the mission, along with the solitude of being hidden away in the hideous building had weighed heavily on them all, and they were due to head to Budapest the following day. As the gin began to flow, so did the relief of this part of the mission coming to a close.

The conversation soon steered away from Singh and Amos's bravery and Sam's horror to something more intimate.

Foster made a point about Brady's bravery in returning from the brink of death.

Hun ribbed her for her bond with Amos and intimated it went beyond friendship.

Blake chastised Hun for his snoring, which had echoed through the building every night.

They drank.

They chatted.

They laughed.

Without realising it, Blake had once again led the team in the needed direction, and as Foster said her goodnights, he understood that the parts of the mission he could control were the ones he needed to focus on. It was his ability to guide as well as command that earned such loyalty, and he thanked his team sincerely for their sacrifices.

Hun stumbled drunkenly to the hallway, and both Brady and Blake watched in amusement as he tumbled into a storeroom with the guarantee of an awful final night's sleep. Blake finished his drink and turned to Brady, who looked a little confused.

'Everything okay, son?'

'I was just thinking, how do you think Pope will react when he realises that you're full of shit?'

'I'll excuse the language...' Blake tapped his finger against Brady's glass. 'But what do you mean?'

'You'll give him leeway with the police? Come on... even you don't have that pull.'

'I had to offer something, didn't I?' Blake shrugged.

'We were asking the man to willingly walk into hell. Remember, this isn't his fight.'

Brady shrugged, finished his drink with one big swig, and then rested his hand on Blake's shoulder.

'That's the thing. It's his fight now. And I guarantee you, he made his mind up the second he saw them photos.'

With a gentle pat goodnight, Brady lifted his hand and headed across the room towards the door. Blake took a moment and called after him.

'Do you think he's a good man?' Blake asked. Brady stopped, took a moment's contemplation, and shrugged.

'I dunno. But I judge a man by his actions, and I'll say this. I can't think of anyone else I'd bet on to make it through.'

Blake nodded, and Brady turned and headed towards the darkness of the corridor. Blake watched his field agent disappear out of sight and then sighed with a grimace.

'Me neither.'

He stuffed the dirty glasses into the sink and then marched towards his own quarters, ready to leave this part of the mission behind.

All he hoped was that Singh, Amos, *and* Pope would all be meeting them in Budapest.

Although the intention of solitary was to punish, Sam had actually appreciated the respite. It had been two days since Kostic and his men had attempted to brutally murder him in the prison yard, and Sam knew there would be consequences for his handiwork.

Two men were dead.

Another two in the prison hospital.

Kostic's power in the prison was palpable, and with his neo-Nazi beliefs powerful enough to draw desperate men to his cause, Sam was certain the man would have been rallying another wave of overeager murderers to visit Sam once more.

But they'd been kept at bay.

After Sam had been hauled from the prison yard, he'd been dumped into the dark room once more. The beating he'd sustained from Kostic's crew and the malicious guards had left his body bloodied and bruised, but he was alive. He found a few hours of sleep, only to be awoken by the thudding of metal against his door, and then three guards entered to give him another swift beating. He pulled himself into a ball, hands over his head, as they rained down with boots and fists.

A message from Kostic?

Perhaps.

But that was the worst of it, and despite only receiving one bowl of watery porridge for his entire segregation, Sam was still relatively relieved with the outcome.

With no food in his system, Sam hadn't needed to use the hole in the corner for anything other than a piss, and even then, the smell just blended in with the stale, dank smell of the prison underbelly. His eyes had become accustomed to the dark, which was little use when the room was void of anything worth looking at, but it at least made his time awake more pleasant. By his rough estimation, he had a day or two left to get by, and if it was spent in the dark confines of the solitary cell, then he'd have survived.

But there were still the trials.

The chance to fight against men with nothing to lose.

Unless Singh had held up her end of the bargain, there was no way he'd be given a chance to fight. His actions, along with Kostic's sway on the prison, would leave him rooted to the darkness, and then he would have to hope that Blake and his team had another plan to get him out.

If not, then he'd be swallowed by Sremska Mitrovica

and Blake would have no other choice but to wash his hands of the whole thing.

He'd have to leave Sam in the deepest, darkest hole in the planet, and Sam would have walked in of his own volition.

The hatch on the door flew open, casting a strip of light into the room that felt blinding. As Sam grunted and threw up his hand, a head appeared at the opening.

'Mr Cooper?' It was Goran. 'Mr Cooper are you alive?'

'For now,' Sam replied drolly and pushed himself up to his feet. He approached the hatch, and as the burning of the brightness subsided, he could just about make out the worry on the guard's face. 'Nice to see you.'

'I wanted to let you know the trials will be tonight.' Goran shook his head. 'It is maybe a chance for you?'

Knowing that Goran had no idea of Sam's true identity or reason, Sam played along.

'Trials?'

'Strazar Kolarov.' Goran lowered his voice and took a quick scan of the area. 'He holds them every year. Inmates can volunteer to fight, and winner gets chance to leave prison. It is disgusting.'

'You mean we can fight for our freedom?'

'No. Winner gets taken by some rich person to a tournament. That's all we know. But they never come back, so either they are free or…'

Goran's voice trailed off, and Sam nodded his understanding.

'Well, it sounds fun.' Sam shrugged. 'Sign me up.'

'That's the thing. This year, the trial is different. The trial is for you.'

'Excuse me?'

'Word is, someone has made offer to take you straight to tournament.' Goran looked around once more, his paranoia hanging from him like a necktie. 'But Strazar says it would cause uproar in the prison…'

'I can imagine.'

'So tonight, buyer wants to see you fight.'

'Why are you telling me this?' Sam asked, approaching the door.

'Because guards are angry. Strazar has kept you in here because of potential money he will make if you win. They aren't getting a cut, so I want you to be aware—'

'They might try something.'

Goran sighed. His eyes told Sam that he'd had enough. Enough of the violence and the constant threats to his safety.

'I have to go.'

'Wait…' Sam called after him, and Goran returned to the hatch. 'I just wanted to thank you for the other day. For unlocking the cage. You saved my life.'

'Trust me…it is not saved yet.'

'Well, you gave me a fighting chance.'

The guard nodded and just as he went to close the hatch, he turned back to Sam, who had returned to the wall, and was lowering himself to the ground once more.

'Can I ask you question?'

'Go for it, Goran,' Sam said with a grimace as he sat.

'Who are you?'

Sam chuckled.

He'd asked himself that a few times during his time in the dark. He wore many hats.

A grieving father.

A dangerous vigilante.

A trained killer.

A hero.

But stripped back and reduced to the barebones, locked away in the most dangerous facility in Europe, where the currency was fear and deprivation, he was only one thing.

The only thing he could be if he had any hope of surviving.

With a wry smile, he looked back up at the hatch and Goran's expectant face.

'I'm a fighter.'

Goran nodded. The hatch closed, and Sam was shrouded in darkness, ready to fight for his life once more.

CHAPTER FIFTEEN

The same sense of foreboding fell over Singh as her car passed through the final metal gate. The drab brick work of Sremska Mitrovic was soaked by the downpour, and the building loomed large, casting the forecourt in a cold, dark shadow. The autumn evening was a mix of sunshine and heavy rain, with the dark clouds winning the wrestling match for control of the sky above. Singh peered through the raindrops that slammed into the window of the car and felt a chill race down her spine at the sight of Strazar Kolarov. The man stood, hands clasped at the base of his spine, while one of his subordinates held an umbrella over his head.

It wasn't the man's stature that didn't sit well with Singh. Nor was it the fact the man clearly took glee in monetising his prisoners as sellable assets.

It was the uncompromising look at the expendability of human life, the same way General Wallace had viewed the world.

But, as the car came to a stop and Amos shot her a knowing glance from the driver's seat, the real reason she felt sick became apparent.

Directive One had treated Sam in exactly the same way. Months of investigation into Balikov's plans had led them to this one and only chance to catch him out in the open, but in doing so, Singh knew she'd put Sam in the worst possible position.

They had sent him to hell.

Made him expendable.

As she stepped out of the car and met Balikov with her own practised smile, her heart broke at the thought of letting this man hold Sam's life in his hands.

'Mrs Al Ansari. Such a pleasure to see you again.' Kolarov snapped his fingers, and another guard appeared, opening up another black umbrella and holding it over her head. She nodded politely. 'I trust your journey was good?'

'As pleasant as expected,' she responded dryly, maintaining her character and slight accent. 'Shall we speak inside?'

'Of course. This way.'

The head of the prison turned and stomped across the stones to the open door, where two guards stood to attention. Singh followed confidently, shadowed by Amos, who made an effort to eyeball every single guard on the way past.

A few looked away.

Others were clearly struggling to hold their contempt for the well-dressed black man they had to open doors for.

His eyes twinkled with the clear message of *'try me'*.

There was a palpable excitement passing among the guards, which Singh understood was due to the trials. Gambling was another vice that was commonplace within the prison system, and the guards were thrilled at the idea of placing high stakes on which inmates would be beaten to within an inch of their lives. Beyond their excitement, the prison felt quiet.

They passed the door to Kolarov's office, and Singh shot a glance back to Amos, but didn't break her stride.

'Are we not watching from your office?' she asked, raising her well tweezed eyebrow.

'Oh no, Mrs Al Ansari. I thought you would want the best seat in the house.'

The strazar flashed her a greedy grin, no doubt already counting the promised cash she would part with once she had her fighter. As they ventured further into the prison, a distant hum began to filter through the air. It grew and grew, and Singh quickly understood it was the roar of the prisoners who were already in situ. A large auditorium had been repurposed as a fighting room, with cages placed around the seating areas to protect the open space in the centre of the room. The concrete floor, despite someone's best efforts with a hose, was stained with old, faded blood, a memory of fighters past.

It made Singh's skin crawl.

Kolarov led Singh and Amos up a flight of stairs and through a narrow walkway, where they emerged onto a balcony that overlooked the entire room. It was ten feet above the highest row of seats, and all of them were partitioned off by thick, metal bars. A safety precaution for the strazar and his guests to enjoy the *'show'* in peace.

'Please.' Kolarov gestured with his hand. Singh nodded and stepped onto the balcony, where all eyes fell on her. The rabid, thirsty mob all began calling to her, many of them making lewd gestures as they did.

Thankfully, Singh didn't understand, but she was certain none of them were offering a romantic meal for two. One prisoner, in the cage beneath, had begun to climb the bars, a fruitless attempt to get closer to her, and two guards set upon him with their metal batons. Singh watched, unmoved, and Kolarov took the seat next to her.

'Forgive them. Many have not seen a woman in years. And none of them have ever seen a woman such as yourself.'

Singh waved off the compliment and glanced to Amos, who stood stoically by the entrance to the balcony. Beside her was one more empty seat, which she eyed with caution. The initial wave of excitement had receded, and an uneasy hush fell across the room. A door on the far side of the auditorium opened, and two guards appeared, followed by a well-built prisoner, who was rolling his shoulders and clearly psyching himself up.

A roar of approval echoed from the baying crowd.

Singh leant in to Kolarov.

'Is this the challenger?'

'One of many, I presume.'

'Many?'

Kolarov turned with a cruel smile.

'My dear, there are many men who want to leave this place.'

'But I am only interested in one—'

'I know…' Kolarov lifted his hand to silence her. 'But like I said, this night is all these men have. So your man will need to fight like he has never fought before.'

Singh frowned, her displeasure clear.

'I trust you have held up your end of the bargain. He has been kept safe?'

'As can be.' Kolarov shrugged. They both knew it was too late for her to hold any power over proceedings. 'However, I will say, the guards have not been happy at the preferential treatment.'

Before Singh could respond, the door to the balcony opened once more. Amos stood to attention, but Kolarov turned and waved him down.

Singh felt her stomach knot.

Artem Alenichev.

As Balikov's right-hand man entered, he wore a smirk that told Singh he was there to specifically make her feel on edge. Despite their meeting seemingly going well the other day, Singh instantly felt the pressure of the situation rise, and she took a calming breath before standing and accepting his advancing hand.

'Mr Alenichev. A pleasant surprise,' she said with a practised grin. He returned in kind.

'Please. Artem.'

He kept his eyes on her as the strazar welcomed him, and the awkward greeting was interrupted as another door opened. The response from the room was entirely different. Never had she imagined that a room built for death, in a structure made for worse, could ever turn more hostile.

But all eyes were on the second door, as two more guards walked out, only this time, their prisoner wasn't in the midst of a warmup.

His wrists and ankles were shackled. They pulled him forward by the chain.

The blood thirsty crowd slammed their hands against the metal partition and spat through the bars.

The prisoner looked around nonchalantly, his eyebrow sporting a fresh cut. His shirtless body rippled with muscles, and was littered with scars, bruises, cuts, and tattoos.

The entire room was a hotbed of violence.

A smile spread across Kolarov's face.

Singh felt her heart stop for a second as Sam looked up at her.

Artem watched intently.

Her fighter had entered the trial.

The guards waited for Sam to remove his shirt before they shackled him, both uttering something in their native tongue that Sam didn't understand. From their tone, he assumed it wasn't complimentary, and he'd hoped that Goran would have been the one to fetch him. In the dark, it was impossible to know who had been attacking him, but judging from the hostility of the guards, they were the likely culprits. With his wrists bound together, he let them fall against his waist; the shackles connected by two feet of solid chain. Standing either side of him, they marched Sam out of the dark bowels of the basement, and up the stairs towards the prison.

A deathly silence had fallen across the facility.

Sam followed the guard through the empty corridors, glancing at the vacant cells as they passed. The guard following would give him the occasional shove, but it was nothing worth responding to. Eventually, the roar of a crowd began to echo, rising in volume with every step as they descended a staircase towards a large outbuilding, which Sam assumed was the arena of battle.

He'd survived.

A week had passed, and despite a few attempts on his life, the lack of food and the occasional beating from the guards, he was still standing. What's more, Goran had insinuated that Singh had done her job.

Sam was in the trials.

All he had to do now was fight.

The rhythmic shunting of the blood-thirsty mob slamming their hands against metal echoed loudly on the other side of the door, and Sam felt his adrenaline begin to bubble within. Throughout his years fighting crime and corruption, he'd found himself on the other side of a fight to the death on countless occasions.

Oleg Kolavenko.

Farukh.

Edinson.

Bowker.

Kovac.

It had been just over a month since he'd battled Laurent Cissé in the kitchen of the Ducard estate, where he ended the man's life with a shard of glass.

Countless men. Countless deaths.

But he was still standing.

Sam Pope was born to survive.

One of the guards threw open the door, and Sam's senses were pulverised by the light and noise. The floor was stained with faded blood, and all around, the inmates slammed their palms against their metal partitions, all of them screaming for Sam's blood. The sound reverberated like a heartbeat, and vile slurs and wads of phlegm rained down from the audience. Guards lined the sides of each section, arms folded, ready to snap into brutal action at a moment's notice. Inmates were readily placing bets with one another, all of them hoping for Sam's demise.

Across the auditorium, one of the inmates Sam had seen in the food hall was waiting. Like Sam, he was shirt-less, but his muscular frame wasn't adorned with the history of war.

It was covered in swastika tattoos.

One of Kostic's crew and the man locked eyes on Sam, and a silent promise of death was shared between them.

One of the guards shoved Sam forward a little further, and Sam glanced up to the balcony that oversaw everything.

Amara.

Next to her was Strazar Kolarov, the man who had read Sam the riot act after the brawl in the courtyard, but who had ensured Sam's arrival at this fight. By locking Sam away from the prison, he'd kept Sam from Kostic's revenge, but in doing so, had angered the rest of the inmates and the guards.

To Singh's left sat a well-groomed man, who kept his eyes on Singh as she caught Sam's gaze, and Sam could only speculate as to who he was.

Somebody dangerous.

Finally, the guards brought Sam to a stop and presented him to the inmates. A ferocious wave of boos consumed the auditorium, and Sam cast another glance to Singh, who kept her composure and cover by not reacting at all. Beside her, the Strazar seemed to be enjoying the spectacle.

One of the guards walked to the middle of the fighting grounds and gestured for silence, which surprisingly, the inmates respected. He laid out the rules.

Sam didn't understand the language.

But he understood the situation.

The last fighter standing would be given the chance to leave the prison.

The ultimate carrot at the end of the stick.

Sam's only concern was how many people were willing to fight for their freedom. The guards raised their hand to Sam's challenger across the auditorium to signify the start of the fight.

The man responded with a vile salute, one which drew cheers and mimicking from countless prisoners.

They turned to Sam, who lifted his wrists for them to unshackle him.

Both guards sneered, turned, and marched quickly towards the exit, leaving Sam to glare after them with his wrists still bound.

The onlooking crowd cheered, and Sam shot one more glance to Singh, who was trying her best to quell her concern.

Sam tested the strength of the chain a few times, snapping it tight to confirm his range of motion, rolled his shoulders, and turned to his opponent, who began to charge.

It was time to fight.

CHAPTER SIXTEEN

FIFTEEN YEARS AGO…

'Get up!'

General Wallace's voice boomed louder than the thunder that was rocking the clouds above, and Sam felt his arms wobble as he tried to push himself up. The rain was crashing down upon his head, washing away the blood that was gushing from his split lip. With his ribs and kidneys screaming for mercy, Sam managed to stand, peering at Wallace through the swelling around his eyes.

'Again, sir,' Sam demanded, feebly lifting his fists to a few chortles from the surrounding gang.

All of them were wearing balaclavas. It was a necessity, as part of the Project Hailstorm initiation meant Sam wasn't allowed to know who of the other members of Wallace's elite task force were hammering him with expert fists. One of them shrugged, took a few steps across the muddy field, and threw a punch, which Sam managed to weave under, before responding with one of his own, taking the man off his feet.

A few of the other masked men took a few steps forward, but Wallace threw his arms out, blocking their path.

Sam raised his split eyebrow in surprise.

'You're still willing to fight?' Wallace asked, seemingly impressed with the beaten soldier before him.

'Till the last breath, sir.'

Wallace nodded his admiration.

'Very good. As you were.'

Wallace stepped aside, his military boots squelching in the mud. With a roar of intimidation, accompanied by another crack of lightning and roll of thunder, the masked group charged forward at Sam, who managed to throw a few punches, before a fist struck his jaw, sending him spiralling to the right. A hard uppercut crunched into his stomach, and as he toppled to the mud, a knee struck his face, sending his world spinning.

He curled up.

He put his hands over his head.

And the fists and boots thundered down on him worse than the rain from above.

Then it was over. Simultaneously, all the masked men took a few steps back, surrounding Sam in a circle, and they stood, arms behind their straight backs and their heads high.

All at the command of Wallace.

Sam spat blood into the mud and rolled onto his back, welcoming the cold rain as a counter to the pain that had engulfed him.

He thought of Lucy.

He thought of his father.

People who he loved and had loved.

All Sam had ever wanted was to follow in his father's footsteps and serve his country with distinction and pride. Make it a safer place for those who inhabited it, and while his father did it behind a military desk, Sam had been doing it behind the scope of a rifle.

Now, he had the chance to do more.

Help more people.

Protect the world.

Wallace had extended the invitation to him, and Sam had recalled how the man had been there the day his father had passed away. He *had recounted the good times he'd spent with Major William Pope, and from that moment on, Sam looked at Wallace with respect and trust.*

To join Project Hailstorm wasn't just an incredible career opportunity.

It was an honour.

The heavy steps of Wallace squelched through the mud and his imposing figure loomed over Sam, shielding him from the downpour. With a grunt, the man extended his meaty hand and Sam took it, gratefully being hauled to his feet.

He could barely stand.

The pain of his beating threatened to snatch his consciousness.

Wallace stood to attention, casting an approving eye over his newest recruit, and a cruel smile cracked across his face.

'Stand down, everyone,' he commanded, before resting a hand on Sam's shoulder. 'Is that enough?'

Sam spat blood onto the torn-up mud beneath them.

'No, sir.'

Wallace held up his hand, commanding his men to stay back, before he rested it on Sam's shoulder.

'You're a fighter, Pope.' Wallace grinned. 'Never lose that.'

A flash of lightning and Sam's memory faded to black.

Sam's mind snapped back to the auditorium, just as the ink-covered neo-Nazi charged forward, his teeth bared and his intent clear. The crowd roared with approval as the man ate up the ground between them, and a few feet from Sam, he let out a roar of anger and swung his fist.

Sam pulled his hands apart, tightening the chain that bound them, and then swerved his body, allowing the fist to flash a few inches past his cheek. Then, he looped the chain over the man's forearm, crossed his arms to snap the chain tight over the man's arm, and then turned and hauled with all his might.

The sudden shift in direction caused the chain to snap the bone of the man's arm, and he roared in horror as the pain jack-knifed through his body. A hush fell over the watching inmates, and Sam used the momentum to yank the chain forward, flipping the man over his shoulder and letting him slam against the hard concrete with a sickening thud.

Dazed, the man mumbled under his breath, but as he tried to sit up, Sam stamped forward, drilling the bottom of his plimsol into the man's jaw, snapping his neck to the side and crushing his head against the stone beneath.

The man twitched through the final moments of his life, then went limp.

A roar erupted from the stands, and Sam stepped away from the body, riling up the inmates with a blood-curdling scream of fury. He shot his eyes up to the balcony above, where Singh watched calmly, maintaining the façade. Then he looked to strazar Kolarov and motioned to the chains.

A chant of 'MORE!' echoed from the stands.

Strazar waved his hand, and the guards rushed to the door, beckoning through another inmate, who enthusiastically raced into the auditorium and headed straight at Sam. As the man's speed increased, Sam planted his back foot and absorbed the man's weight into his stomach as he collided into him. They stumbled back a few feet, but Sam held steady, and as the man threw a few wild punches, Sam took control of the situation by drilling his elbow down onto the top of the man's skull. As his attacker dropped to one knee, Sam looped the chain over the man's neck, stepped behind him, and then drove his knee between the man's shoulder blades.

The crowd once again exploded in a blood-thirsty roar of approval as the inmate gasped for air, the metal chain crushing his throat as Sam wrenched back harder. In a bid to preserve energy and offer something close to mercy, Sam dropped backwards, allowing gravity to take him to the concrete below, and the metal chain to snap the man's neck.

Another one down.

Strazar Kolarov stood, followed swiftly by Singh and the unknown gentleman, all aghast at Sam's proficiency. The man in charge of the prison nodded at his guards, and they opened the door once more, allowing another opponent through. This time, one of the guards handed the violent inmate his metal baton, and the prisoner grinned and turned his gaze to Sam. As Sam steadied himself for the incoming attack, one of the guards rushed towards him, baton in hand, and swung it as if he was aiming for a home run.

The metal smacked the back of Sam's leg, buckling his knee and sending him falling forward. The inmates, thrilled by the fighting they had witnessed, jeered the guard, with many spitting through the bars and screaming.

Sam's opponent didn't turn down the opportunity.

Quickly, the inmate scurried to Sam and drove the baton down, as if he was chopping away at a tree stump, and Sam lifted his hands to try to block the blows with the chain.

One of them got through.

The baton split Sam's eyebrow clean open, sending him crashing to the concrete and splattering the stone with a fresh coat of blood. The man scrambled on top of Sam, trying to press the metal baton to his throat, and as he managed to wedge it under Sam's chin, Sam could feel his air supply diminishing.

Fight, Sam. Fight.

Sam tried to bat away the man's hands, but his potential murderer shifted his body weight, applying more pressure, and his eyes were wild with excitement.

Sam gasped.

Scratched.

Clawed.

He managed to wrap one hand onto the side of the man's skull, and with all his might, he jabbed his finger into the man's eye socket. The man howled with agony, but Sam pushed harder until his finger was warm with blood and the pop of the eyeball confirmed he'd blinded the man.

Screaming in agony, and with a hand pressed to his blood-soaked face, the man rolled to the side, and Sam caught his breath and then sat up. Aching from head to toe, he stood, lifted the metal baton, and to the delight of the crowd, shut the man's lights off with one swift blow to the temple.

Sam stood, exhausted, and he looked up at the wild faces of the perverse crowd. Blood and dirt soaked his naked torso, and just as he was about to lift his arm in victory, a silence fell over the auditorium.

Walking down the steps of one of the caged areas was Ivan Kostic. A few of the guards exchanged awkward glances, as the irate gang leader marched down towards the floor, making a show of removing his own shirt to reveal a plethora of tattoos snaked across his sturdy torso. Flanked by two more loyal soldiers, Kostic approached the door to the cage and demanded it be opened.

The excitement in the room rose swiftly, and as the guards looked to Kolarov for guidance, Sam gestured that his hands were bound. Conflicted, Kolarov dismissed Sam's call for assistance and forbade the guards from opening the gate. But the man's greed backfired as his disgruntled staff rushed to Kostic, fiddling with the gate to welcome in Sam's doom.

Goran raced across the auditorium, and swiftly stuck his key in the lock of Sam's chains and twisted it at the same time as Kostic burst through the gate.

Sam's chains fell to the floor.

'Thank you,' Sam said, his voice drowned out by the crowd. As Goran ran for his life, Sam lifted up the chain and wrapped it completely around his right fist.

Kostic's first goon went down after one punch, the metal obliterating the man's jawbone on impact. The other man fared better, catching Sam with a few sneaky jabs, but Sam cut his right hook off with an elbow to the face, a chain-wrapped uppercut to the ribs, and then a ferocious uppercut that took the man off his feet.

It was just Sam and Kostic.

The veteran criminal smirked, seemingly impressed with the carnage he'd witnessed. Sam stood, panting for breath, the right side of his face coated in blood, and both fists raised.

Still fighting.

Kostic reached into his back pocket and retrieved a curved serrated blade, and waggled it mockingly before pointing it at Sam.

'This is *my* prison,' Kostic yelled, spit flying from his venomous words.

'Not anymore,' Sam responded. Kostic's eyes widened with fury, and the man charged forward, slashing his blade manically in Sam's direction. Sam weaved away from the deathly strikes, and then cut Kostic off with his forearm, then rocked the prisoner with a right hook wrapped in metal.

Kostic hit the ground hard.

Silence.

The sight of the most powerful man in the prison scrambling away, blood dripping from his lip, was one that had shaken the prison.

One prisoner cheered. Then another and another, and as Kostic pushed himself to his feet, he stared at the crowd in disbelief as they cheered his demise. He swore at them. Threatened them.

But they chanted *'MORE!'*

With his pride disintegrating as quickly as his hold over the prison, Kostic once again lunged at Sam, desperate in his attempts to wrestle control of the situation. After a few pathetic slashes, Sam slipped under one of them, and flipped Kostic over, dropping the elder criminal onto the concrete, before driving his foot into the side of the man's jaw, dislocating it from the skull.

Another cheer from the stands, as Sam stood over the man who had ruled with such fear and depravation. Now, as he looked up at Sam, with blood streaming from his useless lips and mercy in his eyes, the man was a ghost.

An imitation of what he once was.

Kostic reached out lazily for Sam, who stepped away, and Kostic slumped forward onto the concrete. Triumphant, Sam turned to face the balcony, where Singh stood and applauded, joining in with the celebration of the five-man demolition. Kolarov stood and reluctantly clapped, while the man on Singh's other side watched on with interest.

Singh's eyes widened with fear, and before she could scream, Sam turned, just as Kostic, with all his strength, thrust the knife towards Sam's stomach.

A collective gasp echoed around the auditorium, and as the two men struggled on the spot, Kostic grunted in exasperation as Sam tightened his grip around his wrist, holding the blade a mere inch or so from his own stomach. Slowly, Sam managed to push the blade away, overpowering Kostic and with enough distance from himself and the blade, the drove his thumb into the pressure point above Kostic's wrist.

The involuntary spasm caused Kostic to drop the blade, which Sam caught swiftly with his other hand, and then swiped upward. The blade sliced open Kostic's throat like it had been unzipped, and a spray of blood flicked across the auditorium as the man dropped to his knees. Gargling and begging for breath, Kostic held a hand feebly to his opened neck, before crashing to the ground. As the last of his life left him, he heard the cheers from the stands, who were celebrating his stranglehold over the prison coming to an end.

Sam dropped the blade and let the metal chain slide from his hand. He looked up at Singh once more and nodded.

He'd survived.

Now he was ready to walk out of hell and into some place worse.

CHAPTER SEVENTEEN

The power that money had over something as substantial as the prison system sickened Singh to her stomach, but she suppressed any urge to stop the process. The greed of strazar Kolarov had been clear from the beginning, and as the man sat at his desk, doing the necessary changes to eviscerate Jonathan Cooper from existence, he did so with a smug grin on his face. According to the strazar, Cooper had earnt his freedom, and therefore, the prison records would include Cooper in the list of deaths it would need to register with the government.

There would be no mention of the trials.

Seven men, including Cooper, were killed in a violent prison break attempt that strazar Kolarov and his guards bravely shut down.

He would be considered a hero.

The money Singh had parted with would grease the hands of those who needed to look the other way.

Nobody would know what she'd witnessed. That desperate, violent men were given the opportunity to tear one another apart for a glimpse of freedom, and while she warmed herself with the knowledge that they were doing it as a way to get to Balikov, she couldn't help but think of those who had competed in years gone by.

Thrown into the colosseum for Stravar's entertainment and financial gain, knowing the only way out was to kill.

Kolarov hummed to himself as he sent off the final documentation, as if it was a routine task, and she glanced towards Amos who rolled his eyes. Throughout the entire mission, he'd played his role to perfection, refusing to rise to the underhanded racism that Kolarov threw in his direction.

He was there as Aysha Al Ansari's personal security, and he never spoke or moved out of turn. He'd just watched everything as it unfolded.

As had Artem Alenichev, who had insisted on overseeing Cooper's release process to ensure that Singh's fighter would be in the tournament. The threat of Balikov's wrath was enough for Kolarov to promise a smooth transition, and as the Strazar put the finishing touches on Sam's path the freedom, Alenichev focused his gaze on Singh. She returned it with little interest, but Singh couldn't help but feel the man's stare was one of accusation.

'Was it everything you had hoped?' Alenichev asked, taking a sip from his water bottle.

'It was interesting,' Singh responded. 'I look forward to watching some *real* fighters.'

Alenichev chuckled and placed his water bottle down.

'Yes, your chosen fighter was quite something.' He raised an eyebrow. 'A fine choice. You certainly have an eye for a good fighter. Especially one who had only been in the prison for such a short time…'

Singh snapped her glance back to Alenichev, asserting some authority.

'If I recall, Artem, it was *you* who suggested I shop

locally.' She turned to Amos, who nodded, then back to Alenichev. 'In fact, you recommended this prison.'

'I did.' Alenichev nodded. 'I guess you could call it fate.'

'I guess you could.'

Singh let her comment linger as the two held their gaze. A smile crept across Alenichev's face and he sat back in his chair, seemingly satisfied. Right on cue, Kolarov tapped the keyboard a few more times and then sat back in his chair with a triumphant sigh.

'All done. Jonathan Cooper is now registered as a dead man, death by fatal stabbing.' He wiped his hands together. 'No one will come looking for him. He's all yours.'

'Good,' Singh said firmly, standing and adjusting her dress. The two men stood respectfully, and Kolarav waddled his bulky frame around the desk and extended his hand. His greedy face was twisted in a horrid grin.

'A pleasure doing business with you.'

'There was little pleasure to be had,' Singh said dryly, accepting the hand and shaking it once. 'These men are not animals, no matter what they have done.'

'Oh, if you knew what most of them had done, you would beg to differ.' He grinned and turned to Amos. 'As for you, you're a quiet boy, aren't you? Sturdy though.'

He extended his hand once more, and Amos glanced to Singh who nodded. Amos stepped forward and clutched the hand forcefully, and as he shook it, he squeezed it just enough to make the Strazar wince and take him down a peg. Without a word, Amos stared the man in the eyes, underlining his strength, and then stepped back. With the Strazar shaking his hand painfully, Singh turned to Alenichev.

'I trust you will be in touch.'

'Of course.' He handed Singh a business card. 'Please call that number when you have arrived at your accommodation in Budapest, and we will hand deliver your invitation. Remember, failure to accept that invitation will expel you from the tournament.'

'Quite.' Singh turned to leave. 'I trust there is somewhere to store my fighter when we get there?'

'Excuse me?' Alenichev frowned in confusion.

'You do not expect me to put that man up in the Párisi Udvar do you?' Singh was laying on the entitlement a little thick, but it was working. Alenichev chuckled and agreed.

'Yes, perhaps a man of his *talents* doesn't quite deserve such luxury.' He looked at Amos. 'Put him in the same place as your help. That should be sufficient.'

Singh looked to Amos, who nodded. Satisfied, she shook Alenichev's hand, offered her goodbyes, and then headed to the door, which one of the guards opened for her. Amos followed, and as they stepped out into the corridor, Alenichev followed.

'Mrs Al Ansari,' he called after her. She sighed and turned.

'Yes?'

'Just a friendly reminder about the delicacy of this. Mr Balikov is a very private person for a reason. I trust we can count on your discretion.'

'I don't need to be dictated to, Mr Alenichev.' Singh made a point of dropping the casualness too. 'You need not worry.'

'Good.' He regarded her carefully. 'The last thing you would want to do is make an enemy of Balikov.'

Amos took a step between Alenichev and Singh, and the man stepped back, holding his hands up as a show of neutrality. But the threat was clear.

A man like Balikov, a dangerous and powerful terrorist, didn't wield the power or privacy that he did without men like Alenichev hunting down every threat. Singh had every avenue closed off. Hun had established not just Sam's life through the prison system as Jonathan Cooper, but also her life as Aysha Al Ansari, and although she was certain Alenchiv would run his finger across every single seam of her story, she was confident it was watertight.

With Alenichev's threat hanging in the air between them, Singh flashed a confident smile at Balikov's man.

'See you soon, Mr Alenichev.'

Leaving the man to watch her leave, Singh turned and followed the guard towards the exit. Amos fell in line behind her, and as their footsteps echoed through the grim, narrow corridors of the Sremska Mitrovica Prison, she counted them down, wanting nothing more than to put as much distance as possible between herself and hell on earth.

It had only been a week, but it had felt longer.

Sam sat on the metal bench that ran the length of the wall of the holding cell, and he rested the back of his head against the brick. His face was a memorial of pain.

His right eye was swollen shut, and the purple bruising spread down across his cheek. His eyebrow had been crudely stitched shut, but the pain was still constant.

He smirked with split lips, the blood clotting and scabbing over the vicious cut.

Sam had been through hell.

But he'd survived.

After he'd killed Kostic, the guards swarmed upon him like an army of the undead, dragging him to the ground and hauling him through the auditorium, where the crowd had continued to chant for him. His display of brutality, killing five men to win the trials, would become legend inside the corridors of the vile prison, and as he'd been taken back to solitary, he'd heard some of the guards talking excitedly.

He didn't understand them, but as there were no cheap shots or wild swings of the baton, Sam understood that they too were just as impressed as the inmates.

But more importantly, he'd freed the prison from Kostic's rule.

The man had run the prison with fear, the loyalty of his men far outweighed the power of the law, and the guards knew that Kostic could click his fingers and have their lives ruined.

Families killed.

For over a decade, the man had killed and raped who he'd wanted, and the guards, like the prisoners themselves, could do little but keep their heads down and hope that Kostic's attention lie elsewhere.

Now it was over.

It had been a few hours since Sam had slit the man's throat when the door to his cell opened, and Goran stepped into the room, a smile across his face.

'It looks like you are a free man, Cooper,' he said with a grin. 'Well, as free as you can be.'

Sam smiled and stood, willingly placing his wrists together for the shackles. Goran shook his head.

'I don't feel that is necessary. Follow me.'

Obligingly, Sam followed the guard from the room and down the corridors of the prison. A few guards were positioned en route, and one of them even offered Sam a nod of respect as they passed. The nearer they got to the exit, the brighter and cleaner the prison became, and Sam felt like he was scrambling up the final rocks to the freedom, with the fires of hell nipping at his ankles. After Goran filled in some paperwork, he stepped through a secure door and Sam followed, where Goran guided him to the holding cell. As Sam stepped through, he turned back to the guard as he closed the door.

'Goran. I just wanted to thank you. You didn't have to do what you did, but you saved my life.'

The young man smiled.

'Everyone deserves a fighting chance.' His smile faded to a confused squint. 'Tell me…who are you?'

'He's the man who made me a lot of money.'

The Strazar's voice exploded into the room, and both men turned to the bulky man as he strode towards the door. Goran nodded his goodbye to Sam and then left as Kolarov approached the bars, a victorious grin across his face.

'I have never seen anything like that,' Kolarav cooed. 'You are quite the fighter, Mr Cooper.'

'I'm just glad to be leaving.'

'Yes. Mrs Al Ansari was most keen to have you.' The Strazar rubbed his hands together. 'I should have charged double.'

The Strazar pulled open the door to the cell and stood to the side, indicating for Sam to leave. Sam stood and marched forward, and the Strazar stopped him with a hand on his shoulder.

'When you are done with that bitch, feel free to come and visit me. We could make a lot of money together.'

Sam shrugged the hand away and squared up to the Strazar, who suddenly folded in on himself a little.

'If I get the chance to come back here, I'll feed you to those men in there. Then you'll understand what a desperate man is really capable of.'

After staring into the soul of the now worried Kolarov, Sam turned and headed to the door, where Goran was more than happy to lead him to the exit.

It was a walk he was more than happy to make.

Something didn't feel right.

Alenichev was sitting in Kolarov's chair, his feet on the man's desk and any respect he had for the man well and truly gone. One of the guards stood watch on the door, but Alenichev had already made it clear to the man who truly held the power. Balikov had the power and means to reduce the Sremska Mitrovica to rubble, with every prisoner and guard in it.

But Kolarov's greed wasn't the reason for Alenichev's agitation.

It was knowing there was something he couldn't see.

When he'd first met Mrs Al Ansari, he'd reeled off the usual spiel, running through the price of entry and using the well-rehearsed charm that made Balikov's job easier. When there was someone to schmooze or put in their place, Balikov would often turn to Alenichev, and let his silver tongue or his fiery temper draw a line under it quickly. It was only when things needed a more personal touch that Balikov would intervene. *Boytsovskaya Yama* was a reasonably easy event to monitor, with the usual suspects from the rich underworld paying for their seats at the table, and often bringing unfortunate fighters to their deaths. It was the perfect combination of toxic masculinity and power, where these men would cheer on the death of a helpless, desperate man for their own entertainment.

It never usually mattered. Marko Balikov would always be the final fight and he would always win.

Then, each year, the same rich and powerful men would bring more money to the table and more lambs to the slaughter, all while rubbing shoulders with Balikov and opening doors and throughways that would otherwise be closed. If Balikov needed an official in Albania to look the other way, he'd just position the Albanian billionaire at his table and that would be that.

Poslednyaya Nadezhda would not be denied, and while Alenichev didn't harbour the same feelings of pride or duty to the *Motherland* as Balikov did, his loyalty to his boss was unbreakable.

But it was constantly under review.

There could be no mistakes. Balikov's existence in the shadows had been over two decades of hard work, which had allowed him to move all the pieces he needed into place, and Alenichev's brilliant mind was a key part of the arsenal.

He snuffed out threats.

He made everything run like clockwork.

There could be *no* mistakes.

Which is why he'd felt a little shaken after his initial meeting with Mrs Al Ansari. A name of such wealth and importance had never registered on his radar before, but every digital avenue he'd investigated had returned nothing but legitimacy.

Her father owned one of the most powerful oil reserves in the world.

The Ansari name was steeped in the new history of Qatar as a world power.

Everything was there. Everything added up.

But not to Alenichev.

He had observed Mrs Al Ansari during the trials, watching with intrigue as she coldly watched prisoner after prisoner fall to the fighter she had her eye on. A man, not of Serbian nationality, who had only just arrived in the prison.

Again, the digital footprints all made sense, and there were a host of prison records for Jonathan Cooper that correlated his incarceration.

It was just a coincidence.

Such a thing, Alenichev had long since known, didn't exist.

With the uncertainty bubbling in his gut, he stood, straightened his jacket and walked around Kolarov's desk and to the high window that overlooked the prison forecourt. His eyes fell upon Aysha Al Ansari, standing beside her militant personal security guard and the luxury vehicle. She looked resplendent in a designer dress, and to all the other eyes on her, she looked the picture of sophisticated beauty.

But there was something off.

Something about how she carried herself, the way she moved and spoke.

With a level of precision.

As if trained.

The door to the prison opened, and Alenichev watched as the guard led Jonathan Cooper to his new 'owner', and the lack of restraints caused Alenichev to arch an eyebrow.

The man had brutally murdered five men less than a few hours ago.

Yet Mrs Al Ansari was happy to meet with him with no chains? There was no doubting her personal security could handle himself, as the man oozed military, but again, the whole situation felt a little off centre.

As if one frame out of all of them was slightly off kilter.

Mrs Al Ansari introduced herself to her fighter, then gestured to her security guard. No doubt a threat of what was to come if Cooper acted out.

Cooper seemed calm. Too calm.

Alenichev watched the fighter slide into the back of the luxury 4x4 and the guard slam the door shut. He then opened the passenger door for his employer, before taking his place in the driver's seat.

Cooper was unshackled in the back.

It seemed too risky.

Too polite.

As the engine hummed to life, Alenichev pulled his phone from his pocket, opened the camera app and then zoomed in.

He snapped the license plate, just as it began to move, the car leaving a cloud of dusty as it rumbled over the gravel and headed toward the sequence of thick, metal gates.

He'd see them in a week's time at *Boytsovskaya Yama*.

And by then – he gave a silent promise – he'd have figured out what the fuck was going on.

CHAPTER EIGHTEEN

Steeped in its grand illuminated majesty, the Parisi Udvar Hotel dominated the street that ran through the centre of Budapest. One of the most structurally beautiful buildings in the Hungarian capital, the luxury hotel was a magnet for the rich, powerful or famous, and the building shot to the sky with a beautiful glow that demanded attention. The building was offset from the main road, conquering an entire corner of the city, with a boulevard running down its right-hand side which was littered with benches and taste-fully selected foliage.

It was truly stunning to witness, and as Singh's driver pulled to a stop by the entrance, a smartly dressed host opened her door and welcomed her to the building. Singh nodded curtly, aware that until she was in her room, she was still very much in character. After the flight from Belgrade to Budapest, Sam and Amos had left in a hired car, while Singh had located the well-dressed man holding a placard with *Mrs Al Ansari*. The drive had been pleasant, with the night sky falling across the beautiful city that exploded into life with light and energy. A beacon of tourism, Budapest had become one of the most popular hotspots, and as the nightlife began to grow, Singh could feel the city pulsating with excitement. Her driver removed her bag from the car and handed it to the host, who ushered Singh up the steps and into the grand foyer of the hotel. The ceiling arched into a magnificent display of glass and gold, and the high walls were interspersed with wooden columns and detailed carvings. Rows of tables and chairs ran one length of the room, with some of them filled by scattered guests, either working or reading.

Singh checked in without a problem, and the bellhop swiftly took her case and led her to the lifts that would take them to one of the two penthouses at the very top of the hotel.

The luxury was not something Singh was prepared for.

Her suite was twice the size of the flat she'd once owned in Canon's Park, on the outskirts of London. The living area was the size of a school hall, with leather sofas arranged in a neat formation around the cinema screen-sized television that was affixed to the white wall.

Everything, despite its basic, white colouring, was ludicrously expensive, and Singh took a few moments to walk around the penthouse and breathe it in.

It wasn't what she was there for, but it was an opportunity to experience a side of life that was reserved for only a select few. With the tournament starting within the week, Singh gave a satisfied smile at her residence for its duration.

She generously tipped the staff member, who scurried from the room, and she swiftly removed her headscarf. Although she was not religious in any way, much to her parents' chagrin, she found it distasteful to wear such a meaningful garment for any longer than she needed to.

She made her way to the bathroom, and began to fill

the freestanding, curved bath with warm water and the complimentary bath salts. As the heat in the room rose, and the aroma began to waft around her in a comforting hug, she undressed and lowered herself into the water. As she submerged her head beneath the bubbles, she held her breath and tried to let the stress leave her body.

But it clung to her like a parasite.

She thought about how dangerous her every move was, and how it was clear that Alenichev was beginning to suspect something.

How one tiny mistake would most likely end her life.

The danger Sam was in.

The danger she'd put him in.

How she'd betrayed him.

She pushed herself out of the water and gasped for air, the water splashing over the curved edge of the bath and spattering the tiles below.

Knock. Knock.

Singh took a moment to collect her thoughts before registering that someone was at the door. She called out to them to wait a moment and leapt from the tub, quickly patted down her naked body with a towel and then rushed to her suitcase. Once she'd slipped into some clothes, she marched to the door and peered through the peephole.

Blake.

With a sigh, Singh pulled open the heavy door, and Blake stepped into the room. Wearing a navy polo shirt, white chinos, and white trainers, he looked like the usual rich mid-life crisis that worked as his cover. He'd booked out the other penthouse suite, giving Directive One the entire top floor of the luxury hotel. Under his own alias, Blake had presented himself as a high profile guest, and his request for the CCTV on the top floor to be disconnected had begrudgingly been accepted.

Hiding in plain sight was his reasoning, which made sense. But Singh also knew that Blake had a taste for some of the finer things in life and would have been more than happy with their accommodation.

'Good to see you, Singh,' he said with a grin, and looked around the suite, impressed by its scale and design. 'This is pretty nice, isn't it?'

'It's a bit much.'

Blake waved a dismissive hand.

'Look, if the government isn't willing to back us up on this, then they can at least put us up somewhere nice.' He turned to her and offered her a concerned smile. 'How you holding up?'

'I'm fine,' Singh replied unconvincingly.

'Yeah, one of my many annoying talents, Singh, is being able to detect bullshit.' He lowered himself onto the arm of the nearest sofa and folded his arms across his chest. 'What's going on?'

'I'm worried—'

'Look, we're keeping an eye on Alenichev and if we think he's acting on his suspicion that you're not who you say you are, we'll pull you out.'

'I'm not worried about me. I'm worried about Sam.'

'Pope?' Blake frowned with exasperation. 'He's a big boy, Singh.'

'I know. But you didn't see what he had to do...'

'Kill criminals?' Blake shrugged. 'That's kind of his thing, isn't it?'

'This was different.' Singh shook her head. 'I've seen him before. When we saved Jasmine Hill from the Kovalenkos, Sam killed some people to save my life. To save her life. It was...war. Does that make sense?'

'Sort of. He was doing what he did best.'

'Exactly. This...this was different. He was led out to the place to fight like an animal and...'

'You feel guilty?' Blake stood and approached her and then placed his hands on her shoulder. 'I understand.'

'I know, deep down in my gut, that stopping Balikov is the *only* thing that matters, but I've put Sam in a place where only the worst of humanity could survive.'

'And he survived.'

'He's not the worst of humanity, Blake.'

'No, he's not. Annoyingly, there is a nobility to the man that I can't help but respect.' Blake looked her in the eyes. 'But the man is a wanted criminal. No matter your personal feelings toward him, he has killed dozens, if not a hundred, men. Even some women. On some level, he might be a good man, but he's still a criminal. A killer. You remember that, and maybe you might not be so hard on yourself.'

Blake patted her on the shoulder and then headed towards the door.

'But I feel like I betrayed him,' Singh said sternly.

Blake shrugged as he opened the door.

'Ask yourself this…if Sam had found out on his own about Balikov, and the things he's done, and then discovered his only route to the man was to get into *Boytsovskaya Yama*, what would he have done?'

Singh sighed and nodded. Blake's distaste for Sam was grating, but understandable.

'What he normally does. Whatever it takes.'

'Like I said. Nobility.' He offered her one final smile. 'Get some rest, Singh. We've got a busy few days ahead.'

Singh stared at the door after it closed for a few moments before she turned and made her way to the minibar in the far corner of the room. Remembering her cover, she scowled as she returned the gin to the fridge and settled on a mineral water and then stepped out onto the balcony. A wind whipped against her instantly, and she pulled her jacket tighter. As she looked out over the incredible city, she sipped her drink and thought of Sam.

He was out there, somewhere.

But not free.

Soon, he'd be stepping into a world just as dangerous as the one she'd plucked him from.

Blake was right. Given the choice, Sam would always do the right thing. But in doing so, she was worried she was pushing Sam too far to the side of his world where he couldn't come back from.

There was only one way for Sam to survive what was to come.

And that was to do what he always did.

Without permission. Without hesitation.

Without remorse.

And that was to fight.

The hostel on the east side of Budapest was as cheap as the price suggested, but compared to the solitary confinement block in Sremska Mitrovica, it was luxurious. Sam had travelled back to Belgrade with Amos and Singh, with his former flame briefing him on the progress she'd made and the confirmation of their place within *Boytsovskaya Yama*. Sam was pleased to be freed from the barbaric prison, but any excitement he had was curtailed by the reality of the tournament.

He'd have to fight people worse than he'd encountered within the Serbian prison, and considering these men would all have won their own trials, it meant they were handy.

It meant what had come before would be a cakewalk compared to what was to come.

Amos had offered Sam a few compliments, as well as a

few wry digs regarding the fights he witnessed, which eased the tension that slowly filled the car on the journey to the airport.

Singh had apologised.

Sam had accepted it.

But the fact remained, she'd used his most painful memory as a way to exploit him into doing her bidding.

She'd also rendered him expendable.

There were some things you couldn't come back from, and in the very dangerous world that they both now existed in, trust was one commodity that couldn't be traded.

It was earnt once.

It was lost once.

And that notion sat coldly between the two of them, as the stunted conversation petered out and all three of them fell silent, their thoughts on the mission ahead. To keep up appearances, Singh took a separate flight to Budapest, pampered to the hilt, whereas Sam and Amos were crammed onto a commercial flight with poor air conditioning and worse food.

But it all tasted fantastic. A mile away from the gruel he was served once a day for the past week.

Whilst Singh was welcomed to Budapest by a well-dressed chauffeur, they were met at Budapest airport by Foster, who briefed them on the next steps and then handed them the keys to the hire car, which was put against an untraceable name. In the back of the car were pre-packed bags for both of them, full of fresh clothes, toiletries, and a pistol each.

The brief was clear.

They had five days until the tournament began, and they would need to lie low, train, and be on high alert. Singh had reported to Blake that she felt a tremor of suspicion from Balikov's right-hand man, which meant they needed to be careful.

Amos took care of everything, encouraging Sam to eat well and rest better. The ordeal of Sremska Mitrovica soon caught up with him, and while his bruises faded, the trauma of the situation came and went like small waves lapping at the shore. Every day, Amos would ensure they ate a hearty breakfast, with Sam's appetite erupting at the sight of every plate of food.

Then they would train.

On one of the side streets near their hostel, Amos had found a boxing gym which he'd signed them up for. The owner wanted a minimum of a month's membership, which Amos was happy to pay. For hours, the two men would spar, often gaining an audience from the other gym patrons who were enthralled by the fighting expertise on show.

Blake stopped by once, under the pretence of a fellow gym goer, and he checked in with Sam to ensure he was well. Despite their cagey beginnings and opposing moral stances, Sam found their friendship growing.

They also met Singh once for lunch, where their performances were once again put on, with Amos roughly shoving Sam every once in a while, knowing full well he'd get a receipt the next time they stepped between the ropes.

Singh was nervous, but determined, and after a few days of good food, better sleep, and focused training, Sam had decided to give her a break. She'd received the hand delivered location for the tournament, and Brady and Foster were already scoping out the area under the guise of a travelling couple. Hun was busy running through as many firewalls as possible to gather as much intel he could.

All they knew for certain was the time, the place, and that Balikov and his champion would be there.

And that Sam would need to be ready to fight again.

Sam gave his assurances and as he went to leave, Singh threw her arms around him, the veil slipping slightly and then she stepped away, dabbing at her eyes as she left them.

Now, on the eve of *Boytsovskaya Yama*, Sam sat in the dingy bar of the hostel, looking around at the innocent people who were joyously drinking and laughing as the monotone electro-pop hummed quietly from the cheap speakers.

Groups of young men and women had collided, all of them flirting and throwing back alcohol as quickly as their inhibitions.

Sam thought about his younger days with Theo, and watching in awe as his best friend would charm every woman who came their way.

Theo had died for what he believed in.

Sam was willing to do the same.

And if they were not able to stop Balikov, then the innocence and happiness he was watching from across the bar would be under threat.

Thousands of people would die.

Millions effected.

Balikov, and the rest of *Poslednyaya Nadezhda*, wanted to disrupt the world, and Sam knew in his heart he would fight until its final beat to stop that from happening.

Amos returned to their table with two bottles of beer and a grin on his face. A few young women were looking over at him with a smile on his face. Sam shook his head.

'You're supposed to be working.' Sam joked.

'I am working. I just make it look effortless.'

Amos cracked a grin and then handed Sam the bottle.

'I don't drink.'

'It's non-alcoholic,' Amos said curtly. 'I've read your file.'

The two men clinked their bottles and then drank quietly for a few moments. The women waved goodbye to

Amos, and then joined the rest of the group, immediately enveloped by the alcohol and loud enjoyment. Sam turned to Amos, who seemed content with his thoughts.

'So what's your story?'

'I don't have one.'

'Come on.' Sam leant forward across the table. 'Ex military?'

Amos grinned and shook his head.

'There is no story before Directive One. That's the rule.'

'Oh, bullshit.' Sam slammed his hand on the table. 'You've got files on me. You know what I've done, what I've been through. I know where Singh's from. Hell, I brought her here with me. Blake, Brady, and Foster, they scream government. Hun, well…he's from a world of his own. But you…you look like a soldier.'

'If I tell you, will you drop it?' Amos said with a frustrated sigh.

Sam saluted.

'Scout's honour.'

'Marines. Well, ex-marine.' Amos grimaced and took a sip of his beer. 'Best of the best. Then one day, a decision was made that put my brothers in the firing line. I went against orders…was given my marching orders.'

'You did the right thing,' Sam offered.

'You're damn right I did.' Amos's fist clenched. 'But they didn't see it that way. You know how it is, Sam. Fat old white men making decisions behind desks that put men like us in front of guns. They fight wars for money and resources and leave us to fight for our lives. I wasn't going to let my family die so some self-indulgent politician could bump his rating by a few points. Then Dom found me…'

'Dom?' Sam said with a raised eyebrow, surprised at the closeness of Amos and Blake's relationship.

'Director Blake.' Amos quickly corrected. 'He gave me

an opportunity, and I will always be grateful for that. So do me a favour…don't fuck this up.'

'I wasn't planning to,' Sam said with a smile. 'Otherwise, I'll be killed.'

'True.' Amos smirked. 'But then you've had a good teacher…'

The two men chuckled, and Sam lifted his bottle to Amos once more.

'To doing the right thing.'

'To doing the right thing,' Amos replied, and they clinked bottles once more and allowed the silence to calmly surround them. As Sam finished off the last of his bottle, he glanced at his new friend.

'So, what's your first name?'

'Nunya,' Amos replied swiftly, finishing his drink.

'Nunya?' Sam frowned.

'Yeah. Nunya business.' Amos slapped the table as he stood. 'One more drink, then bed. We got a big day tomorrow.'

As Amos left Sam to contemplate his terrible joke, Sam finally realised that the weight of the situation had been lifted. Amos reminded him of Theo, and their banter was easy and natural. The lure of Blake's offer was becoming slightly stronger, and Sam knew that the camaraderie between soldiers was stronger than any bond formed.

But there was no point looking to the future.

There was only tomorrow.

Boytsovskaya Yama.

The Fight Pit.

And Sam knew that he was fighting for his life.

As the evening continued with the light-hearted banter, neither Amos nor Sam noticed the car parked across the road, where one of Alenichev's men was sitting. The same man who'd been sitting outside the gym the day Blake had stopped by.

The same man who'd followed them to their lunch with Singh.

The same man who'd documented everything he'd seen, and as he started his engine and pulled away, the same man who was excited to return to Alenichev with proof.

Proof that Alenichev, as always, was right.

CHAPTER NINETEEN

Balikov's luxury apartment sat atop a marvel of modern architecture. The ice-white building loomed large over the edge of the town, situated on an overlook that offered a stunning view of Budapest. The curved building enclosed eighteen luxury apartments, with Balikov's penthouse the cherry on top of a multi-million dollar cake.

Floor-to-ceiling windows led out onto a balcony that stretched the entire length of the building, and as he sat and looked out over the city, he lit a cigar and took a triumphant puff.

It was one of the many properties that the oligarch had across the globe and was one of his more recent. When discussions with a Hungarian politician led to the plans for *Boytsovskaya Yama*, Balikov knew then that he needed a safe house for his annual trip.

As always, Alenichev had made the required arrangements, including the security detail and the young woman that was currently recovering in his bed. As he'd advanced in his life, Balikov's sexual needs were not for sexual gratification, but for the power. He enjoyed throwing money at another human being and then being able to do as he pleased. Whether it was rough intercourse, or some form of degradation, it filled him with a sense of importance.

People were things to be bought.

Everything had a price.

That was how the world worked, and it was his mission to remind its inhabitants. His country had been ostracised for threatening to fulfil its potential, and he harboured resentment for the world who put up the blockades. His disdain was also levelled at the current government, who bent too easily at any show of power and had lost sight of what made Mother Russia so powerful in the first place.

And he wasn't alone in that thought.

Poslednyaya Nadezhda truly was the final hope for his country, but Balikov saw their mission as worldwide. By tearing down the fragile constructs that protected people at every level, he would usher in a new world order, one built on strength and fear. Watching weak people being celebrated or called a hero for the most inane acts would be a thing of the past, resigned to a time in history when the world grew weak.

In his mind, he wasn't a hero.

He was a necessity.

The first few tests of the nuclear weapon he'd been financing had been successful in their application, but not in their design. Already there were multiple government agencies poring over the destruction that had been caused, but Balikov's connections had been able to mask these 'events' as mishaps from neighbouring power plants. All the weapons tests had been carried out within a short distance of an easy excuse, but it highlighted the necessity to be able to launch without detection.

To slowly release a nuclear weapon across multiple targets would be simultaneously the most impressive and devastating attack the world had ever known.

There would be hundreds of thousands of deaths.

Millions of lives, damaged beyond repair.

International relations would spiral and the world would turn on itself.

That was where *Poslednyaya Nadezhda* stepped in.

The promise and the plan to rebuild, yet this time, it would be done on Russian power, not Russian politics.

They would take and demand, then rule with fairness wrapped in fear.

That was the true potential of the *Motherland* and it was something he'd given the past two decades of his life to achieve.

And they were so close.

Three of the entrants to *Boytsovskaya Yama* were aligned with his cause, with the message of a new world beginning to be heard by other countries. Powerful men with vast wealth and influence, who had supported his cause, who would take seats at the top table when the time came.

Current democracy and political structure would be eradicated, not by *Poslednyaya Nadezhda*, but by the people who would be left in the aftermath. The people who would turn to the weak and underqualified leaders, and then tear them apart when they offered no response. Then those who laid the groundwork, men like Balikov and his clientele, would be there to guide the world however they saw fit.

Another smug puff of the cigar and his thoughts turned to his son.

Marko.

The man had all the opportunities that Balikov himself had never had, and there was never any chance of him squandering them. When Balikov watched his own father crumble under the oppressive state and die a broken and poor man, he'd been just sixteen years old.

Too young to make a difference and too young to understand how.

But as the years rolled by, the empathy he'd felt for his father soon turned to shame and he used it as fuel to press his foot down on the throat of the business world. Marko's role model was a man of power, a man of substance, and the repercussions of failure had been crystal clear from the get-go.

Marko would be cut out.

Expelled.

Forgotten.

And that dagger hung over the young man, turning him from a meek, spoilt teenager into a killer, and the man's year-round dedication to *Boytsovskaya Yama* filled Balikov's heart with pride. He was afforded the best coaches and nutritionists the world could offer, and there wasn't a fighting discipline that he hadn't mastered. They had spoken of him entering the MMA leagues, but Balikov was hesitant to allow his son to receive such exposure. Marko would climb fast, and that would alert people to his backstory and could shine a light on Balikov himself. Marko understood, and although he would compete in numerous underground fights throughout the year, Balikov ensured his son's bank account stayed eye-wateringly full as long as he focused on *Boytsovskaya Yama*.

And Marko did so.

No questions asked.

Once again, the power of being able to throw money at someone, even his own son, was a feeling that Balikov enjoyed greatly.

The weakness in their family lineage had died with his own pathetic father, but Balikov had once again guided something to greatness. Watching Marko step into the pit and beat the life from the dregs of society, no matter how big or how desperate, was a cherished moment that had forged their bond. It would begin again tomorrow, and

Balikov, with his cigar in hand and grin across his face, couldn't wait.

'*A moment of quiet, sir?*'

Alenichev's voice cut through Balikov's train of thought, but he didn't turn to face him.

'*A moment of reflection.*' Balikov turned on his chair and gestured to the seat beside him. He then reached for the bottle of vodka on the plush oak table and poured two shots into separate crystal glasses. He handed one to his loyal friend and toasted. '*Novvy mir.*'

'*Novvy mir.*' Alenichev echoed.

Both men threw back their shots, toasting to the new world they sought to create. Alenichev took his seat as Balikov once again reached for the vodka.

'*I trust all is well,*' Balikov said firmly as he passed across another drink. Before he drank his own, he puffed on his cigar.

'*Arrangements have been confirmed, sir.*'

'*Please, Artem. You need not call me sir.*' He smiled cruelly. '*Mr Balikov will suffice.*'

'*Of course, Mr Balikov. All sixteen fighters have arrived. All transfers out of the prison systems have been handled. These men are ghosts...*'

'*Expendable.*' Balikov's eyes glistened with excitement.

'*Quite. Although, I do not come here tonight to share such fine vodka over good news.*' Alenichev sighed and rested his hands on the table. '*I am not convinced by Mrs Al Ansari.*'

'*The Qatari whore?*' Balikov spat. '*A woman, especially one from that country, is stupid enough to think she can sit at our table. I was glad to take her money. Don't worry yourself with her, Artem. She is a stupid woman who will learn her lesson when she brings her fighter to his death.*'

Alenichev twitched anxiously in his chair and then threw back his shot. Balikov could feel the man's unease, stood and reached over to pour him another drink. As he poured one for himself, he stayed standing, a classic power move to assert his authority.

'You worry about her fighter?' Balikov asked in an accusing tone.

'*Worried. No. But I saw firsthand what he is capable of and…'*

Balikov's fist shook the table as he drove it down onto the wood.

'There is nobody capable of defeating my son. Nobody. Marko Balikov is a warrior. These men, these pitiful, vile excuses of humanity, they pale in comparison. They are brought here purely so I can watch the heir to everything I have built, destroy them with his bare hands.' Balikov took a breath and straightened his shirt. Instantly, he was calm. *'Do not be concerned with what a desperate man is capable of. Be concerned with what a trained man is.'*

'I do not doubt Marko for a second. My concern is that Mrs Al Ansari is not who she says she is.'

Balikov stopped for a few seconds, ran his tongue against the inside of his lip and turned to the view of the city.

'Explain.'

'There is nothing concrete, but…'

'No evidence?'

'No, Mr Balikov,' Alenichev said, also standing from his seat. *'But there was too much coincidence. She springs from nowhere, with a name that has never passed us before, but is one that is embedded in Qatari business. Then her fighter just so happens to be transferred to the prison the moment she gets accepted into Boytsovskaya Yama.'*

Balikov nodded.

'You do not believe in coincidence.'

'No, Mr Balikov,' Alenichev stated confidently. *'I do not.'*

Balikov's eyes drew thin.

'Me neither.'

Alenichev walked around the table and stood beside his

boss, taking in the breathtaking view of the city that they would bathe in blood.

'For years, you have made me a wealthy man on the promise that I eradicate problems for you. I fear there might be one here. I had both Mrs Al Ansari and her fighter followed. They travelled separately, and her fighter—'

'Mr Cooper,' Balikov confirmed. Alenichev nodded.

'Yes, Mr Cooper…has been placed in a hostel not far from the tournament. Her personal security guard has been sparring with him…'

Balikov frowned.

'That is odd.'

'And they received a visit from this man.'

Alenichev turned his phone over to Balikov, who glared at the photo of Dominic Blake.

'Do we know this man?'

'My guy said that he spent two hours in the gym and exercised like a pro. But they were engaged in numerous conversations and the man seemed friendly with both the security guard and Cooper.' Alenichev whipped through to another photo. This one seized Balikov's attention. *'Is it normal for your entrants to be so friendly with their fighters?'*

The photo was candidly taken from the back of a restaurant, and it showed the striking Mrs Al Ansari with her arms wrapped around the impressive figure of Mr Cooper.

Balikov ran a hand over his smooth scalp and then handed the phone back to Alenichev. Clearly rattled, the billionaire poured another vodka, knocked it back, and then poured another. He turned to his confidant in fury.

'What are you doing to confirm this?'

'Like I said. I do not believe in coincidence.'

'You know this man? From the photo?' Balikov demanded, his infamous temper boiling to the surface. It was an expe-

rience Alenichev was not only familiar with but also a master in handling.

'I have the FSB looking into it.'

'Tomorrow, I want you to bring them to me and I will take the truth from them, piece by piece, if I have to.'

With the alcohol starting to take control, Balikov woozily reached for the vodka, his hand wafting lazily as if he was swatting a fly. Alenichev stepped forward, calmly lifted the bottle, and poured them both a final drink.

'May I suggest an alternative?' He handed his boss the drink. 'There is something here, I am certain. But we do not have the questions that will get us the answers. Not yet, anyway. She is keen to meet you, so why don't we delay that?'

'Boytsovskaya Yama is my tournament.'

'Exactly.' Alenichev knocked back his shot and slammed the glass down. 'Don't let them turn it into anything else. Stay away tomorrow, and it will rattle her. I will stay by her the entire time and whether she likes it or not, she will slip up.'

'And then?'

'And then you can teach them your lesson about hungry dogs.'

The two men exchanged fiendish grins, and Balikov gave a half-drunken chuckle and threw back his final shot. Stumbling slightly, he approached Alenichev, and rested a meaty hand on the man's shoulder.

'You are a good soldier, Artem.' He lowered his voice. 'I know you will not let me down.'

'Never, Mr Balikov.'

Balikov patted the man affectionately, and then carefully plotted his route back towards the doorway of the balcony. Smoke wafted from the remnants of the cigar that had dropped to the floor, and Alenichev pressed his foot down to extinguish it. As Balikov reached the threshold, he turned, steadying himself with the frame.

'Oh, and as for Mr Cooper.' A sadistic smirk took control

of his world-weary face. *'Please make sure his first fight is extra special.'*

Alenichev nodded, then watched as his boss stumbled through the penthouse, before he returned his gaze to the immaculate skyline. There was a reason Balikov had paid him millions over the years.

Because he was the best problem solver that money could buy.

As he treated himself to another shot of the premium vodka, he could feel that they had a very big problem.

And he would find out what it was.

Whatever it took.

CHAPTER TWENTY

The drive out of Budapest took forty-five minutes, and Sam sat idly in the back of the rented car while Amos took the wheel. Following the explicit instructions that Alenichev had delivered to Singh, Amos ensured that they stayed as close to the car in front as possible. Singh was being driven to the venue also, except hers was a luxury vehicle, with compliments from Vladimir Balikov himself. Blake wasn't thrilled about the idea, originally assigning Brady to be her driver to have another body in the vicinity, but Singh had been adamant she would be okay.

It had clearly irritated Amos as well, and the man, usually so calm and collected, uttered under his breath whenever a car indicated and then bullied its way between them.

After forty-five minutes, Amos followed the other driver off the slip road of the motorway, and then through a series of increasingly derelict roads. Sam looked on, digesting the view of ever-increasing poverty.

This wasn't a place where the police looked the other way.

It was a place they didn't know existed.

To hold such an event, and keep so discreet, Sam could only speculate the vast sum of money Balikov parted with to grease the wheels to ensure the smooth operation.

Police.

Politicians.

Border control.

Prison services.

There were so many pillars of civilisation that would have to turn a blind eye to allow such an inhumane tournament to take place, and it made Sam sick to his stomach. Institutions designed and created to uphold the law would be swimming in blood money, while the rich and powerful watched desperation rip itself apart.

Singh's driver turned off the pothole-riddled street and onto a dirt road that ran the length of a barren wasteland, with dust swirling in the wind.

'Well, it's off the grid,' Amos uttered, more to himself than to Sam.

They drove for ten minutes in silence, before the structure loomed large in the distance. Not dissimilar to the temporary Directive One HQ in Serbia, the monstrous building had been abandoned for years. The stone had faded and cracked over time, and any potential window had been boarded up, with the wood now rotten to the point of disintegration. As the two-car cavalcade approached, two men stepped forward, their arms wrapped around assault rifles and their demeanours cold. Singh's car stopped, and her driver spoke in Hungarian.

It was enough.

One of the men waved the two cars through, and as they passed, Sam clocked the *Magyar Honvédség* crest tattooed on the inside of the man's forearm.

Hungarian Defence Forces.

Most likely ex-serving mercenaries, who were guns for hire to the highest bidder. If Balikov wanted elite protection, he had it, and Sam clocked another four armed men patrolling the front of the building. A line of luxury cars were parked across one side of the forecourt, alongside a few premium coaches that had shuttled in a wave of paying spectators. Singh's driver was directed to the official parking lot, while Amos was instructed to round the abandoned building and approach the back entrance.

Only the rich were treated to the warm welcome, and as soon as they approached the other prison transfers, one of the soldiers directed his rifle at the car and yelled at Amos to step out.

'Don't move,' Amos said as he stepped out, and Sam watched as the man patted Amos down and then removed his firearm. Amos spoke to the man slowly, pointing towards Sam, and the man nodded and marched Amos to Sam's door. As Amos opened it, Sam had the rifle pushed into his face.

'Get out of car, motherfucker.'

The man's English was broken, but the threat was clear, and Sam stepped out, his hands up and he stood next to Amos.

'He wants me to cuff you,' Amos said.

'Fuck off,' Sam snapped. He turned back to the soldier. 'No cuffs.'

The man spat on the ground and stepped forward, allowing the rifle to swing from its strap. He launched forward and rocked Sam with a hard punch to the stomach. Sam stumbled back slightly and gasped for breath.

'You, no talk.'

'Easy,' Amos said, stepping between the two men. Taking the move as an act of aggression, the man swung a fist at Amos. Instinctively, Amos weaved underneath, snatched the arm in mid-flight and then twisted it up behind the mercenary's back. The man yelped in pain, and

Amos slammed him forward, pinning him to the bonnet of the car.

The commotion drew two guards and both of them trained their rifles on Amos.

'Why don't we all just calm down?' Amos said calmly and then looked at the soldiers. 'You can put your guns down.'

'They will kill you,' Amos's captive sneered. With a sigh, Amos reached down and took his handgun from the man's belt and pressed it to the back of his skull.

'Tell them we're good.'

'You are crazy.' The man began to panic.

'*Tell them!*' Amos snarled, pressing the metal as hard as he could against the man's skull. Worried, the man yelled out in his native tongue, and his two comrades lowered their weapons. Sam watched on, impressed at Amos's control of the situation. With the guns lowered, Amos stepped back and slid his weapon back into its holster on the inside of his jacket. 'That wasn't so hard, was it?'

The mercenary pushed himself off the car, spun and squared up to Amos, who didn't flinch. After a few intense seconds, the man scoffed and stepped back.

'Fine. No cuffs.' He then held out his hand. 'But rule is no weapons.'

Amos turned to Sam, who shrugged. Reluctantly, he reached back into his jacket and handed over his gun.

'I want that back.'

'Oh, I'll make sure you get it,' the man said with a wry smile. The threat was obvious, and Amos rolled his eyes.

'Shall we?' He motioned to the door, and the mercenary whistled loudly, and three more armed men swarmed towards them. He motioned for Amos and Sam to follow, and as they did, Sam could see the group of armed men all gagging for someone to step out of line. To them, he was just a vile criminal, and due to the unfortunate history and rather rife racism that ran through the country, Amos wasn't someone they wanted to respect. As they approached the entrance, the mercenary turned with a horrid grin across his face.

'Let's take the tour.'

The back door to the facility creaked open, the inside shrouded in darkness. The man stepped through, followed by Amos.

Sam took one last look at the outside world before he stepped inside, knowing his only way out was to win.

As her driver was guided by the armed guard to a shaded parking spot, Singh peered out through the tinted window. She watched as Amos slowly rounded the building and disappeared out of sight. The driver killed the engine, along with the air conditioning, and as he stepped out of the car, Singh took a few deep breaths.

This was it.

There was no going back.

As her door was pulled open, she adjusted her head-scarf and stepped out into the early afternoon, the heat of the sun offset by the cool breeze that swept around the facility. Instantly, she could feel all eyes on her. As Alenichev had said, there had never been a woman entrant for *Boytsovskaya Yama*, and some of the guards seemed quite taken with the striking woman who had stepped out of the car. A few of the other guests, all of whom had been welcomed personally by Alenichev, had made their way through the front of the building towards the reception, and the driver signalled for Singh to follow him. A side door had been opened, where two armed guards were shepherding a group of fifty excitable patrons, all of whom had paid big money to watch the underground carnage.

The thought of it flipped Singh's stomach.

There were those with the means to make these desperate men fight. And there were those with the means to watch it gladly. As they approached the door, Alenichev stepped out, resplendent in a tailored navy suit with a thin, grey pinstripe. His hair was combed neatly into a side parting, and his eyes sparkled with excitement.

'Mrs Al Ansari,' he said with a warm smile. 'It is a pleasure to have you with us, and I wanted to personally apologise for the way our last rendezvous ended.'

The man was a powerhouse of charm, and Singh could see how he could effortlessly disarm most. She extended her hand to him.

'Consider it forgotten.'

'Please, this way.'

Alenichev turned and ushered her into the building. On the outside, the abandoned factory was a ghastly aberration, thankfully lost so far away from humanity that the residents could forget about it. But once through the door, it was clear that Balikov had spared little expense.

The floor had been carpeted in maroon, and well-dressed waiters walked among the rich and powerful with trays of champagne on offer. Alenichev took two and handed one to Singh.

'Welcome to *Boytsovskaya Yama.*' He toasted.

'I don't drink alcohol,' Singh said firmly, and handed it back. The man looked disappointed with himself.

'Of course. How rude of me.' He clicked his fingers at one of the waiters. 'Please get Mrs Al Ansari a non-alcoholic beverage of her choice.'

'Water is fine,' Singh offered helpfully.

As the young man scurried away, Singh looked around at her fellow competitors. All of them were as she expected. Old. White. Overweight. They were men of considerable power and wealth, and considering the

191

company they kept, they were willing to spill blood to keep it. A few of them were in mid-conversation, while a few others cast a disproving eye in her direction.

'Am I not welcome here, Mr Alenichev?' Singh asked, gratefully accepting the water from the returning waiter.

'Please. Like I said before. Artem.' He flashed his smile again. 'And you have paid the entry and found a fighter, which means you have as much right as these men to compete. Forgive them. Many would never have seen a woman such as yourself before.'

'Qatari?' Singh asked, laying on her accent. Alenichev shook his head.

'One so stunning.'

Singh felt herself inadvertently blush and cursed herself for doing so. She looked around the room and noticed Amos being marched through by an armed guard. They locked eyes, and he nodded to her, before making his way across to the far side of the room, where he stood to attention. Scattered around the edges of the vast, open foyer were numerous private bodyguards, all of them unarmed but ready to jump into action at a moment's notice.

'I trust my fighter will be fine,' Singh said.

'Ah, Mr Cooper.' Alenichev nodded. 'Yes, all fighters are shown to private rooms where they will be kept before the fights. As you can appreciate, we do not roll out the carpet for men of such…history.'

'That is good to know. There are many armed men.'

'Well, we do have sixteen of the most dangerous criminals ready to fight for their lives. Plus, some of those in the cheap seats may get a little excitable.' Alenichev sipped his champagne. 'We can't take any chances.'

Another wave of waiters emerged, all of them carrying trays that were adorned with rich, expensive hors d'oeuvres. Some of the men latched onto them with greedy fingers, while Singh politely declined. As she stood, she couldn't help but feel Alenichev's eyes on her.

Peering.

Searching.

As the last of the entrants made their way into the building, the metal door slammed shut, bringing all conversation to an abrupt end. Alenichev made his way to the front of the group, clapping his hands in appreciation of them all.

'Ladies and gentlemen, thank you. As always, it is Mr Balikov's personal pleasure to host *Boytsovskaya Yama*, and he is thrilled to see some regular faces, as well as some new.' Alenichev looked to Singh, as did everyone else. 'This is an event of power. An event of survival. For those of you who know the rules, they will be adhered to at all times. For our newest guest, I say welcome and please appreciate the delicate process we have here. No phones. No discussion with the outside world. Any bets placed between competitors shall be handled personally and offsite. Any disruption or any attempt to assist the fighters without permission will result in expulsion from the tournament, and severe penalties. Is this clear?'

A few murmurs of agreement echoed. Singh nodded. Alenichev, with a grin on his face, clasped his hands together.

'Mr Balikov sends his apologies for not being here today, but he will endeavour to be here for the semi-finals. As a token of his apology, he has arranged some *entertainment* for you all in your private booths between fights. I'm sure you will find his tastes very satisfying.'

Singh looked at the ghastly men, who may as well have licked their lips at the thought of the young women awaiting them. Alenichev continued.

'As always, enjoy the event. May the best fighter win.'

A light round of applause echoed and then the gaggle

of wealthy men began to disperse, all of them being led to their own private rooms to enjoy the fights and the company of a vulnerable woman. Singh watched on in disgust, and Amos marched to her side.

'Where is Balikov?' she whispered.

'I don't know.'

'Something is off...' Singh broke into a smile. 'A fine speech, Artem. Although I must say, it is a shame Mr Balikov will not be joining us.'

'He does send his personal apologies to you, Mrs Al Ansari. However, as we appreciate your tastes may differ from our usual clientele, and due to him feeling terrible about missing the preliminary rounds, he has asked that I personally accompany you to your booth and steer you through your first tournament.'

There was an underlying threat to Alenichev's voice that was offset by his charming grin. It was clear that he wasn't asking for permission, but Singh knew there was a time to snap into action, and it wasn't now.

'Please, I am sure I will be fine.'

Alenichev took a step closer to her. His face still locked in a grin.

He spoke through gritted teeth.

'I insist.'

Amos took a step forward and Alenichev stepped back, eyeballing the man with an appreciation of the damage he could cause. The threat had ramped up the tension, and then it was sliced in half as he once again clasped his hands together.

'Let's go, shall we?' He turned and led them towards the stairs. 'I must say, I am very excited to see Mr Cooper in action once more. Very excited indeed.'

'I believe he has what it takes to win,' Singh said.

'I hope so.' Alenichev stopped at the door of the stairwell that would take them to their private booth. 'Mr Balikov is *very* keen to see him in action.'

'Likewise.'

Alenichev's smile twisted cruelly.

'Let's hope he can survive.'

With that, he threw open the door and headed towards the flight of stairs. Singh flashed a glance to Amos and then followed. Although she was climbing up the staircase, Singh couldn't shake the feeling that they were tumbling further down a dark hole where the only thing at the bottom was death.

CHAPTER TWENTY-ONE

Alenichev's crew had done a good job of keeping the fighters separated, and as Sam and Amos had been led to Sam's holding cell, they didn't catch a glimpse of anyone else. In their eyes, Sam was still a prisoner, just one dangerous enough to fight his way out, which meant keeping a gun trained on him made sense. Once they'd shoved Sam into the small, windowless room with nothing other than a bench for comfort, the mercenary told Amos to leave. The cells were a few levels underground, through a circuit of dimly lit corridors. The rooms, repurposed as holding cells, were similar to the concrete cubes of prison, with no CCTV, no sunlight, and no way out beyond the thick, steel door. A few guards roamed the corridors, but the mechanical locks of the doors ensured their safety. Each fighter would be led, by gunpoint, to the fight pit, and the survivor would be led back the same way.

Begrudgingly, Amos did as he was told, and he and Sam shared a knowing nod as he departed.

This was it.

Singh would already be working her way to Balikov, which meant all Sam had to do was stay alive long enough for them to pull him out. There was no concrete plan, as the tournament was shrouded in such secrecy that they would need to operate on instinct.

Once Singh could give confirmation to Blake of Balikov's presence, he'd be able to pull the necessary strings to have the building swarmed, and the man pulled out.

Dead or alive.

But that would be harder now as they realised that Balikov's security was armed and well trained.

It could be a bloodbath, and the last thing the continent needed was bloodshed and rising tensions between the UK and Russia. Especially on another country's soil.

But that was Blake's problem to deal with, and Sam refocused his mind on the task at hand. Surviving Sremska Mitrovica was one thing. This was an entirely different playing field.

Sixteen fighters, all plucked from the most dangerous corners of the world, all of them having proved their prowess to their rich benefactors and a baying mob of bloodthirsty onlookers.

It meant that when Sam's name was called, and he was led to the pit, the man he was facing wasn't some desperate criminal who saw him as an opportunity for freedom.

He would be facing someone who had already earnt theirs. It was a barbaric concept, pitting these dangerous men against each other for the enjoyment of the rich and powerful. There would be only one of them left breathing by the end of the tournament, and there was no guarantee that the winner would face anything other than the end of a gun.

Singh needed to do her job.

So did the whole of Directive One if Sam was going to make it out alive.

And Sam needed to do his.

He needed to fight.

From down the hallway, he heard one of the guards bark something in Hungarian, and then the sound of a door opening. As one of the fighters was led from his cell, Sam heard the doors slam shut and then five minutes later, the faint sound of a cheer.

The tournament had begun.

Although the bloodthirsty crowd was small, the excitement between them was incredible. Rich old men who had everything the world could offer. To them, the usual means of entertainment were too accessible, meaning the ability to champion a fighter in a brutal, exclusive tournament held the allure they craved.

It made Sam sick to his stomach, and while he knew the men he would be fighting were plucked from a darkness they deserved to be in, he wished he could turn his attention to the grotesque benefactors.

The untouchable people who made such an event possible.

The privileged crowd who had paid to watch.

The cheering pulsed through the building like a dim hum, then exploded into a big cheer as the fight came to a violent conclusion.

Sam clenched his fists.

Those people had just watched someone lose their life, and the only emotion they mustered was excitement.

A sharp buzz rang out, and the mechanised lock of his door snapped open. Sam turned to face the guard, who stepped in with his weapon drawn. Sam held up his hands to signal his cooperation, and the guard that Amos had embarrassed stepped in.

'You. Englishman. Time to go.'

Sam followed the man out of the door, and the other guard followed, his gun trained on the back of Sam's skull. The corridor was dark and narrow, as were the stairwells, and the guard strode quickly towards the door at the far end. As they approached, Sam could hear the excitement of the fight pit growing in volume. They stopped by the door, and the guard turned to him.

'Ready?'

Sam lifted his T-shirt over his head and dropped it on the floor, his muscles riddled with scars and tattoos. The guard nodded, impressed, and then threw open the door.

The blinding light caught Sam a little off guard, but he blinked through it and stepped into the pit. There was no cage, as he had expected. The fighting arena was surrounded by high brick walls, offering no opportunity for escape. Across the top, overlooking the carnage, were private boxes, and Sam looked up at all the wealthy psychopaths who were watching with glee. A few with scantily dressed women beside them. Others had practically naked young men with them.

Whatever they wanted, Balikov had catered for them.

One side of the wall was opened up, fitted with crude benches where another fifty or so onlookers watched with excitement.

Paying spectators, who couldn't afford a fighter but could afford a front row seat to the blood bath.

All eyes fell on Sam, and he noticed a few impressed glances being shared between them. As he looked around, his eyes finally fell to Singh, who stood as their eyes met.

Beside her was the same man as at the prison.

Alenichev.

Singh's eyes widened in a brief flicker of panic, before she began applauding, keeping in character.

Alenichev watched intently.

Sam nodded to Singh and then began to roll his shoulders, limbering up as the door across the fight pit opened.

A roar of excitement echoed from above as the behemoth of a man stepped through. Sam shot a glance to Singh, who gasped at the size of the brute, and Alenichev chuckled. Over the years, Sam had faced some larger men, such as Edinson and Oleg Kovalenko, but this was different.

Moses towered over them.

The man had the build of a professional wrestler, and his black skin was covered in faded tattoos. A deep scar ran from his forehead to the back of his ear, and by the look in Moses's eyes, murdering another man was second nature.

And he seemed pleased at the opponent before him.

Alenichev stood and clapped his hands loudly, and all eyes turned to Singh's booth. The other onlookers were shaking with excitement.

Alenichev threw his hand down.

'Fight.'

A wave of cheers erupted from above, and Sam began to circle the pit, his eyes locked on Moses, who just marched towards him with little fear. As he got with a few feet, Moses launched forward, trying to snatch Sam in his unbreakable grasp. Sam weaved underneath, and Moses spun and threw a wild fist, which Sam ducked.

The crowd cheered.

Singh felt sick.

Moses chuckled, and then beckoned for Sam to strike him. Sam obliged, rocking the man with a brutal right that did little but move his head to the side. Sam threw another, but Moses leant forward and shoulder-charged Sam, taking him clean off his feet and onto the hard dusty concrete below. As soon as Sam hit the ground, he felt the extreme weight of the man on top of him, and the vile crowd roared their approval.

Sam struggled as Moses tried to wrap his enormous hands around his throat, and with the man struggling to pin Sam down, Sam threw his knees up into the man's spine.

As one of them connected with a kidney, Moses

groaned and loosened his grip, and Sam looped an arm over the man's head and pulled him down, locking in a triangle choke that Amos would have been proud of.

As Sam wrenched as hard as he could, trying to cut off the man's air supply, Moses growled in anger, and to the thrill of the crowd, began to lift himself off the ground. Sam tried to throw his bodyweight back, but the man's strength was unrivalled, and he pushed himself to his feet, lifting Sam into the air with him.

With his opponent clinging to his neck, Moses took a few steps and then swung Sam as hard as he could, slamming him into the solid brick wall of the pit and let him drop to the floor. As he gasped for breath, Moses angrily booted Sam in the stomach and then lifted his arms to the crowd, who all applauded his show of strength.

All except Singh.

Sam pushed himself to all fours, coughing through the pain, and Moses charged and threw another bare foot into Sam's ribs.

But Sam dropped flat to the ground, the foot speeding past him and as it collided with the solid stone, Sam could hear the shattering of bones.

It was followed by a howl of agony, and as Moses rocked back, trying to clutch at his decimated foot, Sam swivelled, and with all his force, drove his foot into the man's other shin.

The bone snapped cleanly, piercing the skin and sending a spray of blood across the ground.

A collective gasp of shock echoed from above, and Alenichev stood, impressed with what he was witnessing.

Moses fell like a tree in the woods, slamming hard against the concrete and sending a cloud of dust up into the pit. The giant had been felled, and as he writhed in agony, his hands reaching for but not touching his obliterated legs, Sam pushed himself to his feet. He stretched the pain from his spine and then marched towards his opponent. One of the onlookers screamed for mercy, watching as Sam was about to eliminate him from the tournament. Moses had barely registered Sam's approach, the pain and shock beginning to take over his body, and Sam knelt beside him and with some effort, lifted him to a seated position.

Then, without hesitation, he placed a hand on the top of Moses's skull and under his chin and snapped his neck in one swift twist.

The man slumped to the side. He was dead before his head hit the ground.

Sam stood, shooting murderous glances at the watching mob, and then turned and headed back towards the door. The thought of fighting for their entertainment bubbled the bile in his gut, but he satisfied his guilt with the knowledge that his unfortunate opponent had been plucked from a life of violence. Amos had placated Sam with the knowledge that every fighter brought to *Boytsovskaya Yama* was a killer. These men had no hope of a life outside of a prison wall due to the horrors they'd inflicted to get there.

Sam may have killed Moses in cold blood, but it was nothing compared to the damage the man had caused.

The world wouldn't mourn him.

And Sam didn't regret the blood on his hands.

As he approached the door, the guard opened it, a look of surprise on his face but before he could commend Sam on his fight, Sam barged past him and marched back towards his cell, with the sound of the crowd chanting for more.

As the door closed behind Sam, Alenichev stopped applauding and turned to Mrs Al Ansari, who was also standing. Her eyes were locked on the motionless corpse of the man her fighter had just defeated, and he scanned her face for any signs of remorse.

Any shred of doubt.

But the woman seemed a picture of calm and she turned to Alenichev and grinned, seemingly pleased with the performance of her fighter.

'That was very impressive,' Alenichev said. 'He really is quite the fighter, isn't he?'

'I had my doubts about this tournament, but I must say, Artem, it is quite thrilling.' Singh had to swallow the vomit in her throat. Watching a man being killed, especially by someone she cared about, was enough to turn her stomach. 'It is a shame that Mr Balikov was not here to see it.'

'He would have been as impressed as I am, I can assure you. And if this Cooper can make it past the next round, then he will be able to fight for Balikov.'

'Can I speak to him?' Singh asked as she summoned the waiter forward. She took a bottle of water from him and sipped it.

'Cooper?' Alenichev frowned. 'You want to speak to this man? That is highly unusual.'

'I don't see the problem. I paid good money for his release and for his entrance to this fight. I think that buys me the right to explain that to *my* property. Don't you?'

Alenichev peered into Singh's eyes, daring her to let her guard slip. There was something about this woman that still wasn't sitting right, and in the years in which he'd helped facilitate *Boytsovskaya Yama*, never had one of the entrants wanted to speak to the vile humans they had marked for death. It was beneath them.

'I don't think I can agree to such terms.' Alenichev

waved his hand. 'It is too dangerous down there for a young woman.'

'I must insist.'

Singh stood straight, asserting authority through her body language. It was an impressive yet futile act. Alenichev sighed and rolled his eyes.

'Mr Balikov will find it most strange, but as you said, you have paid the required money. I will go with you, of course.'

'There is no need…'

'On this, *I* insist,' Alenichev said with a smirk.

'My personal security is more than capable of keeping me safe.' She gently stroked Alenichev's arm. 'Besides, I wouldn't want anything to happen to you.'

The strange turn caught Alenichev off guard, and he stepped back from the beautiful woman. Again, battling the vomit that threatened to erupt at any moment, Singh offered him her most flirtatious smile.

A promise for something better.

If Alenichev was rattled, he didn't show it, and he turned back to the fight pit, where Moses was being hauled from the murder scene. He pulled his phone from his pocket, lifted it to his ears, and barked some orders in his native tongue. He hung up the call, pocketed the phone and then nodded his approval.

'Fine. Go. But make it quick.'

Singh headed to the door, closely followed by Amos. Once they'd stepped from their booth, Alenichev took the phone from his pocket once more.

There was a message.

He opened it, and the photo engulfed his screen and caused his eyes to bulge.

He tapped the sender's contact details and lifted the phone to his ear.

It answered after the third ring.

Alenichev felt a wave of triumph wash through his body as his face contorted into a twisted grin.

'Bring him in.'

Alenichev hung up the phone, took a victorious swig from a champagne glass, then turned to the onlooking crowd, who were ready for him to introduce the next fight.

CHAPTER TWENTY-TWO

From the moment Artem Alenichev had met Aysha Al Ansari, he'd been suspicious. The first meeting was the usual sales pitch, where he would size up the financial legitimacy of the potential entrant as well as whether they would be a good ally for the cause. Considering her bold and brash attempts to topple the male-dominant hierarchy within her own culture, Alenichev had found her fascinating.

It wasn't until he had his contacts look deeper into her background. Hers was a name he'd never encountered, which was a strange outcome considering Balikov had links to multiple oil companies. At some point, the Al Ansari name should have registered, and although his men found a legitimate trail of business and financial records, all readily available, a red flag had been waved in Alenichev's face.

For years, it was his instinct that had made him such a force for Balikov, and although he could handle himself physically, it was his mind that made him such a dangerous foe.

Something didn't sit right.

Which, when Alenichev said it, meant that something *wasn't* right.

All the independent contractors at Alenichev's disposal were ex-FSB, with some of them even serving when it was known as the more infamous KGB. The best of the best, with ties to the most powerful men in the country, all of whom owed these men favours.

Alenichev would call them in.

After his trip to Serbia to watch Mrs Al Ansari's chosen fighter wipe the floor clean with the worst Sremska Mitrovica had to offer, Alenichev's concerns grew.

A random Englishman who had been transferred to the prison a week prior had suddenly become her prized fighter.

All the documents were checked.

Jonathan Cooper was as real as a digital footprint could provide, with a long history of violent crimes. The man had been shunted from dark hole to dark hole, with no prison able to handle him.

It was all there, presented to him after hours of investigation and multiple favours called in.

But Alenichev wasn't sure.

It was why he had both Al Ansari and Cooper followed after they left Serbia, with a tail placed outside both of their respective residence. It was how he was able to attain the images of the man meeting with Cooper and Al Ansari's personal security in the gym, as well as the damning photo of the woman hugging her fighter like an old friend.

There was more to their relationship.

This wasn't just a series of coincidences falling in line to give this woman a chance to win *Boytsovskaya Yama*.

It was planned.

And it was why, despite the supposed Mrs Al Ansari and Jonathon Cooper being inside the tournament facility, that he had his men stationed at their hotels. One of them had already turned the hostel upside down to find a shred of evidence, but it had proved fruitless.

But Fedor Zhirkov, a man the KGB had once nicknamed 'The Torch' for his ability to shine a light on anything, had been more successful at the Parisi Udvar Hotel. Whoever Al Ansari was, she had expensive taste, and Zhirkov had been meticulous when searching her room. There would be no trace of his presence, but then there was no trace that she was anyone other than who she said she was.

It was a dead end.

But not for Zhirkov. The man's pride in his own reputation demanded he stake out the hotel for as long as he had to, and then came the moment that a few dots connected.

He saw the man from the gym.

Although Zhirkov had not been tailing Cooper, he'd seen the photos, and he was certain that the man he saw entering the Parisi Udvar was one and the same.

Why would the man who spoke to Cooper on one side of town also be staying in the same luxury hotel as his benefactor?

Zhirkov made some calls to the Kremlin, asking for the photo to be identified and then called Alenichev with the update. It would take a few hours to get a name to go with the face, but Alenichev's gut had been proven right.

'Bring him in.'

With the target in the hotel, Zhirkov called in a few heavies, men who owed him a favour, and the four of them made their way into the hotel. He flashed a badge to the terrified looking woman on the desk and gave her a vague explanation about an Interpol investigation. The manager tried to intervene, but Zhirkov threatened him with the baseless promise of a few years in prison for obstructing them.

Buckling under the pressure, the manager gave them the room.

It was the suite opposite Al Ansari.

Another coincidence had just fallen into place, and with their MP-443 Grach handguns strapped to their holsters, the four men called for the elevator, entered, and headed up to fix a growing problem.

'How do you know he won?' Blake asked, running his hand through his thick hair. Hun sat opposite him on one of the armchairs, the laptop sitting on his lap and the side table littered with empty cans of energy drinks.

'I've been able to hack a phone within the vicinity and I have the audio. It's a bit crackly, but I heard the people talking about Cooper.'

'Well, we'll debrief with Singh when she gets back this evening. But thank you.' Blake hated to admit it, but he was worried about Sam's safety. 'Keep me posted.'

'Will do.' Hun moved the laptop. 'Mind if I use your bathroom?'

'Do I have a choice?'

Hun cracked a smile.

'Not with all these energy drinks you don't.'

Chuckling, the technical wizard disappeared across the suite and into the bathroom as Blake lifted his phone. He tapped out a message to Brady, updating him about the mission. There were things he wanted to discuss, and within a few seconds of sending it, Brady replied.

I'll be up in two.

Brady, Foster, and Hun had their own rooms on different floors of the hotel. It gave them enough space to not be seen with each other, but also the ability to meet in the communal spaces, as well as in their own rooms. Blake's suite was big enough for them all to meet comfortably, and just as he was about to fire a message off to Foster to join them, a knuckle rapped against his door. He shook the doubt away and walked to the door, chuckling as he opened it.

'Christ, Brady, you move like…'

A fist cut off Blake's sentence, the hard bone crunching into his mouth and sending him stumbling back into the room. As the room spun and blood dribbled down his chin, Blake managed to regroup quickly enough to block the next fist that was thrown to his face, but unable to stop one of the other intruders drilling him in the stomach with a sucker punch. He gasped for air as he dropped to one knee, and he looked up as Zhirkov stepped in, seemingly pleased with the work of his men.

'You're coming with me,' he said in impressive English, and Blake spat blood at the man. He sighed, and nodded to the nearest goon, who excitedly lifted his fist.

A laptop crashed into the back of the man's head, and a terrified Hun dropped the machine onto the man's limp body.

'Hun! Run!' Blake yelled, as one of the other goons made a move for him. As Hun scurried off into the suite, followed by a blood thirsty mercenary, Zhirkov stepped over the fallen henchman and slapped Blake with the back of his hand.

'If you resist, I will start taking fingers.' Zhirkov showed Blake the knife and then motioned for him to get up. The remaining henchman zip-tied his wrists together and the two of them marched Blake to the door. The director tried to arch his head back to locate Hun, but the other henchman couldn't resist the chance to test Blake's jaw strength with another right hook.

'*Dostatochno!*' Spat Zhirkov, annoyed at his employee. They roughly pushed Blake from the suite into the hallway, just as the elevator pinged. Zhirkov held the woozy Blake by the arm, and as the lift door opened, his eyes widened.

Brady analysed the situation quickly, and his hand instinctively whipped his Glock 17 from his belt, just as the henchman rushed forward. He pushed Brady's hand upwards, the gun unloading a round into the roof of the elevator, and the two men jostled for the advantage, their muscular frames shaking the lift from side to side. Zhirkov swiftly turned Blake towards the stairwell and pushed him through, as Blake yelled back to Brady to get to Hun.

Brady heard the order and immediately thought of his friend. Hun was an annoyance at times, but he wasn't a fighter.

As the two men struggled in the confines of the elevator, Brady managed to get a steady footing, and then drove his other boot into the side of the man's knee. It buckled, sending the man to the side, and Brady drove his elbow into the man's temple, instantly shutting him down.

The man collapsed onto the floor, and Brady hit the ground button, lifted his gun from the floor, and stepped out of the lift before the doors closed. With his pistol raised, he stepped into Blake's suite, his eyes immediately drawn to the large man who was stirring on the floor. Blood gushed from a gash on the back of his skull, and as he tried to push himself up, he muttered Russian under his breath.

There was no Hun.

From somewhere in the suite, Brady heard a sickening

crash and the sound of shattering glass. Keeping his gun up, he hurried across the room, sending the bleeding henchman back to unconsciousness with a vicious knee strike en route.

The sound of struggling grew louder, and Brady stepped into the master bedroom and without hesitation, squeezed the trigger twice.

The first bullet hit Hun's attacker in the shoulder, sending him staggering back.

The second blew out the back of his skull, sending a visceral spray of red up the wall.

The man dropped dead. Brady lowered his weapon and rushed to Hun, who had been moments away from being strangled to death. The man had straddled Hun, pinning him to the bed with his superior weight and judging by the bruising already showing on Hun's throat, had been seconds away from finishing the job.

Hun gasped for breath; his face littered with small cuts.

The room was covered in broken shards of glass, and one of the mirrored wardrobe doors had been completely obliterated.

Hun was hurt.

But he'd live.

Brady tucked his gun into his belt and whipped out his phone and called Foster. She answered on the first ring.

'Brady, what's…'

'They have Blake. Stairwell. Get going.'

'What the fuck?'

'Go. Now. I'll catch you up.'

He hung up without explanation. There was zero hierarchy besides Blake within Directive One, but it was an unwritten agreement that Brady was next in line, as much as he hated to admit it. Foster would obey any order given, and he just hoped she had enough time. Brady rushed to

Hun and helped him sit up, as the young man coughed painfully as he caught his breath.

'I think I had him.' Hun joked as Brady helped him slowly to his feet.

'Yeah, it looked like it.' Brady smiled. 'We have to go. Now.'

'There's another guy in the front room…'

'Already taken care of,' Brady said confidently, as he looped his injured friend's arm over his neck to steady him. They took a few careful steps forward.

'Wait,' Hun snapped, and then leant down and picked up his sports bag. That was crammed with laptops and other pieces of tech that Brady couldn't name if he tried. They stumbled through the doorway and into the front room, where the man laid motionless among a puddle of blood and computer parts. Hun nodded proudly at the wreckage. 'I did that.'

'I thought you were against violence?' Brady smirked.

'I am. But sometimes you just have to be a hero, you know?'

Brady rolled his eyes and the two men moved as quickly as they could to the stairwell, pushed open the door and began their descent to the exit. As they passed one of the open windows, Brady heard the roar of a motorcycle engine from the streets below, and he prayed to a god he didn't believe in, that it was Foster giving chase.

Whatever happened, he and Hun needed to get the hell out of the hotel.

'Good work, Artem.' Balikov's voice echoed through the phone. *'As always, I know I can trust you. Continue with the tournament as normal. I do not want any suspicions to arise.'*

'You want to let Cooper compete, sir?' Alenichev asked, the

phone pressed to his ear. He was standing in a derelict room, one of many that dominated the facility.

'Oh yes. Our benefactors, they have paid money for a show. So let them have one.'

'Well, the man is being brought here as we speak. In a few hours, I will have his name. Once I have his name, it won't take me long to extract his purpose.'

'Then I will extract his life,' Balikov added.

'Excuse me, sir?'

'I have already called for the chopper. I will be with you within the next few hours.'

'Sir, I told you to stay back. Whoever these people are, and whatever it is they want, it is not good for you...'

Balikov's voice exploded with rage.

'This is MY tournament. These people want to try to infiltrate Poslednyaya Nadezhda. They want to try to make a fool of me. Then I will show them exactly who they are dealing with.'

Alenichev sighed and rubbed the bridge of his nose. The differences between him and Balikov were stark, but they both believed in the same cause. The world needed to change, and Balikov possessed the ruthless, bloodthirsty nature that could steer the world in that direction. Alenichev was more a thinker than a fighter, but even he knew that a betrayed Balikov, one who had been challenged by an outside threat, was not a beast that could be tamed.

Balikov wanted blood.

And there were few people in the world who could stop the man from taking what he wanted.

Alenichev took a moment to collect himself and then responded.

'Very well, sir. The tournament will continue, and I will see you soon.'

'Very good, Artem.'

'Just, may I request, that we find out who these people are before we kill them? We need to be thorough.'

Alenichev could hear Balikov's face contort into a crude sneer.

'Artem, my friend. These people are about to experience a glimpse of the new world. They are about to witness the full force of Poslednyaya Nadezhda.'

The line went dead.

CHAPTER TWENTY-THREE

Sam sat on the bench of his cell and took a deep breath.

It shouldn't have been as easy as it was to end that man's life, and Sam knew that what he possessed was both a skill and a curse. Many people would freeze at the pivotal moment, knowing that the act of ending another human's life was inherently wrong. But he was able to look beyond that and appreciate the wider mission. If he didn't kill his opponent, then he would have been killed himself.

Losing his life wasn't something he was afraid of.

His death would mean they would get no closer to Balikov, and innocent people would die.

He could hear the vulgar delight of the crowd echoing through the building, as a man known as Marko was systematically taking apart his opponent in a brutal display of barbarian ferocity.

The roar of the crowd and his own thoughts were interrupted by the return of the loud buzzing, and his cell door opened.

Singh.

She stepped in, offering Sam a friendly smile, as Amos nodded to the guard and sent him on his way. Once the man had stepped out of the room, Singh wrapped her arms around Sam.

'I'm so sorry,' she said softly.

'What for?' Sam stepped back.

'For all of this. It's just…just…inhumane.'

Sam shrugged.

'This is the world people don't see. It's why people like us exist.'

Amos reached out and squeezed Sam's shoulder.

'If it's any help…' he began. 'The man you killed, Moses, was serving multiple life sentences for the murder of a young family and seventeen counts of sexual assault. The world is a better place without him.'

Sam nodded. It was a small comfort, but he appreciated the effort they were going through to not make him feel guilty.

He didn't.

It was all part of the mission.

As Amos retracted his hand, Sam turned to Singh, who looked glamourous compared to the beaten, bloodied state of himself.

'Where is Balikov?' he asked sternly.

'He isn't here.' Singh sighed. 'Alenichev is suspicious, that much is clear. He's questioning everything and whatever I say seems to be constantly under inspection. We've done nothing to give the game away just yet, but we need to be watertight.'

'Is being here a good idea?' Sam looked at them both. 'Surely, I'm just some scummy prisoner you plucked out.'

'I told him you were my property and I can do as I please.' She stepped forward. 'I wanted to see you. Besides, until I get back to the hotel and regroup with Blake, we are all we've got. It's just us three here, so we need to know what's going on.'

Sam looked at Amos who seemed to agree. He rubbed his bearded jaw and then finally relented.

'It's your call. Just be careful, Amara. These people... they aren't normal criminals.'

'You think I don't know that?' She was clearly scared. But Singh was tough, and she didn't fail. 'But we didn't come this far to fail now. Alenichev said that Balikov will be back for the semi-finals, which means you've got to get through one more fight before we even have a chance of meeting him. So I want you to know that the next person they put across from you will be just as bad, if not worse than Moses. I need you to fight, Sam. We'll do the rest.'

The three of them let the silence sit for a moment, all of them making a quiet commitment to the cause. They'd come too far now to back down. Anything other than steering the course would result in death, and even if they did get close to Balikov, there was no promise they'd all walk away from this. After a few more moments, Singh turned to Amos and smiled. He knew what it meant and turned to the door.

'I'll wait outside.' He held out a fist to Sam. 'Good luck, brother.'

Sam bumped it, and Amos stepped outside, speaking to the waiting guard as he closed the door behind him. Sam turned to Singh, who frowned to herself.

'Amara. You've got th—'

'I just wanted to say,' she interrupted. 'I never meant to hurt you, Sam. You know that, right? My life has been a blur for years now, but whenever I find myself with a quiet moment, it always goes back to you. I know it shouldn't, and I know our paths have gone so far in opposite directions that this is the only way they'd intersect. You're a number of things, Sam. But to me...ah, I'm not very good at this...'

Sam stepped forward and took her hand.

'I know. And there will always be a bit of me that thinks another life, another path, we'd have done it together. But that's not who we are.' He looked around at the cell. 'Look where we are. This is the life we've chosen, and I don't regret it. Seeing you fight this fight, this is who you are meant to be. Not with me. Not for me. But fighting for you. And what *you* believe in.'

Singh looked up at Sam, her eyes watering. She gently pressed the back of her hand to his bearded cheek. Then she stepped on her toes and leant in for a kiss.

Sam turned away.

'I'm sorry,' he uttered.

Clearly flustered with embarrassment, Singh overcompensated with her collection of herself.

'No, that was my mistake. I better go…'

Sam reached out and clamped his hand around her elbow. She turned to him and he offered her a sad smile.

'Last year, I met a woman. Mel. She had a little business and an amazing teenage daughter. She changed me for the better.' Sam could feel his words choking. 'But then my life and my decisions put them in danger, so I had to leave them behind. For their own sake.'

'She sounds like an amazing woman.'

'She is. And if my fight ever ends and my path does lead me back to someone, I know it would be to her door.'

Singh moved her arm from Sam's grip and then wrapped her hands around his. She stepped towards him, and this time, she gently kissed him on the cheek.

'In another life, Sam.' She smiled. 'But as for this one, try to get back to her.'

'Thank you.' Sam held his grip on Singh's hand, and then lifted it to his lips and kissed it.

Singh turned to the door and knocked on it twice, and Amos swiftly pulled the door open. He nodded to Sam, and as Singh left, she pulled her headscarf up once more, turned and looked Sam dead in the eye.

'Now go give them hell.'

The door closed, and the lock snapped shut.

Sam could hear Alenichev hyping the remainder of the crowd on. A few of the rich men had stormed out of the facility when their chosen fighter had the audacity to die, while a number of other losers were just happy to indulge in the luxuries afforded to them and watch more of the violent entertainment. They'd paid good money for their front-row seat, and being out of the competition simply alleviated the pressure. The other spectators were on the edge of their seats, the excitement buzzing amongst them like a beehive.

Alenichev's voice rose as he announced the quarter final fight, and one of the guards stood beside Sam, swaying slightly in anticipation. Since Sam's brutal showing in the first round, the guards had softened as if his violence had, in some way, ingratiated himself to them.

The door flew open, and Sam stepped out once more into the pit, the eyes of the crowd on him. Simply wearing his trousers and plimsols, Sam glared up at them, his chiselled physique covered in scars, ink, and bruises. He was an impressive sight to behold, and Alenichev once again kept his eyes on Singh as she applauded from her box. The opposite door opened, and Sam's opponent came racing through, his eyes wild with rage. His nostrils were coated in white powder, and Sam knew instantly that the fighter's benefactor had given the man a little "boost". His opponent was a man named Muller, an ex-soldier from Germany who had beaten his own wife to death and then flourished in prison where the currency was pain.

The man could fight.

He was trained not only as a soldier, but as a boxer, and his impressive frame and speed were a testament to it. He swallowed the ground between them in a few steps, bounded and then leapt, driving a fist down into Sam's face mid-flight and sending Sam back a few feet and the crowd into a frenzy. Sam shook the cobwebs and threw his arms up, blocking the expert combo, before Muller caught him in his ribs with an uppercut and then sent Sam to the ground with a thunderous right hook.

The approval echoed above them.

Muller threw his arms up to them, basking in their adulation as Sam gingerly pushed himself to his feet. Muller eyed him enthusiastically, and Sam spat a wad of blood onto the floor and raised his fists.

Muller was on him again in a flash.

Jab. Jab. Straight.

Sam absorbed the blows on his forearms, but the man's speed made it impossible for Sam to retaliate. Eventually, one of the jabs squeezed through Sam's block, catching him on the nose, before another hook sent Sam spinning into the wall. As he hit the concrete, Muller leapt forward, driving his knee into Sam's ribs, and sending him back into the concrete. His head smacked the brick and sent his brain spinning, and without any means to protect himself, Sam felt his whole body get lifted off the ground as the uppercut connected with his jaw.

He hit the ground hard, his jaw aching, and as his brain finally stopped shaking in his skull, Sam realised he was being beaten to death. His opponent was unrelenting, save for the moments he took in playing to his adoring audience. As Muller circled the pit with his arms outstretched, summoning the cheers, Amos stormed past both Singh and Alenichev in their booth, slammed his hands on the railing of their private booth and yelled out.

'Get up and fight!'

Sam rolled to his side and looked up, his eyes meeting Amos's and he nodded. Although he was shaken, Sam's mind raced back to the week he'd spent with Amos, who had swiftly eliminated any notion in Sam's mind that he knew how to fight. There was being trained in a discipline such as Krav Maga or Muay Thai, but it was a very different process to bring it all together.

Not just when to strike.

But when to defend.

When to give your opponent an inch, and then snatch a mile from them.

Sam wiped the blood from his mouth with the back of his hand and then stood once more. He looked to Singh, who, despite her dedication to the role of Mrs Al Ansari, was betraying it with the worry spread across her striking face.

Alenichev regarded her smugly.

The worry wasn't for the violence she was watching.

It was for *who* she was watching.

If the man was on to them, then Sam knew they at least needed an audience with Balikov to make any of it worthwhile.

As he steadied himself, Sam drew in a breath and blocked out the sound of the fight pit. As he eliminated the crowd and the thumping fists against the railings, a wave of clarity washed over him. His mind raced to the little details, the slight limp in the man's run.

The cocaine remnants around his nose.

The opening he left when he swung his hook.

Sam opened his eyes and met the deranged, sadistic gaze of his opponent, who was stalking him like a predator playing with his food.

Sam beckoned him forward.

The crowd roared, but Sam didn't hear them.

Muller's drug-addled mind had failed to spot the change in Sam's demeanour, and he rushed forward with the same volition as before and swung a punch. This time, instead of blocking it, Sam weaved underneath, and in the process, drove a fist into the man's kneecap. The bone-on-bone impact hurt, but as Sam stepped back up with a broken knuckle, he'd exacerbated the man's weakness. Muller yelped in pain and then limped away, trying his best to walk it off and show no weakness.

But Sam smelt blood.

Muller circled back and through gritted teeth, put pressure on his knee as he threw his bodyweight into the following right cross.

Sam threw his arm up, absorbing the vicious strike flush on his solid, left bicep, but in one fluid movement, drove his right elbow into Muller's throat, and then swung his right foot into the damaged knee.

The scream of pain echoed through the fight pit as the cartilage ripped from the bone, and Muller crumpled to the ground, growling like an animal caught in a bear trap. With the crowd calling for the execution, Sam watched as one of the men stood and waved to Alenichev. Clearly, the man was Muller's backer and motioned to Alenichev that the time was now. A few confused faces shared bewildered glances, before Alenichev nodded and then motioned to the guards below. Sam took a few steps back as one of the guards rushed into the pit, his gun trained on Sam, who held his hands up. Another guard helped Muller to his feet and then, to the delight of the crowd, both the remaining participants and the paying spectators, pulled a hunting knife from his belt and handed it to him.

Muller's backer had paid for a back-up plan.

The crowd applauded the show of wealth and intuition, and Singh remonstrated with Alenichev, who seemed to revel in her dismay.

But Sam stood calmly.

To the crowd, Muller was resilient. But in reality, the man had been crippled and was already defeated.

He just didn't know it yet.

With the blade swinging in his hand, Muller limped forward, screaming at Sam in his aggressive German accent that the end was coming. Sam met him head on, and a hush fell over the crowd as Muller slashed forward with the blade.

Sam dodged, drove his fist into Muller's ribs, and then twisted the man's arm until the tendons in his shoulder snapped like rubber bands. The arm went limp, and the knife dropped from his hand.

And Sam caught it.

The pain was already starting to take control of Muller's mind, and Sam spun the blade round and drove it full force into Muller's thigh, before he twisted it and wrenched it upwards, ripping the quad muscle to shreds.

Muller stumbled forward as the leg went limp, and Sam retrieved the blade and then rammed it as hard as he could into the man's throat. Instantly, the warmth of the blood flowed over his hand and Muller's eyes went wide as he gargled for air. Sam slammed his other hand onto the handle and drove the blade further into his opponent's throat, and Muller backwards onto the ground. As the final few moments of Muller's life bled from him, Sam stood, and a sickening cheer accompanied the man's death.

Disgusted by it all, Sam leant down, plucked the blade from the corpse, turned, and then hurled it as hard as he could up at the man's benefactor. The knife spun through the air, and sliced the man across the shoulder, ripping his expensive suit and drawing blood.

The crowd gasped.

The watching guards drew their weapons.

Everyone looked to Alenichev, who stood, his eyes wide

with fury as he regarded the fighter below. Sam returned the look, defiant to the end.

Singh stood.

The crowd watched on in silence.

Clap. Clap. Clap.

The slap of flesh sliced through the tension and all eyes turned to behind Alenichev, where the unmistakable figure of Balikov appeared. And as he applauded Sam for the brutality of his showing, and his disdain for his audience, Balikov did so with a look in his eye that was clear to everyone.

Victory.

CHAPTER TWENTY-FOUR

As Balikov emerged towards the front of Singh's booth, Sam looked on with worry. Alenichev's stance towards his friend had taken a more aggressive turn, and three armed guards swarmed in, shrinking the space that Amos occupied behind. Sam had felt like he was standing in a wolves' den, and judging by the fear and reverence that the other onlookers held Balikov in, it was clear that the alpha had stepped in.

Sarcastically slapping his hands together in a mocking slow clap, Balikov approached the barrier with a fiendish grin. Pinned to the breast of his sharp suit were two pins, both of them symbolising his beloved country.

As his cruel gaze lingered on Sam for a few more uncomfortable seconds, he turned his frame to Singh, who tried not to flinch.

'Mrs Al Ansari, I presume?' Balikov's English was good, but heavy with an accent. He took her hand and cupped his other over the top.

'Mr Balikov. It is a pleasure to…'

Singh's words were cut off by a squeal of pain as Balikov pressed his hands together, clamping her hand between them and began to crush them. As Singh twisted her arm in agony, Amos launched forward, his hands just grazing Balikov before the three guards latched onto him and hauled him back. Sam watched on in horror as they threw Amos to the ground and drove their boots and fists down upon him with reckless abandon.

Balikov turned to Sam, smirked, and then slapped Singh across the face, releasing her as she stumbled back into the grateful arms of Alenichev. Swiftly, Balikov's right-hand man pulled his MP-443 Grach from inside his jacket and pressed it against her temple. Sam took a helpless step forward, and one of the guards who had been putting the boots to Amos pulled his weapon and trained it on Sam.

Balikov clasped his hands together, a figure of composure among the sudden violent outbreak.

'I hear you are Englishman, so let me make this clear.' Balikov rested his hands on the railing. 'This is *my* tournament. *Boytsovskaya Yama* was designed to pit the worst of the world against each other, to show my supporters that the world *can* survive what is coming. That human nature, when stripped back, will take control. These men, they have all seen the vision of *Poslednyaya Nadezhda,* and their money pays for their seat at the new top table when the moment comes. But they pay *me.* This tournament was designed by *me.* And when people try to make a mockery of it, they make a mockery of *me.*'

Balikov slammed his fist down on the railing, his ring clanging against the steel and shaking the bars. It reverberated around the fight pit, along with his anger. His eyes bore into Sam as he continued.

'I do not know who you people are, but I will find out. This woman here, she will talk. This man on the floor, this black piece of shit, he will talk. The man we took from your hotel, he *will* talk. And then, like you, an insignificant bug that crawled out of a crack in the ground, they will die. It is only their co-operation that will determine how painless that moment will be.'

Balikov snapped his fingers, and the two guards hauled a bloodied and limp Amos from the ground and dragged him from the room. He kept his eyes on Sam as he spoke.

'Over time, they will tell me who they are. But you, you will tell me now, Englishman. Jonathan Cooper is not a man who exists.'

'Come down here and I'll tell you. Personally.' Sam threatened, his fists clenched and his muscles tense. Balikov scoffed at the challenge and then turned and threw a violent punch into Singh's stomach. Alenichev released her as she fell to her knees, gasping for the air that had been driven from her body. Balikov straightened his tie and turned back to Sam, gazing down on him like a god among men.

'Tell me. Or I will start breaking her bones.'

'Don't say shit,' Singh spluttered, and Alenichev hauled back her headscarf and yanked her head back by the hair.

'Keep that bitch quiet,' Balikov ordered and turned back to Sam. 'Final chance.'

Alenichev lifted the gun and pushed it into the side of Singh's mouth, her face contorting in disgust at the taste of the cold, dirty steel.

'My name is Sam Pope,' Sam yelled, standing defiantly against the odds before him.

The announcement sent a shockwave of murmurs through the arena, and Balikov's eyes lit up. Worried glances were exchanged by some of the elite men from their booths. Confusion had spread amongst the rest of the crowd.

'I know this name. You killed very dangerous men. Kovalenko. Kovac. This was you, yes?'

'Friends of yours?' Sam asked. Balikov grinned.

'Associates. Some, potential believers in *Poslednyaya*

Nadezhda.' Balikov applauded. 'You are an interesting proposition. I have business to attend to. Your friend, the other Englishman, he has some important things to tell me. So while I go and take them from him, you will stay here. You will *all* stay here.' Balikov turned to Alenichev. 'If he moves, put a bullet through her cheek. This will not kill her, but it will destroy her pretty face.'

Balikov patted the side of Singh's face, and she grunted her anger. Alenichev pushed the gun further into the side of her mouth and glared at Sam, daring him to make a move.

With his friend's life on the line, his other associates in Balikov's capture, and a gun trained on him, Sam had never felt more helpless.

He wanted to fight back. With every fibre of his being.

But as Balikov stormed from the booth and left the room in a terrified silence, Sam knew he could do nothing but wait for Balikov to return to kill him.

After being stuffed into the back of a car and knocked unconscious, Blake was slapped awake by a grizzled looking mercenary leaning into the car. As the hands reached in and hauled him out, he was unable to break his fall. His restraints had pinned his hands to the base of his spine and allowed him to greet the ground cheek first. He grunted in pain, which only summoned a swift boot to the ribs before Zhirkov pushed him onto his back with his boot and looked down at him.

'You are in trouble, my friend.'

Blake engaged his core and pushed himself to a seated position.

'Friend is a little far, don't you think?'

Another boot caught him on the side of the jaw,

sending him sprawling across the dusty concrete, before two men hauled him to his feet and moved him towards the facility. He had no concept of time, but as he surveyed his surroundings, he assumed he was at the location for *Boytsovskaya Yama*. Which meant he'd been unconscious for at least an hour or so. Zhirkov followed behind the men as they dragged Blake through a side entrance, roughly guiding him through the decrepit corridors. The dim lighting made it hard for Blake to commit any details to memory and, eventually, they rounded a corner where an armed guard was standing. The man shoved the metal door open and stood to the side, and Blake was hauled into the sparse room and shoved onto the metal chair that sat in the middle of it. As he went to say something, one of the guards clocked him with a swift punch, rattling his senses and sending a gob of blood-stained saliva onto the floor.

Woozily, he kept himself seated, and he could feel them removing his zip ties but then fastening him in place. He was locked to the chair, and as his vision began to claw back its clarity, he could see the metal table on the far side of the room.

More alarmingly, he could see the impressive arsenal of tools that were no doubt for the express purpose of extracting information.

Hammers.

Knives.

Scalpels.

A blow torch.

A whole deluxe package of pain.

With struggling against his restraints redundant, Blake calmly turned his head to Zhirkov, who stood against the far wall and lit a cigarette.

'Buddy, can you not do that in here?' Blake asked cockily. 'Second hand smoke is a killer.'

Zhirkov looked at his comrades in disbelief and then

began to chuckle. He pushed himself from the wall and strode confidently across the room, cigarette hanging from his thin lips. He squatted down, so he was eye level with Blake, took a deep drag and then blew it directly into his face. As Blake turned his head in disgust, Zhirkov plucked the cigarette from his lips and then stubbed it out on the back of Blake's hand.

Blake gritted his teeth, groaned slightly, but didn't give him the satisfaction of his pain.

Zhirkov chuckled again, stood, and then shoved Blake's face away from him.

'*Suka,*' he uttered under his breath.

'I trust we are treating our guest with respect.'

Balikov's voice boomed from the doorway, startling Zhirkov and drawing Blake's pained gaze. The oligarch stepped into the room, taking deliberate strides towards Blake, his expensive shoes clapping against the solid, blood-stained concrete below.

Blake watched the well-dressed man approach, wondering how many times he'd done this pre-rehearsed routine and how many unfortunate people had sat in the same seat and wished for a quicker death. Balikov made a gesture of wafting away the cigarette smoke and flashed a disappointed look to Zhirkov, who held up his hand in an insincere apology.

Balikov turned to Blake and leant in close.

'You cannot find the staff these days.'

'I know. It must be hard being a terrorist nowadays.'

'Terrorist?' Balikov chuckled and stood up straight, looming over Blake. 'Is that what you think I am?'

Blake shrugged as much as his restraints would allow.

'I mean, you're planning a nuclear attack. You have fanatical followers. You've nearly got terrorist bingo.'

Balikov slapped Blake across the face, the clap echoing off the wall and commanding silence from the room.

Balikov beckoned for another chair and one of the guards scurried into the room with one, placing it a few feet from Blake and Balikov took his seat. He regarded Blake for a few moments, pulled a handkerchief from his pocket and leant forward, wiping the blood that had trickled from Blake's lip.

A show of respect.

'Mr Blake…' Balikov made a point of showing his captor he knew his name. 'That is your name. Dominic Blake. You have had quite a career. Your government must think very highly of you.'

'Well, seeing as how you seem to know who I am, you can see that I'm not working for the government anymore…'

'Oh yes, your work with MI5 just stops suddenly a few years back. Did they let you go? Was it the death of your family that made you leave?' Balikov flashed a horrid grin at the mention of Blake's loss. 'Or, and this is my theory, they took you off the books to try to find people like me?'

Blake shook his head, and Balikov seemed to revel in his misery. Blake eventually gave him the eye contact he desired.

'That's a nice theory. Do you have any on say…relativity? I hear that's a popular one.'

'You are a very charming man, Mr Blake. But I'm afraid you are also an unfortunate one. You see, I will not just kill you. As much as a man of your credentials deserves a respectful death, I will need to know what you know and where you have sent it.'

'I posted it on a blog online. Top Terrorists dot net.'

Balikov leapt forward and rocked Blake with a solid fist. As Blake breathed through the pain, Balikov stood, rubbing his knuckles.

'You do not understand. My work is not in the name of a god or a religion that separates our world. My work is for the future of our planet. A new beginning, where the strong hold up the weak, not cower from their fragility. A world where the selfish majority know pain like famine and fear, where their convenience cannot be found on a screen in their hands, but by proving themselves. I am not a terrorist, Mr Blake. I am just a man capable of setting this world right. Unfortunately, you will not be around to see it.'

Balikov straightened his tie and headed to the door, nodding to Zhirkov an order to keep Blake where he was. Just as he was about to leave, Blake began to laugh. Surprised, Balikov stepped back into the room and shrugged.

'This is funny to you?'

'You should have killed me when you had the chance. Back at the hotel. Now, you've kept me alive long enough for them to track my location and real soon, you're gonna have the full force of MI5 swarming this place and taking your little plan down with you. How's that for a theory?'

Balikov shot a glance at Zhirkov, and then shook his head.

'Lies, Mr Blake. I think you are bluffing. Only desperate men tell lies, and you are not a desperate man. Just an unfortunate one.' Balikov stepped through the doorway and then spoke without looking back. 'I will be back shortly. Perhaps you can tell me more stories then. When the desperation *does* kick in.'

Balikov disappeared out of the room, leaving Blake to slump in his chair, and hope that his team was as good as he knew they were.

Foster's motorcycle came into view after a few minutes of venturing down the dirt road. Brady pulled the car over and brought it to a stop behind her. She was already standing to the side, her hands on her hips and her red hair flowing in the wind. Hun was first out, throwing open the passenger door and lugging his rucksack with him. Foster stepped to him, resting a tender hand on his face.

'Jesus,' she said quietly. 'Are you okay?'

'Oh yeah, you should see the other guy.' Hun joked. Foster hugged her friend and then turned to Brady, who stepped out of the car and slid his arms into his leather jacket. The stolen MP-443 Grach was tucked into his belt.

'You catch up to them?' Brady asked, his brow furrowed.

'Yeah, another mile or so that way and you'll see the facility. Soon as it came into view, I turned and headed back.'

'Guns?'

'Yup.'

Brady nodded, his jaw tight. For a man who had lost his step in the field, he could feel the thrill of it returning, as if someone was topping up his wineglass. Foster looked off into the distance.

'How many?' Brady asked, his mind analysing his options.

'Rough guess. A dozen or so. Half on watch. Probably similar inside.'

'It's twenty-four.'

Hun's voice interrupted both of them, and they turned. With his laptop open and resting on the seat of Foster's motorbike, Hun was tapping away on the keyboard, his eyes glued to the screen.

'How do you know that?'

'I just pulled up an invoice that had been sent through a few shell corporations for twenty-four strong teams of armed security for today.' Hun wiggled his eyebrows. 'I fight my battles online, baby.'

'Good work.' Brady slapped Hun on the back, who groaned in pain.

'What's the plan?' Foster asked as Brady checked the ammo in his gun.

'We go and get our team back.'

'And Sam,' Hun added.

'And Sam.'

'Foster, how far did you say the building was?' Hun asked, his eyes still on the screen.

'About a mile.'

'How fast can you two run that?'

'Five. Six minutes,' Brady chimed in.

'You've got five,' Hun said, his eyes flickering as his screen ran through lines of code. 'Then you'll only have a few minutes to do your thing.'

Brady and Foster looked at each other, then back to Hun.

'How will we know when you're ready?' Brady asked.

Hun scoffed.

'Oh, you'll know. I'm hacking into the power grid that powers the facility. It's run off three main generators and one backup. Pretty archaic. I'm going to shut it down and you'll have a two-minute window before the grid powers the three main generators back up. Only this time, I've doubled the output.'

Brady and Foster looked at each other and then back to Hun.

'Meaning?' Brady asked.

'Meaning the place is gonna blow.' He looked at them both and offered them a firm nod. His way of wishing them luck. 'Now, chop fucking chop.'

Brady and Foster took off, racing across the wasteland, as the wind kicked up the dust around them, and they hurried across the abyss to face their unspeakable odds.

CHAPTER TWENTY-FIVE

Alenichev had pulled the gun out of Singh's mouth and sat her back in her chair. He kept the gun trained on her at all times, but his eyes fell upon Sam. There was an air of triumph about the man, a smugness that came with being proved right. Singh turned to speak to him, and Alenichev struck her with the gun, opening a cut above her eyebrow before hurling a tirade of abuse at her.

A brown woman having the audacity to infiltrate their operation was enough to boil Alenichev's blood, but he wouldn't act without Balikov's permission.

As he struck Singh, he noticed Sam take another step. Muscles tensed with fury and he smirked at the man. A few of the guns made a show of retraining their weapons on Sam, and the fighter had no choice but to relent. All the benefactors sat in terrified silence, the realisation that their loyalty was to a terrifying man with no conscience. The illusion of power and the promise of a seat at his table had once seemed so tempting, but now, having seen the man shut down the tournament and tackle his problems with force, it had turned the atmosphere cold.

The men who had willingly watched criminals fight to

the death may have been entertained by violence. That didn't mean they were violent men.

Repugnant, wealthy, uncaring.

But not violent.

Those who weren't competing sat idly, the gravity of the situation dawning on them as the regret began to seep in.

The door behind Alenichev opened, and Balikov walked in, still massaging his knuckles. He looked at Sam with interest, but then turned to Singh.

'Dominic Blake is a dead man. Do you understand?' As her eyes widened, he smiled. 'Yes, that name means something to you. Like him, you are government. Which means you are dead too.'

Balikov slapped Singh with the back of his hand and then hauled her up by her hair. As she struggled, he drove a fist into her ribs and then pushed her forward, her upper body looming over the balcony.

'Let her go,' Sam yelled.

Balikov rolled his eyes, then motioned for the gun from Alenichev. Obediently, his right-hand man placed the gun in his grip, and Balikov held it to the back of her head.

'What is your name? I like to know who I send to the afterlife.'

'Fuck you.'

Singh's response was defiant to the end, and Balikov's eyes flickered with murderous rage. But before he pulled the trigger, he looked to Alenichev, who nodded towards Sam. Balikov glared at his right-hand man, but then a cruel smile fell across his face.

'You do not fear for your life. I admire that,' Balikov said as he retracted the gun and pulled Singh back to her seat. 'But do you fear for his?'

Instantly, Balikov turned, lifted the gun, and fired a bullet at Sam. The explosion echoed off the solid walls, and Singh screamed out as the bullet skimmed the top of Sam's shoulder, spinning him around and sending him crumpling to the ground. Thankfully, the bullet had grazed him, drawing blood but not penetrating his body, and Sam gritted his teeth as he pushed himself back up again.

'My name is Amara Singh.' Singh begged. 'Let him go.'

'There we are. The truth.' Balikov handed the gun back to Alenichev. 'Here is the truth. Blake is going to die a long and painful death. Your bodyguard, he will be beaten to death by my guards. And as for you...well, depending on how generous a beautiful woman like you wants to be will determine how painfully I end your life.'

Singh spat at Balikov, and he struck her so hard she fell from her seat. He clicked furiously at Alenichev, who hauled her up and dumped her back in her seat. She woozily swayed, trying to regain control of her senses.

'Why don't you try that with me?' Sam called up, his hand pressed against his bloody shoulder. His eyes screamed a challenge at Balikov, and the oligarch met the challenge with a cold grin.

'Oh, I have something better for you, Sam Pope.' Balikov motioned to one of the guards on the ground with Sam, and the man tucked away his gun and rushed to the metal door. 'You are an impressive man. I know this. But I want to see just how hard you are willing to fight.'

The door opened, and Marko Balikov stepped through, drawing applause from Balikov and Alenichev, and thus, the rest of the room who followed their leader. The guards lowered their weapons and retreated to the doorway, as the specimen that was Balikov's son stepped through. Standing six feet two, he was also a few stones heavier than Sam, but without a shred of fat on his body. The man looked like he'd been constructed in a lab by a team of scientists who had been tasked with creating the ultimate fighter. As he approached Sam, Marko loosely rolled his shoulders and shadow boxed, a cocky swagger that told Sam he wasn't a threat.

Sam looked to Balikov, and then to Singh, who watched in terror through her bloodied eye. Without a word, and with the crowd hushed in anticipation, Marko threw the first punch. Sam weaved underneath and then dodged the next one. Marko took a step back, raised his eyebrows and then launched forward with another swing. The fist bore down on Sam, and as he tried to raise his arm up to block it, the pain in his shoulder betrayed him.

Marko caught him full on, and the punch sent him stumbling back a few steps. Balikov roared with approval and Marko showed no let-up, launching forward with another tirade of blows, a few that Sam were able to dodge but a number that connected.

Two jabs caught Sam in the face. Another brutal hook crunched into his ribs. Finally, Marko leant back and threw a solid right hook that would send Sam spiralling to the ground. But Sam dodged.

As the fist shot past his jaw, Sam spun and drove his elbow into Marko's face, crunching his nose to a bloody pulp and sending him stumbling. Then, to the shock of everyone, Sam drove a solid teep kick into Marko's chest, that took Balikov's son off his feet and he crashed spine-first onto the bloodied concrete below.

'Get up!' screamed Balikov, furious at his son's weakness. Marko scrambled to his feet, his eyes watering from the pain and his face contorted into a vicious scowl as he roared with anger and launched at Sam once more. He swung a few punches that Sam absorbed in his midsection, and then a brutal left cross that Sam bobbed underneath. As Sam moved under Marko's arm, he dived forward, burying his uninjured shoulder into Marko's solid midsection, ran a few steps and then lifted Marko off the ground and drove him down onto the concrete.

One of the onlookers roared with approval. As did another. Balikov shot them a furious glance and then screamed at Marko to fight back, as Sam mounted Marko and began to hammer his fists down upon him. A few of the strikes broke through Marko's guard, and in an act of desperation, Marko reached up and pushed his fingers into the open wound on Sam's shoulder.

Sam snapped back in agony, and Marko pulled a leg free and drove his foot into Sam's jaw, sending both men rolling in different directions. They both got to their knees and their eyes locked, peering through bloodied faces and an acceptance emanated between them that this was to the death.

Every spectator was on their feet, enthralled by what they were witnessing. Singh sat in her chair, shaking with fear at watching Sam fight with everything he had just to stay alive.

Alenichev kept the gun pressed into the back of her skull.

Balikov oversaw it all.

Then the lights went out.

Amos had been dragged through the bowels of the facility, his feet dragging behind him and the pain rumbling through his body like a tremor. Blood dripped from his eyebrow and his mouth, and Amos could barely open his eye. As they descended the staircase, one of the guards let go of him, allowing him to fall the final few steps and followed it up with another boot to his ribs.

Wherever they were heading, there was more to come. Eventually, Amos lifted his head and recognised the cells where he'd visited Sam with Singh, and one of the guards pressed the auto-lock button and the door unlocked, popping open with a clang. The guards spoke in Hungarian, laughing as they shoved Amos into the cell and one of them drove a few more hard kicks into his prone body.

Amos tasted blood.

He spat onto the floor, and a tooth was swimming in the blood that hit the concrete.

The smell of smoke wafted through his cell, and he gingerly turned onto his back and looked up at the guard who was smoking a cigarette and casually stood against the door.

It was the one he'd humiliated in the car park.

'This is going to be a bad day for you.' The man warned him, followed by an ominous laugh.

With considerable difficulty, Amos began to lift himself to his feet. With a groan of pain, he eased himself out of his jacket and began to unbutton the cuffs of his blood-stained white shirt. The guard watched, impressed.

'If we are going to do this, can you at least put out that cigarette?' Amos said through his blood-stained teeth. 'Can't stand those things.'

The guard chuckled, took another puff, and then banged his fist on the door. Another guard appeared.

'Sure.'

The guard flicked the cigarette at Amos, who batted it away, and then charged at his captive. Amos took a step back to absorb the blow, wrapped his arms around the man's waist and hoisted him off the floor and heaved him into the brick wall. The guard hit the concrete hard, and then fell to the metal bench below with a sickening thud.

The other guard was right behind him, catching Amos with a sucker punch, but his next one was met with a head-butt. Amos slammed his forehead into the man's fist, shattering the man's knuckles, and as the man retracted in pain, Amos punched him as hard as he could in the throat. The man gargled, choking on his crushed windpipe, before the first guard leapt onto Amos's back and the two of them fell into the other wall of the compact cell.

Footsteps were growing louder in the corridor as more guards rushed to their location.

But then the lights went out.

And all the cell doors popped open.

Brady and Foster were barely breaking a sweat, thankful that the sun had set on the warm day and the darkness of night at least provided them with a modicum of cover and a slight breeze. The facility had loomed into view pretty swiftly, illuminated by the floodlights that had been constructed around its perimeter, giving the duo a view of the building and the patrolling guards. As they approached through the darkness, they soon became visible to one of the patrolmen, who screamed something in Hungarian.

It was a command to stop.

They ignored it.

The man unholstered his pistol and called to his comrade, who marched across.

In his hands was an AK-63 assault rifle, a locally sourced model of the famous weapon. The guard with the handgun commanded them to stop once more, then lifted his pistol to the sky and pulled the trigger.

A warning shot.

Fifteen feet from the two guards, Brady and Foster came to a stop and raised their arms in surrender.

'We were sent by Balikov,' Brady yelled.

The man yelled back in his native tongue, lowering his weapon, safe in the knowledge he had backup.

'BAL-I-KOV,' Brady repeated, slowly, emphasising

each syllable. The main guard shook his head, and he turned to his friend, mockingly laughing.

Then the lights went out.

An audible panic rose.

Brady's hand whipped to his belt. His fingers smoothly wrapped around the gun like an old friend, and as he pulled the weapon free, he drew it up to his line of sight, planted his other hand around it and squeezed the trigger.

The first bullet embedded in the guard's skull.

The second bullet hit the other guard between the eyes.

Foster sprinted towards the bodies, relieving the guard of the assault rifle as Brady unloaded the rest of his clip towards the other guards who had been drawn by the gunfire.

'I got this,' Foster said as she expertly lifted the weapon, pressing the stock of the rifle into her shoulder to steady herself. 'Get in and get out.'

A burst of gunfire came from their right, and Foster turned and squeezed the trigger, the weapon shooting out three-round bursts of death. Brady relieved the two corpses of their MP-443 Grach handguns, just like the one he'd just unloaded, and with a gun in each hand, he ran as fast he could towards the building, with the sound of Foster's gunfire echoing behind him and the warning from Hun ticking in his mind.

They had a few minutes.

Then it was over.

CHAPTER TWENTY-SIX

The fight pit was plunged into darkness for about ten seconds before the back-up generator kicked in, pumping electricity into the dim emergency lights that ran across the edges of the pit itself. It cast the entire floor in a dull, green tinge, and Sam and Marko were able to lock eyes once more.

Above them, the onlookers were shrouded in darkness, and Sam failed to see Balikov give orders to Alenichev, who promptly left.

All he saw was the ferocious champion stalking him, like a lion circling an injured meal. Marko took a few steps forward and then feigned to throw a punch, before catching Sam in the ribs with a brutal kick. As Sam hunched over, Marko drilled his elbow down onto Sam's injured shoulder, and then caught him with a right hook that sent Sam sprawling into the wall.

Despite the darkness and the raised tension, the onlookers were still cheering, watching with fascination as their champion took Sam apart. There was only one person who didn't want to watch.

But, with Balikov holding her at gunpoint, Singh could do nothing but witness the slow death of a man she loved.

Unable to control his ego, Marko basked in the adulation of the crowd, giving Sam enough time to rebalance. But Marko could smell the blood dripping from his opponent, and after a few of his jabs failed to land, he wrapped his hands around the back of Sam's head and pressed down on it. As Sam arched forward, Mark violently lifted his knees, trying to shatter Sam's skull. Sam got a hand up to hold the strikes back, and on the fourth, he slipped his other hand under Marko's thigh and spun.

Marko swung into the concrete wall, slamming hard into the brick and dropped to the floor. Sam rolled away and slowly fought his way to his feet.

The toll of the tournament was starting to show, and he couldn't even lift his left arm.

But he wouldn't quit.

He would fight.

Balikov spat something in Russian, the fury in his voice a warning to his son. As he struggled to regain his breath, Marko stumbled to his feet and threw a lazy punch, but Sam ducked and returned one of his own. Rattled, Marko charged forward and took Sam off of his feet and rained down on him with elbows and fists that Sam tried desperately to block. But with only one arm, Sam's efforts were in vain, and eventually, Marko broke through his resistance, and caught Sam with a few sickening shots that left Sam laying a bloodied mess.

Marko got to his feet and roared to the crowd, and Balikov stood, applauding the viciousness of his son's actions. Sam was barely moving, and Singh pushed herself to her feet.

'Get up, Sam!'

Her words bounced off the walls of the pit and Sam arched his head to look at her one final time.

Just as Balikov drove his fist into her face.

Sam felt his own fist clench.

Marko paraded around the pit and then looked to his dad who gave an approving nod. To the delight of Balikov's guests, Marko drew his thumb across his own throat, signifying the end of the fight. With considerable arrogance, Marko stepped to Sam's prone body and placed his foot on Sam's cheek. He looked up at his father one last time.

Balikov approved.

Marko lifted his foot and slammed it down as hard as he could.

Sam caught it just before it crushed his skull. A gasp echoed and growling through the pain in his shoulder, Sam pushed back and shoved Marko off balance. Balikov screamed furiously from the darkness above and Marko, clearly rattled, charged at Sam once more and threw his most devastating combo at him.

Sam ducked. Dodged. Weaved.

Then nailed Marko with a hard right and then an uppercut to his stomach. Marko hunched over, and Sam drew his knee up, crunching Marko's face and sending the champion to the ground.

The lights came back on.

The sudden burst of brightness blinded the entire room, and Sam took a few steps back, shielding his eyes with his good arm. Murmurs of confusion filled the pit, and then an ominous rumble shook the building.

'KILL HIM!' Balikov screamed at his son, who was struggling to his feet.

The following explosion wasn't from Balikov, but from somewhere within the depths of the building. The fight pit shook and one of the thick metal beams rocked from its joints and fell from the ceiling. It crashed into the middle of the fight pit, missing the fighters, but another explosion rippled through and the panic set in.

Smoke began to seep in through the cracks in the wall, and more debris began to rain down from above.

Everyone made their way to the exits, and the terror rose as gunshots began to ring out from somewhere unknown. Balikov, his rage taking full control, grabbed a handful of Singh's hair and stomped his way to the exit. Through the chaos and the smoke, Sam looked around for Marko, but found no one.

On the far side of the pit, the door to the corridor was opened, and Sam covered his airwaves with his hand and limped towards the doorway as the fight pit collapsed behind him.

Through the dimly lit corridors, Alenichev walked with purpose. When the power had fallen, Alenichev had done his best to suppress any panic. The building was old, with its power supply provided by old generators that would fail any safety test. These things happened, and when the back-up power source kicked in, he assured Balikov it would return to normal shortly.

But Balikov wanted more assurances and had demanded Alenichev check in on their guest, Blake, and report back when the power was returned. It hurt him slightly that Balikov still barked orders at him at times, but he was loyal to the man, to the cause and the wealth his time alongside Balikov had provided. He took great pride in solving problems for the man, and unmasking the infiltration of the British government within *Boytsovskaya Yama* would go down as his finest moment.

He would be recognised as a hero of *Poslednyaya Nadezhda*, and when the world was rebuilt and history rewritten, the name Artem Alenichev will be lauded as a hero.

The man who saved the mission.

As he rounded the corner towards Blake's cell, he caught a whiff of a cigarette and was greeted at the door by Zhirkov, who was indulging his filthy habit.

'Fedor,' Alenichev greeted him curtly. 'I trust our guest is comfortable.'

Zhirkov shrugged.

'He has a problem with my smoking.' Zhirkov arched his head back into the room. 'And he doesn't shut up.'

Alenichev patted his trusted investigator on the shoulder and stepped by, striding confidently into the room. The British man known as Blake was still strapped to the chair. A few fresh bruises were sprouting across his face. The man was older than Alenichev had expected, but he had the handsome charm of a British spy.

A cliche.

As he approached, Blake looked up at him.

'Mr Blake,' Alenichev began.

'Finally.' Blake smiled. 'I take it you're the brains of the operation.'

'This is meant as disrespect to Mr Balikov?'

'Well, I certainly didn't see any when I met him.'

Blake was cut off with a firm back hand from Alenichev, who composed himself by fastening the button of his jacket and running a hand through his slick hair. He disregarded the chair opposite Blake and instead chose to step slowly around him.

'For a man who is approaching the end of his life, you are willingly giving up your chances for survival.'

'Oh, come on. You guys have no intention of keeping me alive. That's what my team is for.'

'Ah yes, your team. I believe you mean Amara Singh?' Alenichev caught the panic in Blake's eyes. 'A fascinating woman, isn't she? A very good accent, too. But a man like Balikov, he cannot be too careful. That is why he has a man like me.'

All the lights in the room burst back into life, almost blinding Blake as he looked away. Alenichev held his hands out, as if accepting a gift.

'Look at that. Problem solved.' Alenichev made a show of wiping his hands. 'The only problem left is how we should kill you, that lying bitch and that bastard you had play her security guard.'

A faint rumbling sound began to grow, before the entire room shook as the facility rocked in place. Then, the sound of an explosion from somewhere within the building caused Alenichev and his men to stumble, and the lights to flicker once more. Blake stayed strapped to his chair. Furious, Alenichev turned to Zhirkov.

'*Idi i smotri!*' He barked, and Zhirkov sighed, flicked his cigarette and wandered off into the hallway to investigate. Slightly dishevelled, Alenichev turned back to Blake who was smiling. Before he could say anything, another rumble and then the echo of gunfire.

Alenichev shot a panicked look at the other guard in the room and then asked for his weapon. The guard handed over his handgun and Alenichev headed to the door.

'Cavalry's coming,' Blake said. 'I did warn you all.'

Alenichev stepped back and pistol-whipped Blake, before turning to the guard.

'*Watch him. If he says another word, take his tongue.*'

The guard nodded and withdrew his serrated blade. Blake winced, his head shaking, and he rocked back into his chair, thankful that he understood Russian.

Alenichev cautiously stepped out into the corridor as another explosion detonated.

They didn't have long.

None of them did.

When the emergency lights had registered in the cell, Amos took advantage of the sudden black out to readjust his position and wrap his arm around the guard's throat. With the confines of the cell making it impossible for the man to escape, the guard flailed wildly until Amos managed to lock in his grip and fall backwards onto the metal bench, wrenching harder against the man's throat until he strangled him to death.

The guard went limp, and Amos let him drop to the floor.

Beyond the door, he could hear the chaos.

The cell doors had opened, and the remaining fighters had chanced their arm at escape. Emerging from their cells with nothing but desperation fuelling them, they'd laid siege to the guards that had patrolled the halls, and the gunfire and anguished screams told Amos that war had broken out.

As he stood, one of the other fighters ran past. Shirtless, the man's body was coated in tattoos, but even that ink was covered with blood. In his hand, the man held the serrated blade he'd used to gut one of the guards and his eyes fell upon Amos.

All the criminal saw was a man that wasn't dressed like a fighter.

Instead, he saw a man dressed like the people who put him there.

Amos held his hands up to reason with the man, but with a scream of pure rage, the man dived into the cell, driving the blade towards Amos's chest. Amos managed to raise his arm to block the blow, but the man pushed forward, sending them both backwards and the metal bench connected with the back of Amos's knees.

He buckled.

As he slammed onto the bench, the man pressed down with both hands, saliva hanging from his mouth as his eyes widened with excitement. The blade was inching closer and ever closer to the centre of Amos's chest and with all his might, Amos pushed back. Usually, his strength would have won out, but the beating he'd been subjected to had left him powerless.

An easy target.

As the man pressed one final time, Amos managed to drive his knee up into the small of the man's back, knocking him forward and Amos swung his entire body-weight to the left.

Both men toppled off the bench onto the floor, the corpse of the guard breaking their fall, and Amos found himself on top now, his considerable bulk pinning the man to the ground.

The man was wheezing, his eyes begging for mercy, and Amos looked down to realise that the blade was embedded in the man's side. Amos looked back at the man whose feral nature had been replaced by a plea for mercy.

Amos offered him none.

He clamped his hand on the blade and twisted it before plucking it from the man's skin, opening up the wound and allowing the blood to gush across the cell. The man groaned softly as his life left him in waves. Amos stood, stepping over the two men he'd killed, and made his way to the door. Carefully, he pushed it open, blade in hand and looked down the corridor.

Bodies and blood.

A few whimpers of pain emanated from the carnage, with those who were not dead not far from it, and Amos could hear the dying breaths and gurgles of those grasping to the final strands of life.

The lights burst back to life, illuminating the slaughter in all its gruesome glory and the bullet ridden and stab covered bodies were brought to life in vivid detail.

Amos stepped out but was suddenly sent sprawling as an explosion erupted from down the corridor, rocking the entire walkway and causing debris to crumble from the ancient ceiling.

He looked up, straight into the barrel of a gun.

Amos dropped the knife in surrender and held his hands up. But beyond the gun, there was no mercy. The guard that had survived the onslaught was covered in blood, and his body was shaking. The adrenaline of fighting for survival was coursing through his veins like a virus, and his eyes were vacant.

The man pressed the gun to Amos's forehead, and a gunshot rang out.

The man slumped against the wall, the side of his skull missing from where it had been blown out. Amos had closed his eyes, accepted his fate and when he opened them, he saw Brady stepping over one of the corpses, his weapon drawn. As he approached Amos, he handed him a handgun.

'Good timing.' Amos offered, thrilled to see his friend.

Another explosion.

'Speaking of time, we haven't got any. Let's move.'

CHAPTER TWENTY-SEVEN

The corridors had been reduced to dimly lit tunnels of smoke, and as another explosion rocked the building, Sam felt his knees buckle and he collapsed against the wall. He had found an old, filthy rag along the way and held it over his face, doing his best to stop the smoke from infiltrating his lungs.

But he needed to move faster.

His body just wasn't willing.

The fight with Marko had left him running on empty, and every step sent a jolt of pain up his spine and he struggled to keep low. After he'd vacated the fighting pit, Sam had stumbled down a few corridors, unsure of a direction but knowing he needed to find a stairwell. When they had brought him to the tournament, he'd been taken down numerous staircases, which meant while he was underground, he had no chance of survival. The building was being rocked by a series of explosions and each one was chipping further and further into the foundations.

Soon it would collapse and bury everyone within it.

He rounded a corner and saw the bottom of the stairwell, and managed to shuffle across, taking the first few steps before leaning against the wall for support. The wide, open staircase was beginning to fill with smoke, and as Sam climbed further, he could hear the noise of the panicked crowd being ushered towards the exit. A rough, angry Hungarian voice cut through the hysteria, and as Sam approached the top of the step, he spotted a guard standing ten feet down the corridor. The man had his back to Sam, and resting in his hands was an AK-63.

Sam stepped out carefully. He needed to take each step as cautiously as he could, otherwise he was an open target. With the guard overseeing the last of the guests to rush up the stairs, Sam got within two steps of the man before he turned.

His eyes widened with horror.

His arms lifted the rifle instinctively.

Sam's grip was already on the man's sidearm, and Sam slid it from its holster, buried it in the man's gut and pulled the trigger. The bullet ripped through the man's back and sent him sprawling to the ground, his hands pressed on the wound. There would be no hope for him, and as much as Sam wanted to put the man out of his misery, he needed to preserve the ammo. The guards carried automatic weapons and with his shoulder damaged, Sam could only face their force with whatever was left in the handgun. The dying guard tried to speak, but his words caught in his throat as he coughed up a splatter of blood.

Sam stepped by, leaving the man to his slow death in the dark.

He followed the sound of panic down the corridor, and just as he approached the next staircase, he heard the sound of two guards rushing down the stairs. No doubt to complete a final sweep and to call their comrade to safety. Sam pressed himself as close to the wall as possible and lifted the gun. As the first guard rushed past him, he squeezed the trigger the second he saw the next.

The bullet burrowed into the side of the man's skull, sending his body limp and colliding into the wall. The other guard spun round upon hearing the deafening sound of the gunshot, but before he could raise his weapon, Sam took aim and sent a bullet through the centre of the man's chest. He dropped, falling next to the similarly motionless body of his comrade. Sam glanced back down the hallway to the other corpse he'd left in his wake, but the smoke was building, blurring the view with its thick poison.

Another rumble and some of the ceiling crumbled to the ground, falling on the dead bodies and burying them beneath the rubble.

With the gun in his hand and three more deaths to his name, Sam leant his useless shoulder against the wall, and began to climb the stairs, leaving a smear of blood in his wake.

———

With the building crumbling and the panic spreading, Balikov stepped through the smoke, coughing and spluttering over Singh. With one arm wrapped around her throat and the other positioning the gun against her skull, he shunted her through the darkening corridors. The heat of fire could be felt through the walls of the facility, with the entirety of *Boytsovskaya Yama* crumbling to ash.

As had Balikov's patience.

As Singh dragged her heels, he wrenched her head back and threatened a fate worse than death if she failed to oblige. Considering the lengths they'd gone to immerse Singh into his world, and the British spook he had locked in a room, Balikov knew that Singh could be a vital bargaining chip.

They just needed to get away from the chaos.

They scaled another staircase when a figure emerged at the top of the stairs.

Alenichev.

Singh's heart sank as Balikov's obedient associate greeted his boss with earnest concern. As they approached him, Balikov's grip on Singh tightened, and he swung the pistol as hard as he could. It cracked Alenichev across the jaw, sending him stumbling backwards. There was a momentary flash of anger, before the man stayed true to form and stood, adjusted his tie and approached again.

'*This is your fault.,*' Balikov snarled. '*You were supposed to check every detail.*'

'*I begged you to stay away until I had it solved,*' Alenichev protested politely. '*These intruders, they will be dealt with.*'

'*Yes, but not by you.*' Balikov barged past Alenichev, dragging Singh with him. '*Go and get that British spook and meet us by the chopper. You have let me down, Artem.*'

'*I am sorry, sir.*'

'*So am I.*'

The resounding sadness in Balikov's tone was an indication to Alenichev of what awaited. The image of Goran Kalenikov being torn apart by Balikov's hounds took control of Alenichev's mind, and he felt a sudden desperation that was alien to him.

He was always in control.

Always.

'*I can make this right, sir.*'

Alenichev pleaded loudly, and as Balikov turned to face him, another explosion as one of the generators finally reached its breaking point and shook the entire corridor.

All three of them stumbled.

Balikov's grip loosened.

Singh sunk her teeth into his hand.

Balikov screamed in agony as she drew blood, her jaw

locking like one of his attack dogs. As she drew blood, Balikov flapped his arm wildly.

Alenichev saw his moment of redemption.

Without hesitation, he charged forward, slamming the full force of his shoulder into Singh, the impact knocking her away from Balikov and through a doorway that led to an old, abandoned office. Singh hit one of the rotten wooden desks, rolled across the top, and slammed against the floor on the other side.

Balikov handed Alenichev the gun.

'*Finish this,*' he commanded, and then marched towards the final stairwell of the building, gasping for the fresh air of the open world above. Alenichev nodded, thumbed the safety from the Grach, and entered the room.

It was time to eliminate the problem once and for all.

———

With each passing explosion, Blake knew his chances of survival were diminishing. Dying for the cause wasn't something he'd ever been afraid of, as long as his death meant something. With their plan foiled and Balikov making it clear that their identities were known, he cursed himself for putting Singh in such danger.

Blake was the leader of the team, therefore he was the biggest scalp for Balikov. To be able to butcher a leading government agent in the name of *Poslednyaya Nadezhda* would solidify his intentions and galvanise the support that was already rapidly growing.

Dying to stop that, he would have been happy with.

Dying alone in a crumbling building, knowing his team had been taken apart by the people they were trying to stop, would be worse than the death itself.

As the building sent warning after warning to its occupants that it was reaching its final moments, Blake listened intently to Zhirkov and the other guard. Not long after Alenichev had left them, Zhirkov had returned, telling the other man that he wasn't paid enough to kill people.

Neither of them knew that Blake spoke Hungarian.

Now, the two men stood with their backs to Blake. The door closed and their voices lowered.

They were discussing leaving, abandoning their pay checks to escape with their lives. Balikov would no doubt be furious but ultimately, the Englishman dying was an inevitability and burying him in the rubble wasn't the worst thing they could do. If anyone was ever bothered to dig it up, they'd find the bones of a man who didn't make it out.

Another explosion, this one on a grander scale, tipped more sand through the hourglass and Zhirkov stated with authority that they were leaving.

Gunshots.

Both men turned to the door, panicked, and from somewhere down the hall, the burst of an assault rifle echoed. As the gunfire rang out, Zhirkov pulled his weapon once more and waited by the door.

'What are you waiting for?' Blake asked.

'Quiet,' Zhirkov snapped back.

Blake pressed against his restraints and hooked his foot around the empty chair opposite him. With the gunfire roaring loudly beyond the door, he dragged it towards him, the sharp screech of metal on concrete concealed by the action outside.

A random voice screamed something in another language, but then another gunshot brought it to an abrupt end. Zhirkov looked at the other guard, who had gone deathly pale. The man was armed only with a knife, and he clutched it in a shaking hand. For years, the security detail for *Boytsovskaya Yama* had amounted to nothing more than shoving cuffed lowlife's into cells, and dishing out the odd beating.

It was easy money.

Signing up wasn't about putting your life on the line. It was about acting tough and hiding behind the fact you were the one that was armed.

'I can help you guys,' Blake offered from behind them, and Zhirkov yelled for quiet.

The gunfire had stopped. Zhirkov reached out a careful hand and pulled open the door. As he did, Blake kicked the chair forward with all his might, sending the metal seat crashing into the back of the other guard's legs. The man buckled forward, colliding with Zhirkov and sending both men tumbling through the doorway and into the corridor.

Before they had even hit the adjacent wall, bullets hit both men, bursting through their chests like scarlet fireworks.

As both men hit the ground, dead, Brady stepped through the door, scanning the room with his weapon.

'Clear.'

He yelled back to the door and Amos stepped in, his handgun by his side and his face a jumble of cuts and bruises.

'Christ on a cross,' Blake said. 'You look like hell.'

'Feel like it too, sir,' Amos replied, his grin appearing through the carnage.

Brady stepped back to the dead guard in the doorway and relieved him of his blade. As he returned, he cut through Blake's binds, freeing him from the chair. Blake gingerly stood, rubbing his wrists that were red raw.

'Thank you.'

'Don't mention it,' Brady said with a nod. Blake smiled, clearly pleased to see his top agent back in the field.

'Took you long enough.'

'Balikov has Singh…' Amos began.

'I know. He made it clear he means to kill her.'

'I'm not leaving without her,' Amos said defiantly.

'If Balikov has her, then he's taking her out of the building. We need to get out of this place and stop him before he leaves. Or, if he has, we need to find out where the hell he is going.'

'Sir, with all due respect, you assigned me to her as her security,' Amos said defiantly. 'If she's in this building still, I need to find her.'

'He's got a point,' Brady said. Blake frowned.

'Fine, one sweep,' Blake said. 'But you shoot to kill, and you run like the fucking wind when this place really hits its last legs. Do you understand?'

'Sir.'

The marine in Amos shone through, and as he stepped through the doorway, he snatched the handgun from Zhirkov's dead body and disappeared down the hallway. Blake and Brady stepped out.

'Want me to cover him?' Brady asked.

'No, I need you with me. If these guys got out, we need to keep them penned in.'

'Foster's covering up top. We neutralised a few guards on the way in…' Brady shrugged. 'Some more on the way to you.'

'Well, let's not pat ourselves on the back just yet.'

The message was clear. If Balikov and his guests had made it out of the building, there was only so much Foster could do on her own. She needed back up.

Brady led the way, setting off on a brisk run down the corridor, his gun held in both hands down by his side. Blake broke into a sprint, ignoring his injuries as he kept pace.

Another loud explosion rocked the building.

It wouldn't be long now until the entire thing collapsed.

And his heart swelled with pride that if Directive One went down with it, they'd go down fighting.

CHAPTER TWENTY-EIGHT

Not many people got a second chance with Vladimir Balikov. Alenichev had seen countless men, good men who had proven loyal to the cause, make one mistake and be gone. Fed to the dogs as scraps.

To break the man's trust was to sign one's own death certificate and as Alenichev marched into the room where he'd hurled Amara Singh, he knew it would take something special to get it back.

Eliminating Singh and gutting whatever operation she was a part of was his only option.

Ironically, it was *his* final hope.

He had watched the woman clatter into the desk and hit the other side, and with the gun ready to go, he planned on putting a bullet through her skull. The power overload to the facility had caused a few of the lighting fixtures to fall from the ceiling, adding more clutter to the abandoned office. Rows of shaky, wooden desks lined the room and as Alenichev stepped around one of them, he lifted the gun with a grin.

Singh was gone.

Alenichev spun round, and Singh's bony fist caught

him clean across the jaw, knocking him back into the desk. The red mist descended, and Alenichev went to raise the gun, but Singh caught his wrist, twisted it, and drove her elbow down onto his forearm. The weapon hit the desk and clattered to the floor and as Singh went to retrieve it, Alenichev yanked her back by her hair.

'You stupid bitch!' He spat through his teeth and drove a hard fist into her stomach. As he rose his knee to her skull, Singh managed to hook her foot behind his other leg and then shoved her shoulder into his hip, knocking him off balance and sending him crashing through the rotten wood. As he ferociously threw the wood away and got to his feet, Alenichev made a show of removing his blazer and unbuttoning his cuffs. Singh responded by reaching down to the hem of her tight dress, and ripping it up the seam of the leg, freeing herself and setting her stance.

Ready to fight.

Alenichev swung a few wild fists at Singh, and she managed to avoid both, before she caught him with one of her own, and then a big kick to his ribs. Angered, he charged at her, crashing his body into her once more and this time he took her off her feet and hurled her through one of the other desks. Singh hit the floor hard, the feeble wood offering no protection and she felt her lungs empty on impact. Winded, she tried to get up, but Alenichev drove a stiff kick into her stomach, keeping her down.

'You made a big mistake.' He warned her. 'There is no problem I cannot solve.'

Another hard boot sent Singh rolling over in the wreckage, and Alenichev turned his attention to the gun that had been knocked from his grip. The lighting in the room was fading, offering him little help, and as his eyes finally landed on it, Singh managed to leap onto his back, wrapping her arms around his neck and tightening her grip with all her might. Alenichev struggled wildly, stumbling to wriggle free and as they fell backward, they collided with one of the fallen halogen lights. It shattered, and Alenichev gripped Singh's arm and pulled it forward. Using her bodyweight against her, he slammed Singh down onto the remnants of the bulb and she screamed in pain as the shards pierced her skin. Alenichev lifted his foot and drove it down to her skull, but she rolled to the slide, wrapped her hand around a shard of the light and rammed it into his calf.

The debris punctured his muscle, and he roared in pain, and threw a barrage of punches Singh's way. The years of fighting with Amos rose to the surface, and as Singh deflected and dodged the blows, she returned fire with precision.

A jab. Another. Then a big right hook that sent Alenichev onto one of the desks.

He returned, swinging wildly as his leg buckled. She caught him with a knee to the gut and then sent him to the ground with a hard elbow strike. Her eyes landed on the gun, but as she made a step towards it, two more guards stepped in, their handguns raised and their sights on Singh.

Blood dribbled from her bottom lip, and her eyes glared at them with anger.

She wouldn't surrender.

It wasn't in her to.

Out of options, she lowered her fists and sighed. Behind her, she heard Alenichev lift himself from the ground, and with considerable pain, he limped past her, joining the two men who had saved his life. The arrogance of the man made her sick, and he stepped around the desk, stretched downwards and his hand returned with his fingers wrapped around his gun.

'There we are,' he said with a grin. 'Like I said, Mrs Al Ansari, there is no problem I cannot solve.'

'My name is Amara Singh,' she said defiantly.

'There is no honour in lying, Ms Singh.' Alenichev shook his head disapprovingly as he approached her. 'You will do well to remember that in the next life.'

Standing a few feet from her, Alenichev lifted his arm and raised the gun to her forehead. The steel was an inch from her skin, and Singh closed her eyes, knowing she'd fought until the very end.

A bullet exploded through the back of one of the guard's heads, driving him forward and sending him spiralling across the ground. Blood and brain slapped across the floor ahead of him.

Before anyone could react, two more gunshots echoed and the other guard took two to the chest, the bullets hitting him dead centre and rupturing the valves of his heart. A few pumps after hitting the ground, he was dead. With the gun still trained on Singh, Alenichev's attention was briefly drawn to the door, where the bloodied Amos stepped through, his gun raised and his mind clear.

Singh's hands shot out, with one of them clamping down on the back of Alenichev's gun, and the other digging into the pressure point in his wrist. The sudden jolt to his nerve loosened his grip, and Singh spun the gun with her hand, snatching it into her grip and aiming it straight at Alenichev's skull.

It happened in less than a second.

Shocked, Alenichev held up his hands. The colour drained from his face as the realisation of defeat set in.

'Please…we can figure this out…'

Singh pulled the trigger.

Alenichev's head snapped back as a mist of red blew through the room. As he dropped to the ground, Singh lowered the gun.

'Problem solved.'

Amos stepped to her, and she threw her arms around him. They'd been through the wars but had made it this far. Now, they would leave together. Singh held her gun close by her side, covering Amos as they stepped out into the corridor. Another part of the facility crumbled beneath its own weight, and they scurried towards an exit, hoping they would make it out in time.

There was a commotion emanating from the other side of the vast room that Sam had stumbled into. The adrenaline of survival was starting to lose its battle with the pain of his injuries, and as he stepped into the main hall, he felt one of his legs buckle. He caught himself against a pillar, adjusted his footing, and then continued. Strangely, the entire floor of the desolate room had been re-carpeted with a plush, maroon fabric, and trays of empty champagne glasses were errantly stacked on random pieces of old furniture. Beyond, he could see the outside world through the door on the far side, and gunshots and screams echoed.

Calling him to a strange sort of safety.

As a gentle reminder, another explosion erupted, this one only a few floors down, and the impact shook the only part of the facility still standing. Sam held onto the pillar to ride the tremor, and some of the metal beams across the roof dropped to the ground.

The building had minutes remaining.

Gritting his teeth, Sam pushed himself off the pillar and marched as fast as he could towards the door, his left arm hanging limp and his right hand loosely holding the gun.

Smoke and dust swirled around him and clouded his vision.

It blocked off his periphery.

It meant he didn't see Marko's fist until it was too late.

The punch caught Sam in the side of the head and sent him stumbling backwards. Marko dived through the grey cloud and drove his boot into Sam's chest, sending him spiralling over the fallen beam and onto the hard floor.

The gun clattered in an unknown direction.

As Sam hauled himself up with one arm, Marko carefully stepped around the metal beam. The fallen debris from the ceiling had created a smaller fighting pit, and with no baying mob screaming for blood, the two men knew that this was personal.

Marko had never lost.

His father forbade it.

Sam was fighting to survive.

Wasting little time, Marko charged at Sam, drilling his fist into Sam's bullet ridden shoulder before driving his knee into Sam's gut. Another shake of the building and more beams and bricks collapsed to the ground, and Sam hit the ground hard as Marko caught him with a hard uppercut. Marko drove his knee down to Sam's head, but Sam moved. The impact jarred his knee, and Marko, overcome with the fear of losing, cursed his sloppiness.

Sam could barely lift himself up.

He'd been through hell.

The brawl in Sremska Mitrovica.

The trials.

The tournament.

He had fought with everything he had, just to get them close to Balikov.

To stop the deaths of innocent people.

He'd done all he could.

But Sam didn't know how to stay down. He didn't know how to give in.

Sam Pope was built to survive.

Limping slightly, Marko approached and threw a

punch, but Sam ducked and responded with one of his own. Infuriated, Marko charged forward, but Sam spun out of the way, and as he did, he redirected Marko to crash into one of the metal beams. Marko's head hit the metal hard, slashing open his eyebrow, and as he turned back to face Sam, he looked shocked at the sight of his own blood. For too long, he'd run roughshod over *Boytsovskaya Yama*, with his father's resources, turning him into the ultimate fighting machine.

But all he'd faced were men fighting for their freedom back. Freedom that had been taken from them due to their crimes.

Now, he was fighting against a man who fought for only one reason.

Because it was the right thing to do.

Rattled, Marko screamed at Sam to bring it and, as his ego took control, Marko lost his focus. He over-extended his next punch, allowing Sam to weave underneath it, and Sam rocked Marko with a brutal punch to the chest, a kick to the side of the leg that caused him to buckle, and then as Sam drove his fist down into Marko's nose, he swiped the back of Marko's legs with his foot.

Marko snapped backwards, and the side of his head thumped violently against the sharp metal edge of the fallen beam.

There was no getting up from it, and as Sam stepped forward, he could see the thick gash that had split open the side of Marko's skull. Blood pumped out of it, and the impressive man had been reduced to a twitching mess on the floor. With his boot, Sam rolled Marko onto his back and looked down at him.

Marko's eyes were wide, the blood loss beginning to claw at his vision, and as Sam watched the man begin to fade away, the door to the giant foyer blew off its hinges as the final generator reached its limit and detonated. The floor shook, and any remaining glass that sat in the windows shattered. Flames licked through the doorway and above, the twang of cables and the creak of ruptured metal erupted.

Sam pushed himself over the metal beam, and as he hit the floor, he fell next to his handgun. He scooped it up and with the last drop of energy pumping through his body; he rushed towards the door as the roof began to collapse.

Somewhere behind him, a downpour of metal shards fell upon Marko, ripping the shell of a man to pieces.

Smoke filled the room.

Sam lost sight of the door ahead.

Running on instinct and his last legs, Sam closed his eyes as the entire building finally collapsed.

CHAPTER TWENTY-NINE

Desperation was not a feeling that Balikov was familiar with. For so long, his life had been an endless corridor of doors being opened for him, with his untouchable wealth and fervent followers affording him everything he could ever want. Control was a commodity few people ever truly experienced, but he was a man who had always been in control. Always had his way.

When the world became too soft, and his country became too weak, he was the one who built up *Poslednyaya Nadezhda* and championed for change.

He was the one who drew others into his way of thinking.

And he was the one who put plans in place to reduce the world to rubble, to rebuild it in his own image.

But now, that was hanging by a thread. His indulgence of *Boytsovskaya Yama* had always been a vanity project, one where he could flex his authority over life itself by offering the dregs of society the chance of freedom, only for his own son to quash it under his expert boot.

He gave rich, like-minded men the opportunity to revel

in the depravity, to glimpse into a world they were removed from, and he gave them the illusion of similar power.

That they owned the life of another human being.

That they were in control.

It was what had bought their loyalty, and the rush of power was an addictive drug that meant they came back for more. They fell in line, and as long as he drip fed them that illusion, whether it be the annual tournament, or a promise of a future seat at his table, then their loyalty was his forever.

Now, that lay in the ashes of the *Boytsovskaya Yama*, and after he'd left Alenichev to clean up the mess he'd made, Balikov had been marched to the exit by a few of the remaining guards, eager to get the hell away from the collapse of his tournament and the questions of his supporters.

Balikov had never answered to anybody, and he didn't plan to begin.

As the guards led him across the carpet to the exit, he was joined by a few of his guests, all of whom were panicking at the collapse of the fight pit, and the ongoing series of explosions. Balikov ignored their questions, bullying his way to the front of the growing crowd and then he stamped through the door and out onto the gravel of the forecourt.

Two gunshots rang out, and his guards hit the ground, both of them screaming in agony as they clutched their kneecaps, the bullets shattering them on impact.

Foster stood, rifle raised and her eye to the sight, and she screamed at all of them to stay where they were. Balikov's guests all looked to him for a solution. *Boytsovskaya Yama* was sold on its discretion, and for them, being associated with it would bring their wealthy lives to an abrupt end. Balikov sneered at the petite woman before him, but the three dead bodies over her right shoulder and the two anguished guards told him she wasn't bluffing.

The woman's accent was English, meaning she was part of Blake's team. Balikov refused to allow his disdain for them to blind him to their proficiency. They had infiltrated his network and seemingly brought down his security.

But they wouldn't take him.

Balikov didn't know the word surrender.

As the final guests filtered out into a cautious crowd, Foster motioned for them to move away from the doorway and then yelled at them to keep their hands on their heads. Most of them obliged, but Balikov defiantly took a step towards Foster, who readjusted her firearm.

'One more step and I'll drop you.'

Her threat was laced with menace, and Balikov held his hands up in acceptance.

'Do not be foolish, little girl,' Balikov said, speaking over the sound of the crumbling building. 'There is no good way this ends for you.'

'It's over, Balikov,' Foster snapped back. 'Now, hands on your head.'

Balikov smirked and took another step forward. His eyes flickered to the handgun tucked into her belt. Foster lowered the rifle slightly and pulled the trigger. The gunshot sent the crowd into a stifled panic, as the bullet hit the ground less than a foot from Balikov.

A warning shot.

'Do as she says, Vladimir.' Blake's voice interrupted the proceedings, and all heads turned as he and Brady stepped from the doorway, having made their way to freedom. 'It's over.'

All eyes fell on Balikov. The majority of them were terrified. A few were filled with hatred.

Balikov began to laugh. He held his hand up to signal

his intention and then summoned one of the benefactors to join him. Hesitantly, the man did, his white hair dancing sloppily in the breeze. Behind them, the fire blazed throughout the facility and the smoke began to pollute the night sky.

Soon, the authorities would arrive.

And it would all be over.

Still laughing, Balikov reached his hand out to his associate. As the man took it, Balikov used his strength to spin and hurl the man towards Foster.

Instinctively, Foster squeezed a shot off before the man could collide with her, the bullet ripping through the man's thigh and sending him crashing to the gravel and a blood-curdling howl of pain into the night sky.

Balikov was on Foster like a flash, and before Brady could fire off a clean shot, the oligarch had his arm wrapped around Foster's throat and her own sidearm pressed against the soft flesh under her chin.

'Lower your weapon.' Balikov ordered.

Brady refused.

Blake took a step forward.

'This is ridiculous, Vladimir. There is nowhere for you to go.'

'He's right.' Singh's voice chilled Balikov to the bone, the colour draining from his face as if he'd just seen a ghost. Singh emerged through the wreckage, along with Amos. Her face was smeared with blood, her dress was ripped and dirty.

But she was alive.

Which meant Alenichev was not.

Balikov's world was closing in on him, but the idea of surrender was moot. Slowly, he began to walk towards the helicopter that was parked on the far side of the forecourt, dragging Foster with him and pushing the gun against her jaw.

No one would open fire.

There was too much smoke and too much carnage for any of them to take the shot, and as he moved further away from the crowd, Brady and Amos stepped through them, guns trained on him, but their fingers off the trigger. Blake and Singh followed, and Singh lifted her gun.

'Sir, I've got a shot.'

'Stand down, Singh.'

'Sir…'

'Do not shoot,' Blake yelled, his eyes looking to Foster who seemed resigned to her fate. A gap opened up between Balikov and the crowd, and as he approached the chopper, the driver brought the propellers to life. Singh looked to Blake in shock, and the realisation that Balikov would escape fell across the whole team. Foster had failed to secure the helicopter when tackling the guards, and now she was nothing more than a human shield for Balikov to make his getaway.

Singh lifted her gun again, and Blake pushed it down. He solemnly shook his head at Singh, his eyes watering.

An evil grin spread across Balikov's face as he backed towards the helicopter, and a final explosion erupted from the facility and the remaining standing structures collapsed.

It was over.

Foster looked one more time to her team, tears streaming down her cheeks, and then she closed her eyes.

The door to the helicopter opened, and Balikov dragged her to it.

A gunshot rang out, and blood splattered the helicopter window.

As the roof of the facility crashed around him, Sam managed to push himself onto the steps that led to the doorway before he was crushed. He collapsed against the stones, shocked that he'd escaped death at the final second. Up the final eight or so steps, he could hear the commotion and a gunshot ring out, followed by a scream of agony that would last long in the memory.

He could hear Singh.

Her voice was a welcome sound amidst the chaos, and her survival filled Sam with a fresh batch of purpose. With a grunt, he pushed himself to the wall. The blood loss from his bullet wound was ebbing away at him, and he managed to use the wall to pull himself to his feet.

His knees buckled, but he caught himself, and then slowly trudged up the steps, the fresh air of freedom seductively calling to him.

The last few weeks had been spent in confinement, either in the worst hole on earth in Serbia, or under the watchful eye of Balikov's men.

He had fought with everything he had.

Killed without hesitation.

And now, Sam was a few feet from freedom.

Behind him, the facility crumpled to nothing more than flames and rubble, burying the corpses of many and the entire concept of *Boytsovskaya Yama* along with it. Now, leaning against the wall and shuffling slowly up the steps, Sam knew it wasn't over.

Everyone had their back to him as he emerged into the night, the thick smoke offering him a cloud of secrecy.

He saw Amos and Brady, their guns held up, and their eyes focused on the target.

He saw Blake.

He saw Singh.

Sam felt his heart pump at the sight of his friend,

knowing that despite their complicated past, she still held a section of it and most likely, always would.

He feared he'd lost her.

But like him, she was a survivor.

A fighter.

Through the crowd of terrified accomplices and customers, Sam peered across the courtyard towards the helicopter, where he saw Balikov. The man had his arm wrenched around Foster, a gun pressed to her chin, and the smug look of victory on his face. The propellers of the chopper were spinning loudly, the thud drowning out pleas from Blake for him to let Foster go.

None of them had a clear shot.

But without one, Foster would be killed. Dumped out of the chopper, probably with a bullet in her skull, and Balikov would disappear once more. The man had the resources to stay off the radar long enough to build a fanatical group, hellbent on nuclear war.

He had the means and the reason to disappear once again.

As the door to the helicopter was thrown open, Balikov took another step to it, dragging Foster up, and minimising the window of opportunity.

Sam closed his eyes and took a deep breath.

He thought of the first time he looked through the scope of a sniper rifle.

He thought about his father, Major William Pope, and the integrity he instilled in Sam during his early years.

He thought of Lucy.

Of Jamie.

Theo.

Marsden.

Mel.

All the people he'd lost along the way.

Directive One were not his family.

But when you fight and bleed alongside each other, a bond is forged that can never be broken.

He wasn't ready to lose anyone else.

He wasn't done fighting yet.

Sam exhaled and opened his eyes, and with the last remnants of energy that pumped through his veins, he lifted his right hand, drew his expert eye to the sight that ran along the top of the MP-443 Grach, and then squeezed the trigger.

The gunshot clapped through the night sky, sending a shockwave through the crowd as the bullet ripped through the air and buried itself in Balikov's collarbone. Blood exploded from the wound, bathing the side of the chopper, and Foster wriggled free from the man's grip as he clattered into the body of the helicopter before collapsing to the ground. He dropped the gun, his hands clasped to the wound that pumped blood through his fingers. Brady and Amos rushed forward, with Brady ordering the pilot out of the cockpit at gunpoint, while Amos wrapped his arms around Foster.

Blake strode forward, and through the mayhem of the thudding propellers, the anxious crowd and the burning ruins of the building, he gleefully told Balikov that it was over.

Singh stood on the spot and lowered her weapon.

She turned her head to where the shot was fired, knowing full well what had happened. She looked at Sam, a smile spreading across her face.

A smile that portrayed the disbelief that they had survived.

And a smile that was filled with love.

Sam nodded to her, pressed his back to the wall, and slid down until he sat on the top step.

The fight was over.

CHAPTER THIRTY

The events of *Boytsovskaya Yama* became international news. The fallout dominated every major news network and newspaper, all of them throwing their own spin on things depending on what side of the political divide they sat. Nobody was interested in the actual truth.

Just how they could spin it to their own agenda.

One thing that was unanimous among them all was that a cataclysmic event had been avoided, and as the dominos began to tumble, more and more powerful allies of Balikov were revealed and arrested.

Poslednyaya Nadezhda was crumbling.

MI5 had taken a leading role in the investigation, working alongside Interpol and a number of other agencies to ensure that the men who had colluded with Balikov and invested into his warped future, would be held to account.

Many had their assets stripped by their respective governments.

Others were already facing jail time.

Balikov got to witness it all from his cell. He had been handed over to MI5 by Blake, who had agreed that Directive One's involvement should be kept out of the records. Balikov was handed over to the Russian government as an act of alliance, the first brick of a long bridge that needed to be built. Any hope for refuge from his own country was soon eradicated, as Balikov was labelled a traitor, and would face the full force of the law.

Treason was a serious crime and could result in the death penalty.

Until that day, he would rot in a Russian Gulag until he practically begged for the needle.

Blake had spent the next few days on back-to-back conference calls, navigating through the usual political red tape that came with such a widespread incident. There were pats on the back from people who had doubted the need for Directive One and critical comments from those who felt that there were more delicate ways to handle it.

But Blake stuck to his guns.

His team stumbled upon Balikov's plans and when he presented them to MI5, they were shot down. The Foreign Secretary, who was holding onto her job by the thinnest of threads, had told them it was a dead end. Instead of rubbing the victory in their faces, Blake used the success as a means to justify the need for Directive One and, more importantly, the need for the other agencies to work together.

Lives were lost.

They could have been avoided had they acted sooner, and Blake wanted all the decision-making suits who sat behind their desks, to roll around in their own guilt for a while. He doubted much would change, but he had to try.

There would always be those who turned their noses up at the notion that he and his team were given special treatment. An unspoken permission to operate outside of the guidelines.

But those who truly mattered knew the truth.

And that was that Directive One was a necessity.

After all the calls, Blake agreed to a debrief in a few days' time, wanting to give his team plenty of time to recover. He had booked out a number of rooms at a small bed-and-breakfast on the outskirts of Budapest, and had ensured that whatever the team wanted, they could have.

Food. Drink. Rest.

All of it.

Amos had been laid up in bed, recovering from the savage injuries he'd sustained during the collapse of *Boytsovskaya Yama*. A lesser man would have leant heavily on the trauma for a little extra sympathy.

But not Amos.

The man was as solid as the concrete cell he'd fought his way out of, and all he wanted was a little bit of company when he was awake. Foster stayed by his side, their friendship built on years of trust, and while Blake made the odd joke about them being a married couple, their love for each other was purely platonic. Now and then, Blake would knock on Amos's door, and find the two of them asleep on the bed. Her head rested on his shoulder.

Just happy to be alive and to be together.

Brady's renewed purpose had been a bonus that Blake had not seen coming, and the trauma of being shot in the stomach all those years ago had finally dissipated. The man was back to his usual swashbuckling self, with his confidence and charm ramped up to eleven. Despite the swagger, Brady was Blake's most trusted soldier, and the best field agent he'd ever known.

Including himself.

To have him back and fighting fit meant that Directive One's future was assured, and when the time came in the not too distant future that Blake finally stepped away from the life of espionage, he knew that Brady would take the mantle without a hitch.

He was proud of the man.

Hun had been as gracious as he'd expected when Blake had congratulated him on all his work. The man had called himself 'The Walking Inferno' after burning *Boytsovskaya Yama* to the ground, a nickname that had drawn groans and eye rolls. While the arrogance was at times grating, the levity was welcome, and Blake often wondered the effect it would have on Hun if he told him that *he* was, in fact, his most valuable asset.

He had been gutted to miss out on watching Sam in action, and Hun had annoyed both Singh and Amos with his requests for a play-by-play on how he fought. When Sam had finally gained consciousness, it was Hun who had sat by his bedside, commending him on the shot that saved Foster's life and that finally brought down Balikov.

Like Singh, Sam hadn't said much, but had shown an admirable resilience. There would come a time when Blake would need to apologise to Sam for deeming him expendable, but considering the magnitude of what they had foiled, he didn't think Sam would mind.

Begrudgingly, Blake knew that Sam was a hero.

They would be leaving Budapest in a few days, and before they did, Blake knew he would need to let Sam know it.

Until then, Blake kept himself busy, kept his eye on his team as they recovered, and looked forward to their next mission.

'How you holding up?'

Brady leant against the frame of the door to Singh's room, his arms stretching the sleeves of his T-shirt as he crossed them over his chest. Singh was easing herself off of the bed, the delayed aches ravaging her every move. In the heat of the moment, every blow she took had only fuelled her adrenaline. Now, each one felt like it weighed ten pounds.

'I've been better.'

'You've looked better, too.' Brady joked. Singh shot him a glare. 'Come on now. Remember what you said to me when you visited me in hospital?'

'Yeah. And?'

'You don't think it was insensitive?'

Brady's face broke into a cheeky smile, and Singh found herself warmed by his playfulness.

'I think it was accurate,' she replied before grimacing in pain.

'True.' Brady chuckled, and Singh slid her arms into the baggy hooded top and pulled it over her head. 'That's mine isn't it?'

'I don't think so. Aren't all your clothes super tight?'

Singh smiled and as she approached her friend, he opened his arms and allowed her to bury herself in his broad chest. For a few moments, they stood in silence, lost in the embrace that most people couldn't comprehend. It was similar to the bond shared between Amos and Foster.

Once you were out in the field together, once that trust had been established, you became something more to each other. Brady gently lowered his chin and kissed her on the top of the head.

'I'm just glad you're okay,' he whispered, and she squeezed him a little tighter and then stepped away.

'Thanks. It's good to know you're back to being you.'

'Took me a while…'

Singh patted his chest and then stepped past him.

'But you got there. That's all that matters.'

Singh began to walk down the hallway of the bed-and-breakfast, and Brady followed her out.

'Hey, I was wondering if maybe you would want to get a drink?' The usually ice cool Brady looked a little sheepish. Singh turned, shrugged and carried on walking.

'Sure. Give me a minute will you?'

'Where are you going?'

Singh carried on down the hallway, heading to the stairwell that led to the rooftop terrace.

'I need to lay something to rest.'

With that cryptic message of hope left hanging between them, Singh left Brady standing in the hall as she began her climb up the stairs.

The terrace was a modest, concrete clearing on top of the building, but the proprietor had made a somewhat decent effort to make it more appealing. A wooden terrace ran the length of the wall, with greenery slithering up between the pattern and blossoming into some stunning flowers. A woven furniture set was laid out nicely, with a large L-shaped sofa and a few chairs surrounding a nice table. A parasol stood to the side, but the sunset had rendered it useless as the taller buildings bathed the entire area in a cool shadow.

What the patio did offer was a gorgeous view of the city of Budapest, and as Singh stepped onto the terrace, she felt herself gasp at the stunning vista. It was a town rich with history, and under any other circumstances, she would have immersed herself in the culture.

Perhaps she would extend her stay for a few more days?

Perhaps with Brady?

For the first time in a long time, Singh could feel the

spark of possibility igniting within her, all because she'd finally come to a moment of clarity.

Sat on one of the chairs, casting his gaze over the magnificent city, was Sam.

Like her, he'd said little and spent even less time with the rest of the team. Despite the budding camaraderie he'd had developed with the rest of Directive One, he was still the outsider. Brought in to do the dirty work.

Same goal, but different role.

Now that the mission was over, the separation of himself and the rest of the group was becoming clear, and Singh knew that she was experiencing the start of her last conversation with Sam.

She took a few steps forward and then stopped, her stomach turning, questioning her about the decision she'd come to.

'You're not as subtle as you think you are,' Sam said without turning.

'Want some company?' Singh asked, her arms wrapped around her to shield her from the surprising chill of the shadow. Sam reached across and pulled another one of the chairs beside him and patted the cushion. Singh graciously accepted the invite and sat down next to him.

They sat in silence for a few moments, and as Sam watched the traffic moving below, Singh looked at him with watery eyes.

'Sam, I...'

He reached across and took her hand in his. All of his knuckles were scabbed.

'Don't apologise,' Sam said calmly and turned to her. 'I get it. I didn't like it, but I get it. You needed to see it through, and you did. We all did. And that's all that matters.'

'I love you, Sam,' Singh said quietly, dabbing at her eyes with her sleeve. 'But not in the way I thought I did.'

'I know.' Sam squeezed her hand. 'And I love you too, Amara. From the first moment, you pointed that gun at me.'

Singh let out an uncontrollable giggle and took a deep breath. She placed her other hand on his, knowing full well she wouldn't hold it again.

'I just want you to know. To me…you are not expendable.' He turned to her, and she stroked the deep bruise that spilled across his face. 'In another life, Sam Pope.'

Sam lifted her hand and kissed the back of it.

'In another life, Amara Singh.'

Singh readjusted herself on the seat, pulling her legs up and then leant across and rested her head on Sam's shoulder. The two of them sat and watched the sun falling behind the final cloud, mirroring the agreement they had just made. Their lives would fracture off into different paths, but as they sat for that moment, alone and together, they would always remember the moments that their journeys intersected.

The love that they would always hold for each other.

'Tell me about Mel. I want to hear about you being happy.'

Sam couldn't contain the smile, and as he began to describe the times he spent with Mel and Cassie in Glasgow, Singh knew that the longer she could keep the moment going, the more she would cherish.

In the morning, Sam would be gone.

Off to fight the good fight.

And Singh, along with the rest of Directive One, would be off to do the same.

EPILOGUE

A few of the airport security guards glanced curiously in Sam's direction, which wasn't anything new to him. After most of the fights he ended up facing, there was always a period afterwards where all eyes would turn to him.

The stitches in his eyebrow and purple, swollen eye were a bit of a magnet for attention. Walking alongside Blake, they made their way towards the departure gates of Budapest airport.

As always, Sam was travelling light, and had his newly purchased rucksack slung over his shoulder, which was stuffed with a few new T-shirts, underwear and toiletries. Blake had spared no expense in ensuring Sam had the essentials he needed, especially as the man hadn't been home for nearly two months. From bringing down a corrupt potential president to fighting through a Serbian prison, Blake had made it clear that Sam had deserved a holiday.

The least he could do was buy the man a few things to get him started.

Sam took a sip of his coffee and then dumped the cup in the bin and then turned to Blake.

'Thanks for sorting all of this out,' Sam said.

'Don't mention it.' Blake reached into his jacket and pulled out a thick envelope. 'This is yours.'

He handed it to Sam and watched as Sam opened it up and pulled out the passport. He flicked it open, and his good eyebrow arched up.

'Ben Carter?'

'Well, we thought now that Jonathan Cooper is a criminal and in numerous prison databases, we figured you'd want a new ID. Plus, you look like a Ben.'

'Thanks.' Sam chuckled.

'Hun put it all together. Driver's licence, school records, employment records. The whole digital footprint. You thought your previous alias was good. This one is watertight.' Blake leant in close. 'Also, Jonathan Cooper had a pretty big bank balance.'

'A gift from a friend.'

'We made sure Ben Carter got a very generous donation to whatever he had planned next.'

Blake extended his hand.

'You do know you didn't have to lie to me about pulling some strings with the police back home. I'd have done it, anyway.'

'I know. And I may have exaggerated the influence I have.' Blake shrugged. 'We do whatever we can to get the job done, right?'

Sam took Blake's hand and shook it firmly.

'That we do.'

'Oh, I do have something for you, though.' Blake began to pat his pockets and then pulled out a USB drive. 'Hun put this together for you.'

'If it's a playlist, I'm going to be very disappointed.'

'As much as he'd like it to be, I'm afraid it's just a little gift from us to you. A token of appreciation.'

With the hum of the airport surrounding them, Sam turned the USB stick over in his hand, inspecting it.

'Nothing good, I take it?'

Blake did a weighing scales motion with his hands.

'Let's just say that the more we looked into Balikov's backers, the closer to home we got. Now, there are people who are off limits, even to myself and my team...'

'A few cages that need rattling?'

'Perhaps. Like I said, just a little something to keep you busy.'

'You know I don't work for you, right?'

Blake drew Sam in for a hug and patted him on the back firmly. Sam reciprocated and then shot a glance to the board. His flight back to London Gatwick was already boarding, and the time to put all of this behind him had arrived.

He needed to get home.

Find his next fight.

That was all that mattered.

He had sacrificed too much for it to stop now, and no matter how much of a blind eye the world turned to its own mess, there was always someone who needed something.

Someone who needed someone who was ready to fight back. Sam adjusted his backpack, tucked his new passport into his back pocket, and gave Blake a nod.

'Take care of Amara.'

'I don't need to,' Blake replied firmly. Both men were fully aware of the force of nature the woman had become.

'I know.' Sam smiled. 'I hope I never see you again.'

Blake gave a lazy salute and then turned on his heel and marched back across the concourse, fading into the crowd and disappearing. Sam joined the line to go through security, and within the next forty-five minutes, he was crammed into an uncomfortable seat, nursing a lukewarm lemonade and gazing out of the window as the city of Budapest became smaller and smaller.

He was heading home.

Amara Singh and the rest of Directive One will return in:

FALSE DAWN
A DIRECTIVE ONE NOVEL

COMING 2024

GET EXCLUSIVE ROBERT ENRIGHT MATERIAL

Hey there,

I really hope you enjoyed the book and hopefully, you will want to continue following Sam Pope's war on crime. If so, then why not sign up to my reader group? I send out regular updates, polls and special offers as well as some cool free stuff. Sound good?

Well, if you do sign up to the reader group I'll send you FREE copies of THE RIGHT REASON and RAIN-FALL, two thrilling Sam Pope prequel novellas. (RRP: 1.99)

You can get your FREE books by signing up at www.robertenright.co.uk

SAM POPE NOVELS

For more information about the Sam Pope series, please visit:

www.robertenright.co.uk

ABOUT THE AUTHOR

Robert lives in Buckinghamshire with his family, writing books and dreaming of getting a dog.

For more information:
www.robertenright.co.uk
robert@robertenright.co.uk

You can also connect with Robert on Social Media:

 facebook.com/robenrightauthor
 instagram.com/robenrightauthor

Cover by The Cover Collection

Edited by Emma Mitchell

Proof Read by Steve Crawshaw

Printed in Great Britain
by Amazon

28127360R00171